The Diamond Bearers' Destiny

The Unaltered Series: Book Four

Lorena Angell

License Notes

For more titles by Lorena Angell visit
LorenaAngell.com

In memory of

**Susan Bennett
and
Janet Wittman—**

Diamond Bearers and special friends.

Books by Lorena Angell

The Unaltered Series

A Diamond in My Pocket, Book 1
A Diamond in My Heart, Book 2
The Diamond of Freedom, Book 3
The Diamond Bearers' Destiny, Book 4
The Diamond Bearer's Secret, Book 5
The Diamond Bearers' Rising, Book 6
Books 7-10 coming soon!

The Lost Crown Series

Royal Refugee
Royal Resistance
Royal Redemption

Contents

Chapter 1 - Misinterpreted Destiny

I don't know if I want to be a Diamond Bearer anymore.

I finally have a complete Sanguine Diamond lodged inside my heart, containing all the powers the ancient stone can hold, and yet Chris Harding is further away from me than ever before. I can't see Chris's future because he's behind a wall of power-canceling obsidian at his father's government compound. I'm not able to tell if we still have a future together, like the future I saw in a vision three years ago.

It's not that I think I can't go on without Chris, but I feel betrayed by the guy who is supposed to be my destined love. I feel deceived and tricked into thinking everything would be fine once Freedom had been eliminated. I feel like a fool for thinking that becoming a Diamond Bearer would solve my problems and ensure Chris and I would have a future together. The only thing I can figure is the future has been altered, and the vision I saw while bound on the stone altar will no longer come true.

What's worse, it appears Chris has sided with Deus Ex, because together they effortlessly killed Neema, a Diamond Bearer several thousand years old. Deus will need to be taken out to protect the Diamond Bearers, and if Chris is truly aligned with Deus, he will need to be killed as well.

What if I'm the one who is forced to kill the boy who

was once destined to be my love?

I'm holed up in Maine at my parents' vacation cabin hiding from Deus Ex and Chris. An all-powerful Diamond Bearer—hiding.

I'm here with my parents and Duncan, a fellow Diamond Bearer and distant relative. He's my protector, my guardian. I can't read Duncan's mind, so I'm not able to determine what he's thinking.

Maetha ordered me to resist looking for my own future because of my inability to decipher what I see. What I'm left with is a completely helpless feeling. I can't see the future. I can't read Duncan's mind. I don't know how to bi-locate.

So what was the point of all this?

Duncan's voice unexpectedly enters my thoughts. *You are not alone, Calli.*

My eyes meet Duncan's across the breakfast table. The only sound in the room comes from my mother as she crunches on toast and dips the corners in the soft yolk of her over-easy eggs. My eggs are a mess. I have unconsciously drug my fork through the yolks and torn the whites in the process.

I use my thoughts to reply to Duncan. *I know. I'm just feeling overwhelmed and depressed. I don't know what's going to happen next.*

None of us knows all the answers. We're dealing with every day as if it might be our last. You need to work on blocking your mind, Calli.

"Calli, are you going to eat those eggs or mutilate them?" my mother asks.

"Sorry," I say as I set my fork down on the plate. "I'm not hungry."

Her eyes soften, yet show worry around the edges. "You haven't eaten much since you arrived here. I can go shopping today and pick up some other groceries if you like." Her thoughts continue after she stops speaking. *Calli's wasting away. I have to help her.*

"It's all right, Mom. I'm fine." I push my chair back slowly and stand. "I think I'll just go lie back down." I pick up my plate and take it to the sink and push the egg-mess into the garbage disposal. After I wash the remaining yolk from the plate and turn off the disposal, I look out the window, taking in the morning colors as the sun streaks across Sebago Lake.

"Charlotte, how long have you and Allen owned this cabin?" Duncan engages my mother in conversation in an attempt to get her focus off me.

"We bought it when Calli was young. We only looked at it once. The whole setting was magical, really. I just knew we would enjoy many vacations here away from our daily grind and responsibilities."

I note her voice holds more enthusiasm, and Duncan begins complimenting her on her decorating choices, which only buoys my mother's spirits further. He catches my eye as I walk out of the room and sends me his thoughts. *I've got this, Calli. Go meditate.*

His efforts are certainly welcome. My mother worries too much. Two days ago Duncan told me, "She's just being a mom. Someday you'll understand what that feels like." The thought of my own children only brought reality back into focus, unfortunately. Chris Harding was supposed to be a part of my future and the father of our children.

Recent events have me wondering if that will ever be the case.

I walk up the large staircase to the bedroom that has been mine since I was nine-years-old. I remember the many times I've hauled my suitcase at break-neck speed up to my room, ready to shed my clothes, put on my bathing suit, and run out to the lake for a swim. Today, swimming is the last thing on my mind.

I enter my room and sit in the lotus position in the middle of my bed amidst the lumped-up bedding. I have always loved the warm, comfortable feeling the room brings me. The exterior log walls and the flat wood interior have a thick layer of golden-tan varnish which enhances the natural designs in the wood. My mother has decorated my room with all sorts of knotted-wood items like the bed frame, dresser, settee, nightstands, and chair. I rather like the natural feel of all the wood.

When I was fourteen, I felt the room needed a bit of my own personality, so I bought a poster of the periodic table to pin on the wall. By the time we came to visit again, my mother had framed my poster in a custom knotted-wood frame. Her effort to match the décor and please her daughter at the same time still brings a smile to my face.

I close my eyes and focus on my breathing. I need to clear my mind and get these memories out of my head in order to meditate properly. Controlling my thoughts is also essential to be able to bi-locate, according to Duncan. I haven't been able to bi-locate yet.

My mother's laughter filters up to my room from the kitchen, along with the clink of dishes being moved around. My father has apparently returned from his early morning jog, and the three adults are engaged in conversation.

Jonas Flemming enters my mind . . . sort of. The connection I have to Jonas is difficult to explain. I can see everything he sees when I close my eyes. At the moment, he is helping haul boxes, bags, and crates from a docked boat to a concrete building. Palm trees sway with the warm ocean breeze, blowing Jonas's brown hair into his eyes. My initial thought is, *Get a haircut, Jonas.*

An incredible shock follows when he replies, *What? I like my hair. Your mom is worried about you.* He grabs a crate of assorted fruits, turns toward the island, and walks up the dock. *I'm glad I'm already dead to my mom so I don't have to deal with her incessant worrying.*

I hardly think that's a good thing to be glad about.

A knock at my door brings my attention back to my immediate surroundings. "Come in," I say.

Duncan enters and closes the door behind him. He stands in front of me. "Calli, I understand your feelings of helplessness. I've been feeling the same way. Consider the fact that no Diamond Bearer has ever been killed in the history of the world until seven days ago, when Freedom's heart was shot out. Three days later Neema was ambushed, and her heart shot out." He takes a deep breath and runs his hand over his head. I realize he's frustrated, and wonder if it's with me. Then he continues, and I can see I've been too self-absorbed. "Never before has a Bearer been tricked into not seeing their impending, unavoidable death. Furthermore, now the government is aware of the diamonds and knows how to kill a Bearer. But the worst problem by far is Deus Ex. She knows how to kill all of us—well, if the government's special army of Unaltereds doesn't wipe us out first. Deus Ex and Brand's repeating ability was necessary to end Freedom's life. Unfortunately, it could also destroy each and every one of us. Believe me, I feel your pain, Calli."

Though I know I'm being selfish, I blurt out, "I know, but Chris and I—"

He raises his hands, cutting me off. "Let me stop you there. Chris was shown a vision of a girl who would eventually come to his rescue. That vision came true. Does that mean you two will live happily ever after? Not necessarily."

"I saw my own future when the Death Clan died, Duncan. My grandchildren ran to me as I stood over Chris's grave."

"Interpreting visions can be tricky if you don't know what to look for. All it takes for you to have grandchildren is for you to get pregnant and give birth to a child, and then for the child to grow up and produce a child of their own. That doesn't mean Chris will play any part."

"But Chris's headstone declared him a loving husband, father, and grandfather."

"Okay, but the inscription on Chris's headstone might not have been referring to *you* and *your* grandchildren. Were you able to determine if the grandchildren running toward you were his?"

I glance down at my hands and think for a second. "I don't remember. I might have just assumed they were because of the words etched in stone in front of me." I raise my eyes and glare deep into his. "You know, Duncan, you're not helping me feel any better."

"Even if those grandchildren were yours and Chris's, your vision made it clear he had died, right? My whole point is as a Diamond Bearer, you can't get distracted by your fear of losing Chris. You're scared right now because you think you've lost your 'destined love', but in fact he was never part of your destiny."

"What? Why would you say that?"

Duncan sits down on the bed beside me. I unfold my legs and turn sideways to face him. "Maetha gave him the vision to help ensure the downfall of the Death Clan."

"Yeah, but she told me herself that visions of the future can't be manufactured."

"True, but just because Chris saw what he did doesn't mean you two are destined for each other. Anyway, I don't believe in destined love. Any change to the present can create a change in the trajectory of your future, causing you to miss your 'one and only' by a mile, just like a ship at sea. If the coordinates are off by a single degree at the start of its journey, a ship could be off target by hundreds of miles by the time it reaches its destination, depending on how far it has to travel."

"Sheez, you're *really* not helping me feel better."

"Then I need to try harder. Calli, if you're completely tied up emotionally with the idea that Chris is your future, then you pose a risk to all Diamond Bearers. You can't be so fixated. If you can't let the future play out, regardless of your vision, then you're a threat to everyone else."

I can't believe what I am hearing. This guy is as cold hearted as they come! "Haven't you ever been in love?" I ask.

"Yes. Have you?"

"What kind of a question is that?" I stammer in response.

"I believe you're in love with an idea. You did what you needed to do in order to save lives. That doesn't mean you know what love is. True love takes years to build and nurture. It takes compromising and supporting, sacrificing and failing together, and then rebuilding after tragedy. You haven't lived long enough to know what love is."

"Well, Captain Buzzkill, tell me about your experiences with love, so I can learn." Sarcasm comes as second nature to me.

He clears his throat and says, "Before I became a Diamond Bearer, I fell in love and married a Healer. We had ten magical years together and two beautiful sons before I was recruited by Maetha. I didn't understand what I was choosing to do. All I knew was the evil Healer Clan the villagers called vampires threatened the futures of my wife and sons. What I didn't know was my wife was a member of the clan. Later, when I was strapped down on an altar with the diamond on my chest, just like you, I watched my love and her clan try to kill me. Like you, I also saw a vision of my grandchild—of *our* grandchild—in the last moments before the diamond exploded. I felt the burn of the diamond on my chest, but I was relieved that we would live through the event. Try to imagine my confusion as I watched my wife crumble into a small pile of dust. I had read too much into the little I had seen. I didn't look for the not-so-happily-ever-after information.

"For many years after her death, I tried to learn how to bring back the dead. Over time I realized resurrection wasn't possible. My sons grew up and married, and I lived to see my vision come true when I held my first grandchild in my arms. I could sense my wife's blood in my beautiful, innocent grandbaby's body. The vision had come true, and it played out exactly as I had seen it on the altar. That's when I understood completely visions can be misinterpreted."

"You thought you could save her by sacrificing yourself, didn't you?"

"Sometimes we do crazy things out of love. That's what I'm worried about with you."

"I'm sorry, Duncan. I guess you of all people would know exactly what I'm feeling right now. I just wonder where Chris's loyalties lie and what's to come."

"Yes, that's why Maetha assigned me to watch after you. She knew you would—" He pauses and places his fingertips to his temples. "Hang on, Calli. Do you feel it?"

"Feel what?"

"Maetha is sending a message."

"How do you know?" I truly don't feel anything different.

"You have too much floating around in your head to

hear her. First of all, you need to close your mind to block easy access from other Diamond Bearers. It's too distracting to me."

"How do I do that?"

"Mentally decide what you want others to know and what you don't want them to know. In my opinion, I'd say just block everything in your head. Everyone else does. They will still be able to bi-locate to your position. Give it a try and I'll test you."

I make a conscious decision to block my mind from all Bearers and then turn my eyes to his. Duncan's brown eyes have many laugh lines extending from their corners, and deep grooves frame his mouth. He has chosen to look around sixty years old, with more grey hair than brown, and it makes me wonder what age I will decide to look down the road. Currently, I look like the girl from Chris's vision who entered the room and healed his legs, but do I want to look like this anymore after everything that has happened?

Duncan looks deep into my eyes and says, "Very good, Calli. Now feel the diamond inside your heart. Think of it as a piece of a larger stone, a stone that is broken into twenty-one pieces. You have one, I have one, and one isn't possessed by anyone." I figure he is referring to Neema's diamond. "Each piece is unique," he continues. "Once you can feel where other pieces of the diamond are in relation to you, you can identify each of the Bearers. This is how you bi-locate to another position. It's actually two diamonds connecting."

"What was Maetha's message?"

"She wants us to meet her tomorrow at her home on Martha's Vineyard."

In the morning, I stand in front of the mirror in the bathroom after changing into my running suit. My body has matured dramatically since the first time I wore a suit like this. Ironically, I still don't have a Runner's body dimensions. My DNA has not been altered to produce the perfect frame for super-speed running, but the diamond in my heart picks up the slack and makes me faster than any Runner.

I pick up the lucky necklace Chris's Uncle Don made for me and tie it around my neck. The necklace has an Imperial topaz added, charged with the running power, that I can use if I ever encounter a piece of obsidian. Then I put my arms into the heavy bullet-proof vest all Diamond Bearers now wear and fasten the Velcro and snaps. Hopefully, it will do its job if I come in contact with Deus Ex.

Duncan and I say goodbye to my parents and begin our run south. We skirt along the east edge of Sebago Lake and then turn south to I-95, where we run parallel to the interstate, heading down to Boston. Once we enter heavier populated areas, we slow down and jog at a normal pace to blend in. Duncan uses his future sight to determine the best pathway through the city.

As we travel, I think about the story Duncan told me the day before. I'm left with a lot of questions. I wish I had paid better attention when he told my parents his story about the vampires the night we arrived at the cabin. I don't want to admit I didn't listened. I figure he didn't tell my parents about the actual death scene because that might make them wonder if I went through the same kind of thing. Hearing his account makes me think he thought he could save his wife from her involvement in the evil Healer Clan. Yet, he watched her die. I feel sorry for him, and also realize he probably hasn't retold this story in a very long time . . . if ever. My respect for Duncan has grown immensely.

We take the Vineyard Haven ferry to the island rather than run across the open water. Duncan can't foresee a clear path that will allow us to go unnoticed due to the bright sunny day. Running so fast I can run on water is something I never would have believed back in high school. How things change.

Once the ferry docks, we head south.

As we walk along the road past the old-style clapboard homes jammed tightly together, Duncan says, "Maetha doesn't ever use this home for gatherings."

"Why do you suppose she would do so now?"

"I'm not sure. I can only sense a special purpose."

I'll admit I'm tempted to look for the future, but I resist. Maetha's words of caution still linger in my mind. We continue walking through the streets until we turn up a private drive that climbs a small hill. The home comes into view, surrounded by a beautifully manicured landscape. Maetha's home is not a huge house by any means and doesn't scream wealth, apart from its location on several acres of prime real estate with an unobstructed view of the ocean in the distance. I make a mental note of the peaceful feeling I experience while walking up the drive.

As we approach the front door, Duncan halts abruptly and reaches out his arm to stop me. "Wait, wait . . . something's . . . unusual here." He holds his breath while he mentally scans the yard and home for a moment. Then a warm grin spreads across his face. "Unusual indeed. We're in for a treat."

I feel inside my body for any kind of unusual premonition or sensation like Duncan feels, because I can't read his mind to find out what he senses.

A housekeeper opens the door after Duncan knocks.

She guides us through the well-furnished home. I'm not surprised to see nearly all of the furniture and decorations appear to be antiques—an antique dealer's dream come true. The housekeeper silently leads us out the double doors and onto the back patio. Lush thick greenery and shrubs flank both sides of the patio, creating a private sitting area with a breathtaking view of the ocean. Four occupied high-back lounge chairs face away from us toward the sea. I feel inside my body for my diamond and then try to feel for any diamonds in the vicinity. Duncan's diamond naturally surfaces by my side, as does Maetha's and Merlin's coming from the two chairs on the left. The occupants of the two remaining chairs are not Diamond Bearers. The one on the far right emanates a strange force—one I'm not familiar with. The other one next to it gives forth a familiar scent of wood and citrus that reminds me of Chris. The memory of his smell causes my heart to pick up its pace.

The voices coming from the chairs are barely audible from where we are standing until the person sitting in the wood and citrus chair says, "I'll go get one for you." Then he stands and begins walking toward us without looking up.

Chris!

His eyes meet mine. He inhales sharply and freezes in place, completely shocked. His mouth opens slightly like he is trying to figure out what to say.

I'm not any less stunned by the sight of him. He's the last person I thought I'd see here. He's the last person I *want* to see right now. I feel as though tears are going to burst from my eyes at any second. My throat muscles constrict, making it impossible to speak.

"I didn't know you'd be here, Calli," Chris finally says. His mind panics: *Oh no! Why is she here? How do I even begin to tell her what happened? She won't believe me.*

Maetha's voice interrupts our stare-off. "Better grab three, Chris." She turns to me and says, "Come join us," motioning for Duncan and me to sit down. I break eye contact with Chris and walk coolly past him. We pull two more chairs and place them perpendicular to the female stranger and sit down with Duncan positioned near the woman.

Maetha speaks telepathically to me: *Calli, you will have the opportunity to learn his side of the story. Just be patient.*

Why didn't Duncan tell me Chris would be here?

Because he didn't know. I didn't even know until he arrived.

Yeah, well the last time he arrived unannounced, Neema died!

I know, but this situation is different. Try to relax, Calli.

Why is Maetha so calm? I need answers—and what's up with the strange reverse-magnetic force I feel from the woman to my left?

I glance over and look her up and down. I try to read her mind or feel inside her body but can't do either. If she isn't a Diamond Bearer, I should be able to do both. This woman is definitely a person of powers, but not a power I have come across before. She looks to be in her late forties and is rather plain looking. In fact, she looks like a save-the-earth hippie type who drives an old Volkswagen van covered in peace signs and multiple colors of paint. She has long, straight brown hair and tanned skin, and wears a sleeveless sundress over her thin frame. She wears zero jewelry or makeup and has no discernible scent. Her sandals look like they are a hundred years old and made of all-natural materials, like the ones I can find at Aura's Organic Clothing shop near my college dorm.

Chris comes back outside with three tall glasses of ice water. He serves Maetha first, then Duncan, and then me. His proximity to me awakens strong emotions. I need answers! My anger and confusion intensify by the second. His hand shakes as he presents the glass to me, and I am careful not to touch his fingers as I take the glass. I look up into his deep blue eyes and say politely and quietly, "Thank you."

His mind says, *What can I say to get her to understand?*

Maetha says, "Chris sit down. Calli, you are spot-on with your assessment of our guest."

"What?" I half-laugh, half-choke on my response. She read my mind? I guess I haven't blocked well enough.

Maetha continues. "She's a person of powers, although she doesn't own a VW. Calli, I'd like to introduce you to Crimson."

My eyes shoot back over to the woman, who now looks familiar to me. She's still wearing the same clothing and has the same appearance, but *now* I recognize her. She is the lady who taught me how to read lips when I lost my hearing in middle school. I remember her as if it was yesterday. JoAnn Jones, or Jo Jo, as she liked to be called.

"Jo Jo?" I laugh, mainly because I don't really know how else to respond. Jo Jo is Crimson . . . *The Crimson* . . . I can't believe it! She smiles at me, but doesn't speak. I notice Chris is amazed to realize I recognize Crimson.

Chapter 2 - Through His Eyes

Chris exclaims, "She was Jo Jo to me too, Calli! She lived down the street from me when I was a young boy."

"She taught me how to read lips when I lost my hearing when I was younger," I say, almost competitively.

Merlin speaks to my mind. *Calli, Jo Jo has been in all our lives at one time or another before we became Diamond Bearers. She rescued me from the ocean after my ship sank off the coast of France. I sailed with her for three months before she took me home. A few years later I became a Diamond Bearer and met her again.*

Maetha speaks aloud. "Chris's father has been under surveillance for years now, and by way of association, Chris has been watched as well."

Crimson sits forward in her chair and crosses a slender leg over the other. She addresses the group in a soft, serious voice. "Time is of the essence. The threat is greater than ever before, and every moment spent here is one less used to resolve the issue. Calli needs to be brought up to speed, and then we need to be on our way."

Maetha stands and says, "Yes, I agree. Let's leave Chris and Calli alone so he can catch her up on current developments."

I glance nervously over at Chris. He leans forward, his elbows on his knees, and wrings his hands while he stares intently at me. *If she doesn't break my neck first.* The others wander away, leaving only the sounds of the rustling leaves and chirping birds. *I can't believe she saw the whole thing like Maetha said. She would have seen the ring too. She'll probably never accept a jewelry box from me, not after seeing what happened to Neema.* He rubs his face with his palms and says, "Calli, I don't know where to begin."

"Why did you do it, Chris? *How* could you do it?" My heart races within my chest and threatens to explode.

He stands and says firmly, "Come with me."

Reluctant at first, I follow him as he walks to a covered swing further away from the house, where it's more private and secluded. He stops in front of the swing and invites me to sit. I do so, and he sits beside me, but not close enough to touch my leg with his.

I can't get the image of Neema being gunned down out of my head. I feel the same feelings of astonishment and disappointment I experienced that day not so long ago. The pain is still raw inside my mind. Images of Chris dancing seductively with Kikee in Alaska flit through my consciousness and fill my mind with jealousy and distrust. I had compartmentalized his actions in my mind, thinking he wasn't in control of his mind. Now I realize that once he betrayed my trust by killing Neema my suppressed feelings have surfaced with a vengeance.

Chris waits for me to speak. After several long drawn-out seconds pass, he speaks quietly, "Calli, I give you permission to extract my memories. I won't resist you. You need to know the truth." He reaches for my hand.

The truth? What truth could he possibly tell me that would erase my feelings of betrayal? Fear prickles along my spine. I pull my hand away from his slightly. I'm not ready to forcefully yank out his memories. From what I remember of the events the last time I used the power, I felt like I had performed something wrong and extremely selfish. Justin Macintyre's mind extraction had happened by accident when he grabbed me in anger, and I wasn't aware of my actions when I extracted his mind. However, when I used the memory of the Healer, Andrew Stuart, to satisfy my selfish need to see Chris alive, I knew exactly what I was doing. I felt bad afterwards.

My concerns are lessened by the fact Chris has just given me permission to perform the extraction, but I'm not ready.

Chris says, "We'll wait till you're ready then."

"What?" *Did I just project my thoughts into his head?*

"We'll just talk, all right?" He lays his hand back on his lap and stares ahead out to the distant water where a sailboat slowly drifts by. "When you and I had our talk on the airplane after everything went down in Alaska, you told me something that's been stuck in my head ever since. It's why I volunteered to go back and work for my dad. You told me you 'saw a bigger picture' and that it didn't include your short existence. Your words hit me hard. You also said you'd seen a vision of our grandchildren. That blew my mind, honestly. Your revelation cleared out all my depression and helped me come back to my senses. The fact that the vision I had been shown about you healing my broken legs actually came true helped me realize we just might still have a future, and I needed to look for the bigger picture you already possessed."

Oh, dear. Duncan's words about misread visions meander through my head. I quickly dismiss them.

Chris turns his head and looks me straight in the eyes. "Calli, I see the bigger picture now. My world has been chaotic and full of government tests. I was unaware of it, but my mind has been regularly read to interpret what was going on inside my father's facility. Crimson watched me closely all that time, even playing the part of one of my neighbors while growing up. Like I told you, I thought her name was Jo Jo up until last week, when she told me her real name."

He successfully piques my curiosity. "Last week? Before or after Neema—" I can't finish.

"Before. This would be a lot easier if you would just take my hand, Calli."

I move my hand forward, and he takes hold, interlocking our fingers with a gentle squeeze, then he places his other hand on top. His hands are warm and comforting. I feel his rapid pulse through my fingertips, followed by his emotional energy. His mind blossoms like a stop-motion film of a rose slowly opening every last velvet petal. I close my eyes and let my mind sift through his memories. He had said Crimson was one of his neighbors, so I look for that first.

I begin to see a pleasant neighborhood with large broadleaf trees lining the road. The limbs stretch across, overlapping in the middle. The homes are older but well maintained. I can smell the flowering bushes nearby and feel the warm breeze on my skin. I'm amazed at the detail I can visualize through this mind-extraction session. However, I sense the distinct difference—the limitations—within Chris's mind when compared to how I perceive the world with the full power of the Sanguine Diamond.

A small group of boys toting skateboards surround me. They are laughing. Because Chris knows them by name, I do as well. They are Chris's same age: eleven.

A woman I identify as Chris's mother yells in his direction, "Chris, have you fed Ms. Jones's fish yet today?"

"Oh, shoot, no. I'll go do it right now." The memory fills my head as if it were my own, as if I am saying the words and experiencing the events first-hand. A wave of concern floods my body as I worry Jo Jo will be upset that I have forgotten about her fish while she is on vacation. I hop on my skateboard and hurry down the sidewalk to Jo Jo's home. Using the key from the secret plastic rock in her flower garden, I enter through the back door. Once I am inside the house, Jo Jo's fish greet me by bobbing to the surface in anticipation of their meal.

Chris's memory jumps ahead to a date when Jo Jo is home. She's serving cookies and lemonade at her kitchen table. Jo Jo looks the same as she does today. I feel . . . or should I say Chris feels . . . relaxed in her company. She passes Chris postcards, telling about her recent trip to Greece.

I wonder in my mind about the events that unfolded when Chris's running power emerged. A new scene opens up in Chris's mind. He's twelve years old. His hand reaches forward to grab his baseball mitt as his body experiences some uneasy sensations.

I find it extremely interesting to be in Chris's mind, experiencing his past, feeling what he felt—like the ultimate virtual reality—yet unable to alter his actions or heal his ailments.

Chris's stomach flips and rolls with nausea as he slips his fingers inside the stiff leather. He doesn't want his father to know he's not feeling well. That would show weakness, and Chris knows his father doesn't accept weakness. Besides, Saturdays are the best day of the week: the day he and his father play catch. *I'm not going to be sick today,* Chris thinks in his mind.

"Got your mitt?" Chris's father, Stanley Harding, asks. He's wearing a white tee-shirt and pair of tan military pants tucked into his lace-up boots.

"Yeah."

"Good, let's go." Stanley opens the door for Chris. "Wait," he puts his hand in front of Chris to stop him. "Tuck in your shirt. You look sloppy." Chris takes the mitt off and pushes his blue button-up shirt inside his jeans. Chris stands straight and tall, awaiting his father's approval. Stanley looks him over, steps aside, and extends his arm toward the door. Chris leads the way to the empty lot beside their home.

"Why don't you stand by the sidewalk, Chris? I'll take the back fence today."

"But what if I miss the ball? It might hit a car or roll down the road."

"Then you'd better not miss."

Chris's sick stomach clenches again at that thought. He forces a smile and waits for his father to take his position and throw the ball. The muscles in Chris's legs begin to shake slightly. He tries to hold still but soon gives up. Instead he shakes one leg at a time, as if he's limbering up or getting ready for an intense session of catch with his father.

"You need to remind your mother to get your hair cut soon," Stanley says as he gently tosses the ball to Chris.

The ball lands effortlessly in Chris's mitt. "Okay." He takes the ball, winds up, and throws it back to his father.

"Good. Next time follow through with your whole arm and shoulder." Stanley throws a faster ball back to Chris.

The slap of leather on leather, and the immediate stop of the ball inside Chris's mitt, brings a slight jab of pain to his palm. He grasps the ball as an intense wave of nausea flips his stomach. *I refuse to be sick!* He pulls his arm back, takes a step forward, and launches the ball in his father's direction, making sure to follow through with his arm and shoulder.

"Whoa, where did that come from?" His father chuckles as he removes the ball from his mitt after catching it. "I've never seen you throw like that before. Do it again."

Chris's mouth begins to water in anticipation of vomiting. He sees his father wind up to throw the ball back to him but is too slow raising his mitt to catch it. The ball deflects off the top and flies sideways, bouncing down the sidewalk. He hears his father let out a sigh and doesn't wait for the order to go get it. Chris swallows hard and runs after the ball, now two houses down the block. A burst of painful energy electrocutes his legs and he bolts forward at an uncontrollable rate of speed. He passes the rolling baseball, zooms beyond Jo Jo who is trimming her roses in the front yard, and crashes through her next door neighbor's hedge. Chris rolls a few times and comes to rest on his hands and knees. Shaking uncontrollably, he hurls his breakfast out on to the perfectly trimmed grass.

"Chris," his father yells from a distance.

Jo Jo's concerned voice sounds from the other side of the hedge. "Are you all right, Chris?"

Chris coughs and spits, then stands up. His legs shake as electrifying sensations race up and down his bones. He examines his forearms. They're covered with gashes and bleeding lacerations from his wrists to his elbows. *Ouch!*

I think back to when I won the 100m and what my body felt like afterward—nothing similar to this. Then again, I wasn't actually experiencing the emergence of the running ability. Maetha had enchanted me with speed . . . or something like that.

Chris lets himself out onto the sidewalk through the nearby gate. His father jogs toward him and stops in front of Jo Jo where the ball has come to a rest.

"I'm fine," Chris says, embarrassed. He doesn't know what just happened or why he's experiencing such awkward impulses and unsettling stomach issues.

Stanley bends down and picks up the ball. For a long moment he just stares at it. Then his eyes meet Chris's. Something about his expression causes Chris to shrink inside. "No, Chris," Stanley says with slow deliberation. "No, you're not fine."

Two men cross the street, walking briskly toward us.

Through Chris's eyes, I recognize them as Hunters even though they are dressed nicely and are clean shaven. They could pass for undercover cops. Chris, however, only sees their overly large noses.

The taller of the two says to Chris, "Young man that was an impressive run you just made. We'd like to talk to you."

Stanley steps forward. "Excuse me, I don't know what you think you saw, but this boy was about to head home, weren't you?" He nods his head in Chris's direction, giving a firm hint to leave and go home.

Chris looks over at Jo Jo who has her expressionless gaze set on the two men.

Chris takes a shaky step forward. The taller man juts his hand in front of Chris and stops him. "I don't think you understand, son. We need to talk to you right now."

Stanley steps forward, taking an intimidating stance. "Take your hand off the boy. Who exactly are you? And how did you find him so fast?"

The Hunter removes his hand from Chris's shoulder. "Do you know this man?" he asks Chris.

"He's my dad."

"Oh, well that's even better," the Hunter says and then looks to his partner and nods.

The other Hunter moves his hand as if he might be going for a weapon or gun stashed under his jacket, but then freezes. I recognize the freeze from the time Maetha froze everyone in Justin Macintyre's building. At first, I wonder if Maetha is nearby and invisible, but then I remember Jo Jo—aka Crimson—is standing on the other side of the roses. Maybe she has the same ability as Maetha.

Chris looks from the frozen Hunter to his father and wonders why his dad said: "How did you find him so fast?"

A tall, athletic young man appears out of nowhere,

followed by a gust of air which rustles everyone's hair with the exception of Stanley's buzz-cut. I find it interesting how Chris and Stanley react to the sudden arrival, but I understand this man is a Runner and he has just come to an abrupt halt after running. He stands by Stanley and addresses the Hunters. "Not this time, guys."

Stanley takes a step away from the Runner in complete shock. I wonder what he must be thinking.

"You're too late. We got here first," the taller Hunter states defiantly. He turns to his frozen counterpart and demands: "What are you waiting for?"

The second Hunter slowly and awkwardly moves his arm forward. He seems to be distressed and confused as to why his arm is doing what it's doing.

"What's the matter with you?"

"I don't know!" the obviously mind-controlled Hunter shouts.

The Runner extends his hand to Chris, "Come with me, I'll protect you."

Stanley, rushes to Chris and grabs his upper arm. "He's not going with anyone but me."

"And you are . . . " the Runner asks.

Chris looks up at his father, waiting for him to speak. Stanley appears to be struggling with what to say. Chris speaks up: "He's my dad."

"Oh, well then, we need to go somewhere safe. Do you live around here?" the Runner asks Stanley.

Chris glances over at the two Hunters. Both of them seem to be frozen in place. I feel Chris's confusion over their behavior as another wave of nausea tosses his stomach around.

"Sir," the Runner says emphatically. "We need to go somewhere safe where you can call the police if these two Hunters decide to fight for your son. I can then explain to you what just happened with him."

"I already know what happened." Stanley remains rooted to his location on the sidewalk.

Chris's stomach winds up for an encore performance. I completely understand his desire to be inside a locked bathroom when he vomits again.

Jo Jo says to Chris, "This is a good man. Take him to your house, Chris." I recognized Jo Jo's voice sounding *within* Chris's mind, but he thinks she's actually speaking to him.

"Come with me," Chris says to the Runner, as he hurries past the frozen Hunters and his dad.

"Chris, what are you doing?" Stanley yells at him.

"Are you coming, Dad?" Chris doesn't wait to see if his father follows. His nauseous tummy only has just so long before it erupts again.

The Runner follows Chris. "What's your name, son?"

"Chris Harding."

"I'm Ivan Bjorn."

Chris cuts across the front lawn and takes the steps two at a time. He uses great effort to control the movement of his tingling legs. The last thing he wants is to have a repeat occurrence of the crazy uncontrollable run that started this whole mess. He holds the front door open for Ivan. "This is my house. Take a seat, I need to use the bathroom. Sorry."

Chris's memories of the events that follow are patchy. I figure they are unimportant, except for his father's reaction to the whole event. Stanley doesn't look Chris in the eye, won't refer to him as his son, or ask Mr. Bijorn any questions about the Runners. Stanley already seems to know about as much as he wants to know. Chris's young mind is crushed by his father's behavior.

My knowledge of General Stanley Harding helps me

fill in the blanks. I understand why he acts the way he does. I know what he's been studying at his compound. My heart aches for Chris.

Chris's memories jump forward to his arrival at the Runner's compound. Clara Winter isn't the leader yet. Instead the leader is a man named Joseph Grimly, who is a lot nicer to the girls than the boys. Chris doesn't like him. He isn't the only one.

Mr. Grimly sits in the office and informs Chris in a rather uncompassionate manner that he should simply accept his new reality. Concerning Shadow Demons, Mr. Grimly says: "If you don't want to believe me, then be my guest and go walk into the shadows and find out for yourself."

For a boy Chris's age, conflicted with hormones, having only recently exhibited a freakish display of super-human speed, ripped away from his mother's compassion, and dumped in the office of a heartless, insensitive leader of the Runner's Clan, I think Chris takes it pretty well.

Chris's memory pushes forward to a point when the youngest Runners are sent home while a transition takes place within the compound. Chris is excited because his father has invited him to go to Denver for a week. Chris looks forward to spending time with his dad.

I experience the day Chris first enters the military compound in Colorado. He is introduced as Chris, not "my son." The lack of personal attachment hurts Chris, as he realizes his father has labeled him certifiably abnormal.

Freedom . . . or Agent Alpha as Chris only knows him as . . . comes to greet Chris. "You look just like your old man." Then Agent Alpha turns to Stanley and says, "Now, what are the odds of that happening? Your own flesh and blood becoming one of them."

"Take him," Stanley orders Agent Alpha. "Get him

hooked up and draw his blood samples."

Agent Alpha leads Chris to the laboratory and orders a female technician to do the bloodwork. "Once we're done here, we'll go record your speed on the treadmill."

"I already know I run faster than sixty miles per hour."

Agent Alpha says, "I already know that too, but as you are aware, some subjects are faster than others."

"Subjects?"

"All the abnormal ones are called subjects. Not to worry, Chris. When we're done with you, you'll at least get to leave and go home. The other subjects aren't so lucky."

"What happens to them?"

"They are permanent residents of the compound. Relax, we take good care of them," Agent Alpha says to Chris. I note that Chris senses things are not as hunky-dory as Agent Alpha would want him to think.

"Do you have any Runners here?" Chris's head itches. He scratches his scalp.

"Why, are you worried, Chris?"

"No," he answers defensively.

"I think you're worried you might be discovered and revealed. If a captured Runner knew you were here helping your dad, they might rat you out."

"How did you know I was thinking that? Are you a Reader?"

"No. Unlike you, I'm not abnormal."

The technician proceeds to remove a blood sample from Chris's arm. After she completes her job, Agent Alpha takes Chris to the treadmill room.

"All right, let's see what you're made of." He indicates that Chris should get on the treadmill. Chris does. "Your speed will be registered on the equipment in the other room. Begin."

Chris starts jogging at first to get a feel for the machine. Then he pours on the speed like any teenage boy wanting to show off. I experience what it actually feels like to be a Runner—exhilarating. It's as though every cell in his body is lined up, ready to react, awaiting orders from his brain, then executing the order perfectly. Every muscle, tendon, and ligament co-exists in unity. Cartilage floats, cushioning every step. Each individual bone in his feet lines up in anticipation for the next movement ordered by his brain.

Even with the full diamond, I've never felt the same sensations as Chris does.

Chris glances through the open door and sees Agent Alpha and his father standing near a computer monitor. His father points to the screen and says something to Agent Alpha, who nods his head and looks at Chris.

"That's enough, Chris," Agent Alpha says in a raised voice.

Chris slows down, letting the treadmill slow as well. As the machine comes to a halt, he hears his father say: "The subject appears to be faster than any of our previous subjects."

"Yes, but he's also younger," Agent Alpha adds.

"We'll compare the subject's DNA to the others and see if an alteration is occurring."

Chris wonders, *Why is he calling me a subject? I'm his son!*

The following days are spent testing Chris's reflexes, cognitive abilities, performing x-rays, CT scans, and further blood tests. Chris's father continues to treat him as abnormal and a subject. Agent Alpha is the only person in the compound who will carry on conversations with Chris, but they appear to be only for Agent Alpha's own gain.

At one point, Agent Alpha says, "Most thirteen-year-old boys hate their fathers. Why are you so attached?"

"I don't know. I just want my dad back. Since my running powers came out, he treats me like I'm broken."

"You think he doesn't love you anymore?"

"I just wish everything would go back to normal."

"If you want him to see you as his son again, offer to give him information about the Runners and what happens at the compound."

"Be a spy?" Chris asks, definitely shocked by what Agent Alpha is suggesting.

"Look, you're the one whining that your dad doesn't pay attention to you anymore. You need to understand this—your defect scares him."

"I'm not defected!"

"You are to him. So why don't you make yourself useful and pass along information to him? You could give him something he doesn't have right now—someone on the inside."

"I'll get kicked out of the compound if I get caught."

"You can't have this both ways. You can't change the fact you're a Runner, but you can help your father in his research. Besides, a good spy doesn't get caught. But maybe you don't have what it takes."

Chris's young mind can't ignore the challenge Agent Alpha has laid in front of him. His mind yells: *I do have what it takes! I'll show my father I can still be his son and he can be proud of me.*

Chris's memories jump forward. He's fifteen, taller, and more spirited. He sits in Clara Winter's office with two other boys: Andrew and Jordan. His mind tells me Clara was voted into position after Mr. Grimly was kicked out of the clan for inappropriate conduct with a female Runner. Chris and the two boys are being interrogated for their involvement in a hazing accident that caused a clan member named Brett to have his hand bitten off by the Shadow Demons. Chris's mind reveals he wasn't directly involved, but he didn't speak up or try to stop it either.

Clara's demeanor is stern. "This is not a college dorm. We do not participate in initiation rites or hazing. Brett lost his hand because of idiotic behavior from the whole male population of this compound. This is completely unacceptable! You're lucky he didn't die."

Jordan tries to defend the others. "But we weren't the ones who forced Brett to reach into the dark. Why are we in trouble?"

"Because you didn't alert me or any other leader to the danger."

"Yeah, but then we'd get beaten up," Andrew adds.

"Who'd beat you up?" Clara asks intently.

All three boys exchange worried glances with each other. No one speaks.

Clara says, "This is what I'm talking about. You are choosing to protect your own backsides instead of telling me who is bullying other Runners. I need to know who the trouble maker is so we can get back to becoming a functioning unit."

No one speaks.

"Fine, go back to your rooms. Chris, send in the next three on your way out."

The boys turn to leave the room. Chris holds back and sneakily hands a small folded piece of paper to Clara, making sure the other two don't see.

On his way up to his room, Chris thinks about the names he'd written on the paper. He hopes Clara will follow his instructions to interview the rest of the boys before she singles out the troublemakers and dismisses them. He contemplates his duality. Clara doesn't know he's sending information to his father through coded messages. The group of thugs doesn't know he's just "ratted" them out. Agent Alpha was right. A good spy doesn't get caught.

Clara is also right. The compound is not a college dorm. Since moving into the compound at age twelve, he's never felt comfortable. He always looks forward to his "vacations" when he can go home to Kansas and be with his mother. He misses his neighborhood, his old stomping grounds, the familiarity with his surroundings. Of course, his friends avoid him whenever he goes home. Since his "accident" when his powers emerged, they've viewed him as a different kid entirely. However, Jo Jo, who saw the whole thing, hasn't ever treated him any different. In fact, she seems to always know when he's in town.

Chris realizes the bigger reason he likes going home is because he gets to spend time with Jo Jo. He believes she is a Reader because whenever she's around his head itches. Her ability must be how she always knows he's arrived home. Jo Jo is the only person Chris has ever told that he's a spy for his father. He remembers a conversation where she recommended he tell Clara that he's feeding information to his father. He hasn't done that yet, but now might be a good time to do so, even knowing Clara might decide to include him in her "house-cleaning", but maybe that would be for the best. If Clara will let him stay, he'll work even harder to help build a stable, supportive setting within the compound.

Chris decides to wait till tomorrow evening when things, hopefully, will have settled down from the earlier evictions brought on from his tattle-telling. That will be a better time to talk to her.

"Come in, Chris," Clara says when she opens her office door. She closes it behind him. "How can I help you?"

"I have something to tell you."

"Have a seat. Before we get started, I want to thank you for giving me the list of names. If anyone else gave me a list like that, I would have dismissed it, but I trust you, Chris. You're a good kid. You've been raised well. I know handing me that list was extremely difficult for you, but I appreciate your bravery."

Chris swallows hard. This will be tougher than he thought. *She trusts me? Oh boy,* he thinks to himself. He clears his throat and says, "Um, well, I just wanted to help clean out the bad eggs. Brett's injury scared me. I'm happy he survived, but his life will not be the same."

"It's true. I wish the other Runners could have your wisdom, Chris."

"Um, yeah, well, you see, I'm not who you think I am."

"I'm sorry, what do you mean?"

"I need to tell you something that you're not going to like. You know my father is an army general, right?"

Clara nods.

"Well, he studies people with powers, and part of his studies comes from me. I tell him things about the world of powers and abilities. I have since I was thirteen. I couldn't handle how terribly he reacted to my running ability and I thought if I spied for him he might accept me again. At first, I only told him names and ages, but then he wanted more details like the locations of the other clans. He wanted to know about our different missions and deliveries. I began withholding information bit-by-bit because I didn't want any of the Runners to be hurt. I'm telling you this now because I don't want to do it anymore, but I don't know how to stop being a spy."

Clara silently straightens a pencil that lies next to her phone. "Chris, do you know why I trust you? Because I've been tracking your letters to your father. I already know you don't tell him everything. Stan Schlater has been watching you, reading your mind, and he says you are an honest boy who is stuck in a bad situation."

"What? Stan has been reading my . . . wait, how have you tracked my letters? They're written in code."

"Your code-key isn't hidden very well in your room, Chris."

"You've been in my room?"

"Yes."

"I . . . don't know what to say. I think I should be mad that you've been spying on me, but you're the one who should be mad at me for spying on you. Why haven't you kicked me out of the compound?"

"Because Stan says your intentions are good. I've only double-checked your communications with your father to be current on what you're telling him."

"Are you going to kick me out now?"

"Do you think I should?"

"I don't know."

Clara pulls out a blank piece of paper from her drawer. She begins writing on the paper. Chris doesn't know what to think. She completely surprised him with her revelation.

"Okay, Chris, I want you to tell this to your father in your next communication." She hands him the paper. Her message says: The Seers clan is dividing. One group is heading to Oregon, the other to southern California.

"Is this true?" Chris asks.

"No. It's a test. I want to see if your father is paying attention to what you tell him. Chris, this isn't the first time the government has tried to infiltrate our compound. We've just never had someone like you who could work both sides."

"Both sides?"

"Yes. I'm asking that you continue to feed information to your father, but that you do so under my direction. If you learn something from your father that you think would be of benefit to the clan, I would hope you'd pass it on."

"Of course. One thing I know is the government is satisfied hearing we are not training to rise up against them. They like hearing there aren't many of us and that we keep to ourselves. We are not a threat to the United States. In fact, I overheard my father talking to someone on the phone, telling them the government campaign to discredit psychics and fortune tellers, with the help of the media, was effective."

Clara scoots forward in her chair. "The government is involved in actively discrediting metaphysical powers?"

"I guess. That's what I heard my father say."

"Well, that makes sense. They're helping the clans stay hidden from the general population, probably out of fear. The government knows the people would panic if they knew they were surrounded by people with powers. They behave the same way with UFOs and aliens. To prevent mass panic, sightings are quickly disproven and individuals who claim they've been abducted are discredited."

"So, is the government really hiding the existence of UFOs?"

"I've personally never seen one, but considering how the government is handling the existence of superpowers, I have to figure they are hiding UFOs as well."

Chris's memories zip ahead to when he learns how his father reacts to the news of the Seer's clan splitting up. Chris receives a letter written in code from his father stating "where Seers live is of no concern" to him. Yet, Clara interprets this to mean Chris's father is quite interested in everything Chris has to tell him.

I sense within Chris's mind a bitter-sweet emotion. He

realizes he's attained his father's attention and possibly his respect. Except it has taken Chris being a secret agent to reach this point. Betraying his friends and slipping potentially deadly information to the enemy is what it has taken to win his father's love—if this is considered love.

Chris's memory jumps further ahead. He is barely sixteen and has participated in several delivery missions. The information he feeds his father is carefully constructed, with the help of Clara, to protect the clan.

Chris asks the Reader, Stan Schlater, how to protect secrets. Stan's answer is simple: "Don't tell anyone anything you don't want other people to know."

"You mean, except for people you trust, right?" Chris smiles.

"No Chris. No one can be trusted one-hundred percent. A secret spoken aloud is no longer a secret. I was able to read your mind more easily, simply because you'd spoken things about the clan to your father. The memories lingered in your mind right on the surface. They were easy to locate. I can teach you more effective ways to block other Readers from entering your mind."

"Please teach me."

Chris's timeline leaps by a large stride. He is now seventeen, going on eighteen. He has just broken up with a girlfriend from the compound, Shay Gibbons, because she "can't be with someone who won't open up." He is a locked box, and she "needs more from a boyfriend."

If girl-troubles aren't enough, Chris's father presses him for more information about other clans and their leaders. The increased pressure is brought on by Agent Alpha. Chris is tired and exhausted, so he decides to take a break and return home to Kansas. On his way, a woman intercepts his path. Chris knows she has powers simply because she was able to spot him during his run.

"Young man, my name is Maetha. I am a Seer. I knew you would be running this way. I need you to lend me your running ability so I can get to Oklahoma quickly and undetected. In exchange for helping, I'll offer to show you a vision of your future."

"Show me? How would you do that? It's not possible."

"I have the ability to project my visions into your mind."

"Are you a witch?"

"No, dear. I've been affected by the cosmic rays differently than other Seers."

"All right, take my hand and I'll deliver you to Oklahoma faster than the wind."

They begin their run.

I note that Chris trusts this woman without any good reason. It's reckless, in my opinion. But then I consider that maybe Maetha used her mind-control on him. I can't detect anything from his memories indicating he is under her control, though.

When they reach Oklahoma, I recognize the town as the same one where Brand and I had exchanged cars with the dying man, Wendell, on our way to California.

Maetha directs Chris to a coffee shop and sits with him in a private corner of the building. "Close your eyes and let the vision fill your mind, Chris. When you open your eyes, I'll be gone. But if you ever need me in the future, you can find me in the same place as you found me earlier."

Chris closes his eyes and the vision fills his mind. He sees that after visiting his mother in Kansas, he will go to Washington D.C. and meet a powerful Spell-caster named Merlin. Merlin will help him build impenetrable walls around his memories, protecting the damning secrets he possesses. Chris also sees he will become the fastest Runner in the compound when he turns twenty years old.

The vision ends and Chris opens his eyes. Maetha is gone. Chris leaves the shop and begins his run home to Kansas, wondering how and when he'll go to Washington D.C.

Chris's memories jump to Jo Jo's kitchen. Jo Jo is always a good listening ear, and she has great advice about Chris's ongoing girlfriend woes: "Stop trying so hard to find love," she says.

"What else is there in life?" he asks her.

"Everything! Seek out the beautiful qualities of the world and love will find you."

"Huh?"

"You'll figure it out, Chris. Hey, I want to show you something." Jo Jo leads Chris out to her garage and opens the door. Inside, a sparkling new Harley Davidson rests on its kickstand.

"Whoa . . . is this yours?"

"Who else's would it be?"

He laughs and walks to the bike and runs his hands over the smooth leather seat. "Have you ridden it yet?"

"How do you think I got it here from the dealership?" she chuckles.

"Would you take me for a ride?"

"Sure. I can teach you how to ride it if you'd like."

With an ear-to-ear grin, he simply nods his head. I conclude this is where Chris learned to ride a Harley.

Chris's memory moves to dinnertime, sitting at the table with his mother and father.

"You're going with me to the east coast tomorrow, Chris," General Harding announces.

"Pardon?" Chris coughs on his fork-full of food.

Chris's mother says in her usual quiet, timid voice,

"Stanley, Chris was going to take me shopping tomorrow."

"You can take yourself. He and I have business to attend to." Stanley's uncaring mannerism toward his wife unnerves Chris. He's seen this behavior all his life, but now after having relationships with girls, his father's rudeness brings a different type of irritation toward his father and sympathy for his mother.

"I came home to visit both of you," Chris says to his father. The knowledge Maetha gave him, telling him he would take this trip lingers in the back of his mind.

"This is more important that any *shopping* your mother has planned." General Harding turns to his wife. "Go with Jo Jo. She seems to have nothing better to do than ride around on her new toy. Which, by the way Chris," he swivels his head in Chris's direction, "I don't want you riding that thing."

Chris meets his father's eyes in contempt. He knows better than to question his father.

Chris's mother bravely says, "Come on, Stanley, there's nothing wrong with riding a motorcycle."

"If you want to die, perhaps. Those things are nothing more than donor-cycles. After you crash and die, they donate your good organs to smarter people."

Chris flies to D.C. with his father the next day and attends several meetings with him at the Pentagon. At one point, Chris is asked to wait out in the center courtyard while General Harding goes to a top-level meeting that Chris is not permitted to attend.

Out in the fresh air, Chris finds a bench with a man sitting on the far end. Chris sits down. Thoughts about his mother skip through his mind. He hopes she was able to get her errands done. Chris imagines his mother riding on the back of Jo Jo's motorcycle to the grocery store and a smile lights up his face.

"Beautiful day today, wouldn't you say?" the man at the other end of the bench says.

Chris casts a glance in his direction and nods.

"You look like someone who has a lot on your mind. Do you want to talk about it?"

Chris shakes his head and then reaches up and scratches his scalp. He freezes with the eerie feeling his mind has just been read, then lowers his voice and says, "Why would you ask me if I want to talk about it when you can just find out for yourself?"

The man cracks a sly grin. "Young man," the man lowers his voice to match Chris's. "I think you should learn better mind-blocking abilities, especially when you're around these people."

"Who are you?" Chris demands.

"You may call me Merlin, Chris Harding."

Chris reasons that Merlin would have found his name while reading his mind. Chris says, "I've seen a vision of you, Merlin."

"How? You are a Runner, are you not?"

I find it interesting that Merlin is genuinely surprised when Chris announces he had a vision.

"A Seer named Maetha showed me a vision."

"I've heard of her. What did you see?"

"That you'll teach me better ways to block my mind."

"From what I can see, you are doing the best job possible. What I will do for you is place spells upon your mind, blocking the sensitive information that could mean the death of your friends."

"Are you a wizard? I mean, with a name like Merlin, one might jump to that conclusion."

"I'm a Spell-caster. I use spells with nature's will in mind. I can sense nature's balance is threatened by what you know."

"Wait, how did you read my mind if you're just a Spell-caster?"

"You already know that witches and wizards can mimic the cosmic powers to a certain extent. Now, hold still while I fulfill the vision you saw."

Through Chris's memory, I feel the solid, impenetrable walls go up within his mind. I remembered what it felt like to run into these walls from the outside when I tried to read his mind a few years ago. To be in Chris's mind and to feel the inner side of the wall is amazing.

Merlin says, "You're all set. You can add memories behind this wall at any time and they'll be protected too. But, I'd caution you to not make everything an unshared memory. You don't want to close yourself off like that." Merlin stands from the bench and says while slightly bowing, "Until next time."

Chris bows his head ever so slightly in response and watches Merlin walk away. The overwhelming sense of relief Chris feels, knowing his mind is protected and his friends' lives are as well, boosts his spirits.

I pause for a moment to absorb the magnitude of Chris's situation. At sixteen years of age, he's a double agent, helping keep the government at bay to protect the clans. What an incredible responsibility for his young shoulders to carry. Then again, I had some pretty big responsibilities on my sixteen-year-old shoulders once upon a time.

His memories jump to a time when he's nineteen. He's assigned to go pick up a recently discovered Runner in New York. I feel his excitement, as he understands he's being considered an adult or leader within the clan. This signifies a huge jump for him. Plus, if what the Seer promised him comes true, he'll soon be the fastest in the compound.

Clara puts Chris's itinerary together with carefully selected flights that arrive before sunset, and with sleeping arrangements at nearby hotels.

On his journey to New York Chris decides to check in with his father from the Bozeman, Montana airport.

"Hey, Dad," Chris says when he's connected with his father's office.

"What have I told you about addressing me?"

"Excuse me, I forgot. Hello, sir." Chris emphasizes the "sir." He chastises himself for thinking he and his father could ever have a normal father/son relationship. "I'm checking in, sir."

"Good. Did you get the information I asked for?"

"Yes."

"When will you bring it to me?"

"I have an errand to do first, then I'll deliver the package."

"No. Bring the package first."

"I don't have enough time to do that . . . sir."

"I don't care what else you think you have going on! I want that package ASAP or I'll storm the compound and gather the information myself."

Chris considers his flight plan and says, "I'll drop the package in Denver."

"I'm not in Denver. Bring it to my office at the Pentagon."

Chris begins to panic. He knows the detour will cost him time, but he has no other choice. "Yes sir."

General Harding disconnects without saying good-bye, leaving Chris holding a phone in his hand and wondering if he'll ever get out of this situation. He should have called his father before he left the compound. If he'd done so, other arrangements could have been made to pick up the new Runner. Better yet, he shouldn't have called his father at all.

He considers calling Clara to alert her, but decides not to. She may never again give him another assignment if she feels he's too unreliable. He decides to surprise her with his ability to multi-task.

Once his airplane arrives at J.F.K International in New York, Chris deplanes and hurries to the ticket counter. He purchases a round-trip ticket to D.C. that will allow him a short amount of time at his father's office, yet still give him enough time to be able to be back in time to pick up the new Runner.

Chris arrives at the Pentagon and clears security, only to find out from the receptionist his father is in a meeting.

The receptionist says, "Your father left instructions for you to wait until he returns from his meeting."

"When will that be?"

"I don't know."

"I can't wait. I have an appointment to keep. I'll just have to leave this package with you."

"I cannot accept it. You know your father better than I do. He will only want the package delivered from your hand to his."

"I can stay for thirty minutes. After that, I have to leave. Is there any way to get a message to him?"

"I'm afraid not."

Chris grumbles in frustration and sits down on a chair against the wall. He checks the time. In his mind he reviews the location of the boy he's supposed to meet. The Seer foresaw a boy super-speed running down the sidewalk and crashing into a vegetable stand in lower Manhattan. Chris's memory of his own clumsy power emergence comes to mind.

Thirty minutes pass and Chris stands to leave. General Harding enters at the same time.

"Chris. Good. Come with me."

"I can't. I need—"

His father doesn't listen and walks to his office door. He opens it and looks back at Chris. "What are you waiting for?"

Chris exhales in frustration and hurries into the office. "I don't have much time. Here's the package."

"Sit down. I want to go through this with you." General Harding motions to a chair while he takes his seat behind his desk. "You'll be interested to know your flow of information is paying off."

"That's good. Now if we can discuss—"

"My soldiers were able to intercept a group of Seers. We captured all ten of them." General Harding lets out a proud chuckle. "You should have seen the look on their faces. I have it on video from the soldiers' helmet cams."

"Dad, um, sir, I have to go *now*. If I fail in this errand, I might lose my standing in the clan. Here's the package. The names and locations of the people you requested are in there."

Chris stands from his chair and hands the manila envelope to his father. General Harding takes the envelope without comment. Chris doesn't wait to be excused. He turns and leaves the office, knowing his father will view his sudden departure as insubordinate.

Once he clears the building, he opens up and runs to the airport, risking being seen by regular people. He arrives at the airport and finds he's missed his flight. He's incredibly angry and frustrated. How will he get back to New York in time to pick up the boy? The next flight doesn't leave soon enough. The train takes nearly three hours. Running isn't an option. Driving is out. Chris decides to wait till the next flight and hopes there is no delay. Even without a delay, he realizes he'll arrive about twenty minutes past the time he should be there.

As I see his memory-visions, I think to myself that the cursing going through Chris's mind is both justified and acceptable.

Chris ponders his life while he paces the floor of the airport, waiting for the boarding call. He wants out and away from his father's clutches. He hates being tied to this lifestyle. He never asked to be a spy, the duty was imposed upon him through pressure and implication.

The plane boards and leaves on time, heading for New York. Chris can't sit still in his seat. He feels as if he'll explode if he holds still. Soon the plane begins its descent and then lands.

Once Chris is out of the airport, he launches into super-speed running. He has a lot of ground to cover to get down to lower Manhattan. The fear of being discovered or seen is absent from his rational mind. He simply must arrive in time, just in case anyone else is aware of the new emergence of power in the Runner he's trying to reach.

Chris arrives to find police are there to take a report of a kidnapping. Two Nigerian women hold each other, sobbing. A distraught man speaks broken English to the officers, giving the description of the two kidnappers.

Hunters, Chris realizes.

He is only one face in the large crowd of onlookers, but the ache of failure painted over his face apparently makes him stand out—that, and the fact he's wearing a Runner's suit. A stranger comes to stand beside him. Chris pays him no attention, thinking he's another onlooker. Then the man speaks.

"You were too slow, son."

Chris raises his eyes to the man next to him. A long scraggly beard and mustache do nothing to detract from the man's large nose. He's a Hunter. Chris says despondently, "I know." Then he turns and walks away from the crowd. In Chris's mind, he deduces the Hunter was left behind to kill the family if the captive escaped.

Because Chris was too slow, too concerned with keeping his father happy, he knows many lives will never be the same. So much pain and misery lies on his shoulders.

Chris finds a pay phone and calls Clara.

"High Altitude Sports," she answers.

"Clara, it's Chris."

"Good to hear from you, Chris. Do you need me to secure an extra ticket back to the compound?"

Being inside Chris's memory and hearing his thoughts as well as his words, I can say he does exactly what I do: constantly running through things to say or not to say before speaking.

After a brief moment of silence, Chris says, "No. I was too late. I missed him and he was taken by the Hunters."

"Oh dear. I'm so sorry, Chris. Was my scheduling wrong with your flights and hotels?"

"No. This is all on me. I screwed up, Clara." She doesn't answer back and the line goes quiet for a few seconds. Then Chris says, "I'm going to take some time off. I'll see you later."

"It's all right, Chris. Take all the time you need. But remember, you are not the first person to miss a pick-up."

"I know. Bye." Chris hangs up the phone with the thought running through his mind that he's the first to miss a pick up because of his duty to meet with the government task force in charge of rounding up and capturing people with powers.

Chris's memory jumps forward. He becomes the fastest Runner at age twenty, just like he had been shown in the vision. He has slowed down the information he feeds his father and feels immense regret for ever telling him anything, but the damage can't be undone. Following Jo Jo's advice, Chris has stopped trying to find love. Instead, he focuses on the beauty of the world, the complexities of nature, and the operations of the compound. True to Jo Jo's advice, love has found him. The females of the compound all seem to have a crush on him.

I find myself feeling a bit jealous observing these memories in his mind. I don't recognize any of these girls. At least, none of them stand out in my mind because I wasn't at the compound for long and only got to know a small handful of the female Runners.

Chris's memory speeds through the next three years of his life. A couple relationships between Chris and various girls fly by in his recollection, none of which are serious, all of which end over the same reasons: Chris won't open up.

Because of the greatly reduced, tightly-measured information he feeds his father, General Harding issues vicious threats, insisting if Chris doesn't continue helping him, he will invade the compound and kill everyone. The clan's Seer, Donald Rheyes, doesn't see anything of an invasion in the future, so the decision is made to not move the clan. Clara advises Chris to continue keeping his father happy, but to be careful.

Other important issues have developed. Chris meets with Clara in her office to discuss the fact that reports have been made about a boy named Justin Macintyre who is consorting with the Death Clan. Clara says, "Is it possible to follow Justin in your spare time?"

"Follow him where? He doesn't ever take time off. He never leaves the compound."

"Perhaps we should place him on the next delivery team with you. That way you could watch him closely."

"Okay. Let's do that. What do you think is the greatest threat from him talking to the Death Clan?"

"That's a good question, Chris. They already know everything about our clan. Maybe they're trying to co-ordinate a delivery of some kind."

The scene in Chris's mind jumps to a small group, a delivery team, including Justin. They are checking into a motel for the night. Everyone's hair and running suits are wet because they've run through a heavy spring thunderstorm. The sun is low in the sky, but the group still has time before the Shadow Demons surface.

The guys get situated in their room and Justin says to Chris, "I'm going to go get some ice. I saw the machine by the office."

"Okay," Chris says, trying to appear normal. Inside he knows this is probably a moment of opportunity for Justin to make a phone call to his contact.

Justin leaves the room and Chris waits a moment before following him. Chris arrives at the ice machine and to no surprise, Justin is not there. Chris walks around the corner to the office door. Voices travel with the evening breeze from the parking lot beyond the office. Chris carefully approaches the edge of the building and listens.

Justin's voice says: "Why not? I know I could beat him."

A man replies, "Not yet. I'm told Chris needs to re-main in his position for the future to play out."

"Fine." Justin doesn't sound too thrilled.

Chris recognizes the voice, but can't place a face with it. He slides a little closer to the corner to try to get a peek at the two of them. The male's face is turned away, but Chris recognizes him anyway by his large muscular build and military haircut. Max Corvus, a soldier from his father's compound, is talking to Justin. *Why is he talking to Justin? And how did he find us?* Chris wonders. His foot accidentally crunches gravel. Max and Justin both turn their heads in his direction.

Justin grunts in frustration, probably because he knows he's been caught. "You spyin' on me, Chris?"

"Yeah." Chris doesn't try to dismiss his presence. He walks toward the two conspirators. "Why are you talking to *him*?" Chris points to Max.

"That's my business."

"No, you were talking about me, so it's my business too." Chris's mind fills with apprehension. He wonders if Max has told Justin about his spying. Then he wonders if Justin is spying on him for his father? "Tell me what's going on here."

Max pats the air in front of him and says, "Now, now, don't worry, Chris. This is nothing for you to be worried about."

"Really?" Chris doesn't even try to control his sarcastic tone. "Does my father have him watching me?" Chris points to Justin.

Justin takes a step back. "Wait, what? Do you two know each other?" he half-laughs. "And here I thought I was the one with secrets to hide."

Max cracks a devious smile. "Everyone has their secrets. The question is, are either of you going to rat the other one out?"

Chris's mind reels with confusion.

Justin says, "What are *you* involved with the Death Clan for, Chris?"

"I'm not."

"Well then, how do you two know each other?"

Max says, "I work with his father."

"The government? You work for the government? I thought you were—" Justin spits on the ground. "Holy crap, you're a spy, Chris."

"What, and you're not? What information are you

giving the Death Clan?"

"Like I'm going to tell you. What are you leaking to the government?"

"What are you?" Chris asks Justin, then turns to Max and says, "I don't know what you're up to or why you're playing two games, but I can't have this idiot running around telling everyone about me or I'm no good to my dad."

"Oh, I don't think Justin will say anything about you if you don't say anything about him. Am I right, Justin?"

"Yeah."

Max continues, "Justin will continue to let you keep the fastest runner title in exchange for your continued secrecy about his connections."

"Justin isn't faster than me, so that doesn't really matter."

"Yes, I am."

"How do you know? You've never beat me."

"I let you win."

"We'll see about that."

Chris's memory jumps ahead. He sits in Clara's office, telling her about the encounter with his father's soldier. Chris outlines the verbal agreement made between him and Justin.

Clara says, "This won't last for long. I don't believe Justin will keep his mouth shut."

"Well, once he opens it, I'll have to step down."

"I know."

"I'll keep you updated on any other activity."

"So did you find out if Justin is faster than you?"

"Yes. He's faster. But he said if I'd deny his involvement with the Death Clan, he'd let me keep my spot."

"The two of you raced?"

"Yeah. The problem is, I was considering stepping down from the lead position, but now I can't or he'll take the lead. As long as I stay put, he'll be forced to hold back."

"How long have you been thinking of stepping down?"

"Not long. My parents are divorcing and I know my mother could use my help getting the house in order."

"Oh, I'm sorry to hear that."

"It has been a long time coming. She'll be happier, I think. It got me thinking. What's the point to life? I mean, as a person with powers I don't have an optimistic future. If two normal people can't make a marriage work, what chance do I have?"

"These are heavy thoughts you're having. Marrying someone with powers would be a wise choice for you, but it doesn't guarantee a successful marriage. Relationships are tricky under the best circumstances."

"I just need to know if there's any kind of future for me other than betraying my friends on a daily basis and pretending to be someone I'm not. I need to know if I have love and companionship in my future."

"Have you asked Donald for a reading?"

"Yeah, he told me to have a reading done by the Seer Maetha."

"Then I guess that's what you should do.

The scene in Chris's mind jumps to a quiet grassy area in a park. Chris sits at a picnic table with his elbows on the tabletop. Maetha sits across from him.

Maetha says, "Finding love weighs heavy on your mind."

"I only want to know if my life's path has any purpose. Is there anyone out there for me?"

"Give me your hand," she extends her arm across the

table, with her hand open. "I will show you the vision I've had concerning your future."

Chris takes her hand and closes his eyes. His mind fills with the image of a room, like a hospital room, a bed upon which he is lying with two broken legs.

I recognize the vision because I saw the same one when I looked into his mind following the Death Clan's destruction. Chris had said Maetha had given him the vision. I hadn't realized just how significant this event was for him until this moment as I experience his emotions in connection to what he's seeing.

Chris views this vision as meaning he and the girl, whom he recognizes and calls "Calli", are destined to be together. He assumes this event won't happen for a few years because he sees himself as being older in the vision.

As I experience Chris's pure joy through his memories, I begin to understand his seemingly unfounded deep attachment to me shortly after I read his mind at Cave Falls. I hadn't comprehended his emotions before. I mean, how could someone have that kind of certainty about someone else? Now I understand.

I'm momentarily focusing on my own questions, but Chris's memories come back into focus. Realizing he has a destined love, a Healer, who will enter his life down the road, helps him decide to quit his role as a spy. He truly feels like a new person. He vows that as soon as he can, he will begin to clean up his act and reorganize his life. He wants to be ready for the day his Healer walks into his life. He doesn't want to be a closed box or a secret-keeper any longer.

Chris returns to the Runners' compound with renewed energy and learns about a new delivery assignment. A time trial is held, and Kayla Cooper times as the slowest. Chris is slightly bothered by this because he knows Kayla has a crush on him. He adds another girl to the trio, Jessica Harper, as the third member. During the process of completing the delivery, which requires him to hold Kayla's hand to give her speed, Chris senses that Kayla is reading more into the situation than she should. He admits to the two girls that he has been shown a vision of his soulmate. He tells them his heart belongs to his mystery girl. Kayla begins holding hands with Jessica to extract her running power instead of his, appearing rejected.

This particular memory of Chris's sheds more light on events I witnessed while at the compound. It also marks the first time he labeled me as his soulmate. In his mind, the girl named Calli, whom he'd never met, gave his life meaning, purpose, and hope.

When Chris returns to the compound after completing the delivery, Clara pulls him aside and asks him to go investigate the possible disappearance of another delivery trio. A different delivery request had come in the day after Chris, Jessica, and Kayla left the compound on their task. A new group had been selected to run the delivery, only they hadn't arrived yet at the delivery destination. Clara can't help him with the search because she needs to go pick up a new Runner in Ohio.

Chris calls his father first to ask if he is responsible for the missing Runners. When his father assures him he's not involved, Chris heads out and hires a Hunter to help him search. All the while, he stews over the fact Justin hadn't timed as the fastest Runner of the missing trio. Dirk Evans had. The fastest should have been Justin—unless Justin knew ahead of time the trio would be compromised. Chris wonders if it would be so bad to simply expose Justin as a traitor and, in doing so, eliminate his own position with the clan.

Chris arrives at the compound and heads straight to

Clara's office. He catches sight of Justin just before he knocks on the door. Justin has a concerned look on his face. Chris runs his pointer finger across his neck to indicate to Justin he is about to go down, and then knocks on the door.

Clara invites him to come in. Chris enters, noting someone is in her office with her, so he speaks a bit cryptically, to keep from giving away too much information. When Clara tells him the Healers are also missing three members, Chris looks over at the girl sitting on the couch. She looks like she is about to pass out.

I must admit, it is truly amazing to see my younger self through Chris's eyes.

In his mind, he shouts, *What? Calli Courtnae! No, it can't be. She's so young! She's fragile looking.* Chris swiftly scans my face and body. I don't look like the woman he saw in his vision—the woman I would one day become. I wear no makeup to enhance my green eyes, and nothing is noteworthy about my short hair, but I have an iridescent glow that is impossible to look away from. The question comes into his mind, which he then asks Clara: "Why did the Healers send her to deliver the news?"

"Calli is not a Healer. She's a Runner. This is her orientation."

He is almost brought to his knees by the wave of shock, confusion, anger, and disappointment that washes over him. His mind protests, *A Runner? No! She's not a Runner! Calli is supposed to be a Healer!* He struggles to maintain his composure and asks Clara to step out into the hallway. He tries to tell her he knows for certain the girl on her couch is a Healer, but Clara won't listen to him. He looks at me through the window—the timid, frail girl who is supposed to be his destined love, the one who will set his life's path in order—and turns away from Clara and goes to his room.

I experience his feelings through his memories. Chris feels betrayed. His hopes and dreams have crashed in a single moment. Why would the Seer Maetha show him a vision that isn't true? Is it possible there are two different Calli Courtnaes? No, he recognized my high-set cheekbones and green eyes. He knows I am *his Calli,* but will I be his at all? The vision clearly showed me as a Healer who will repair his injured legs. A Runner won't be able to do that. *And no one possesses multiple powers. That is impossible.*

Chris still needs to deal with Justin, continue his investigation into the missing Runners and, he determines, avoid crossing my path. He reasons he doesn't have time to wallow around in his own private misery.

His memories prior to beginning the delivery assignment reveal he looks my way a lot more often than I'd realized. He discusses my presence with a few of the other boys, calling it unusual. He also discusses his vision with Mr. Rheyes, the clan's Seer, who recommends he take me along on the delivery team to keep an eye on me.

Chris fully intends to bring me on the assignment. He doesn't, however, figure I'll be coming along as the slowest and a member of the trio. I find that interesting, just as I found it perplexing that he'd already written and crossed off my name from his list when I saw it in Clara's office.

Once we begin the assignment, my own memory of entering Mr. Bates's office included seeing Maetha the secretary. Chris's memory shows someone entirely different. To his eyes, the secretary is a twenty-something cute girl. I recognize the fact that Maetha used her power to change her appearance in his eyes. I figure she would have looked the same to Justin too, because he knew her as Maetha, the same as Chris—a fact I would later learn.

I am the only one who saw her in her actual form.

Chapter 3 - The Other Side of the Story

Chris's memory jerks forward to the moment in the cave when I stand behind the waterfalls, right after I'd read his mind and discovered how he really felt about me. The cat is out of the bag, so to speak. He knows pretending to be upset with me won't fly any longer, now that I know his desires. His larger concern is that I might discover the darker secrets contained within his mind—the part of his life he'd hoped to clean up before ever meeting me.

His memory jumps to the moment when I display the Healing power by recognizing the cancer inside Jonas. *She's a Healer!* Chris rejoices, feeling as though his vision might actually come true. He thinks perhaps he'd misinterpreted the vision, not identifying that I'll also have other powers when I will heal his legs. He's overjoyed and desperately wants to kiss me. He thinks about it, but then vetoes the notion and takes a step back to put some distance between us before he oversteps his bounds.

I remember the moment well.

Everything changes within his mind whenever he looks at me. Even though I am only sixteen years old—at this point in his memories—my mind and soul are incredibly attractive to him. He is held back by my age, though. The law declares me off limits.

The rest of the delivery journey flies by in his mind, coming to rest at the moment the Death Clan leader accuses me of carrying the real diamond. The old man says it is the reason I have powers . . . my powers come from a rock. A chunk of carbon. Chris's heart, which had been beating furiously in anticipation of being chosen for death, now explodes with complete disillusionment. *Calli isn't even a person with powers. She's just a regular human,* he thinks.

Yet, he still holds on to the vision. He clings desperately to the idea he has something to live for . . . someone to share his life with.

The scene shifts to the clearing. Seeing my dead body through his eyes is almost too much to take in. When I'd viewed the destruction of the Death Clan through Clara's eyes, and then again through the mind-extraction of Mr. Stuart, I'd watched Chris's actions from a third person point of view. However, looking through the window of Chris's mind, coupled with his intense emotional meltdown, I gain new respect for what he's been put through.

In his memory, someone places a comforting hand on his shoulder after the Healers take my body to the tent. He turns and finds Maetha. He yells at her, "Why did you lie to me? You showed me a girl who was supposed to be a Healer, but she's human. She was supposed to be my destiny, but now she's dead!" His emotions are uncontrollable. For a moment, he just lets them flow.

"Chris," Maetha says calmingly, "visions of the future cannot be fabricated. Take heart," Maetha walks away and collects the diamond shards that lay smoldering in the grass. Then she follows the Healers into their tent.

Chris sits down on the grass, surrounded by mounds of dust piles that used to be human beings. He contemplates on what Maetha just told him and comes to the conclusion she had played with his mind before, and he's not going to let her do it again.

Before long, a Healer comes and tells Chris they have revived me.

Chris jumps to his feet and rushes to the tent. My

body lies peacefully, my breathing causes my chest to rise up and down, even though blood covers my body. He places his hand gently on my head, and as tears escape his eyes, he bends down and kisses my forehead. "I'm so sorry," he says. Even though he knows I have no cosmic power, he still has feelings for me—even stronger now that I've sacrificed my own life to save his. Then he turns and leaves the tent.

His memory shows he doesn't leave the clearing at that moment. First he helps with the repairs on the tents to prevent any Demon attacks. After a couple of hours, Maetha addresses the crowd. Her words of explanation don't give him any comfort. She reveals she is a Spell-caster, not a Seer. Those words are the only thing that makes sense in Chris's mind. She talks about the will of nature and how nature always balances itself when choices are stripped away from other beings. The Death Clan had defied nature, she explains, and the course of events that led to this moment had been orchestrated by nature. Her basic message is: If you mess around with nature, it will come back to bite you in the butt.

The crazy twisted turn of events leaves Chris feeling devastated. However he's encouraged that I will be walking around on the surface of the same world as he is . . . even if it's as a regular human.

He sets out on his own for the compound. Once I arrive with Clara, he avoids me. Not because he doesn't want to see me, but because he is still trying to figure everything out. The next morning he watches from a distance as I leave.

His memories jump to a conversation with Clara as she got back from taking me to the airport. Clara tries to explain what Maetha told her about me. Chris doesn't really care to hear what he considers are more lame excuses and explanations, especially from Maetha. His focus is on forcing Justin's departure from the clan.

Soon after, Chris calls a staff meeting in Clara's office.

Chris announces to the group of adults: "I'm resigning from the clan."

Clara is the first to speak. "I'm not surprised, after everything you've been through. We'll need to hold another timed race to see who is the fastest."

"That's why I'm announcing this to everyone. The fastest Runner is Justin Macintyre. He's responsible for the deaths of Michael and Jessica, and the kidnapping of Dirk, John, and Macey. He has been communicating with the Death Clan all along. He cannot be allowed to remain with the clan. I'm formally asking that he be kicked out."

Mr. Evans speaks: "We should bring Justin in to defend himself. These are serious charges, Chris."

"Bring him in." Chris motions toward the door.

A few minutes go by while waiting for Justin to be located, during which Clara updates the staff concerning Michael's and Jessica's families' requests for their things to be boxed up and shipped.

Justin enters the room, his energy standoffish. "So, were going to do this now, Chris?"

"Yeah. It's time. I've requested you be removed from the clan."

"Fine!" Justin steps forward, closer to the center of the group. "If you're going to kick me out for spying, then you have to kick him out as well." He points to Chris. "He's a government spy, working for his daddy."

Mr. Evans asks, "Is this true, Chris?"

Viewing Chris's memories, I realize the only people who ever knew Chris was a spy were Clara Winter, Stan Schlater, who identified the secret in Chris's mind, Donald Rheyes the Seer, and the clan's Healer, Frank Kinsington, and Justin. The staff members had no idea.

"Yes," Chris admits. "I've been giving careful information to my father at his request."

Justin's voice rises with emotion. "His dishonesty is far worse than mine. Now that the Death Clan is dead—"

Chris stands in anger. "You think your slate is wiped clean because you have no one to report to now? Two of our Runners are dead because of you. Three were held captive because you didn't speak up and alert Clara. Don't even get me started on the fact you left a scent trail for Hunters to follow us."

"Oh yeah" —Justin cuts into Chris's rant— "and a new Runner was taken captive because you were too busy meeting with your father to pick him up on time."

"Is that true?" Ms. Coleman asks Chris.

Chris's head hangs low. "Yes."

"See," Justin exclaims, "I'm not the only one with dirt on my hands. The difference is his contacts are always going to be seeking us out."

Chris says, "That's why I just resigned from the clan, Justin."

The clan's Seer, Donald Rheyes, addresses the group. "Whatever information Chris has fed to his father, it hasn't led to an invasion of our compound. As for the capture of a Runner because Chris was too slow with the pickup, many newly emerged Runners have been captured because someone was too slow. It's always a tragedy."

Justin grunts his disbelief. "You're actually defending Chris? He's putting everyone's life at risk and you're defending him?"

Chris asks Justin, "What were you passing along to the Death Clan?"

"What does it matter? They're dead."

Stan Schlater announces: "He was trying to join their

group. He'd been told if he'd safely deliver the upcoming package, he'd be allowed into the group. I read it in his mind prior to the assignment."

Clara says, "I believe it can be assumed Justin would have joined the Death Clan and would have willingly helped them murder many people with powers, including Runners. I don't need to be a Seer to figure that out. I vote in favor of Justin Macintyre's expulsion from the clan."

One by one, hands rise in the air in support of Clara's motion.

In a dramatic fashion, issuing insults and profanities, Justin storms out of the office and leaves the compound with his belongings.

Chris leaves the compound soon after and slowly makes his way across the country to Washington D.C. He uses the Hunter's tent he acquired from the diamond delivery to protect himself from the Demons.

General Harding, isn't happy with Chris's decision to quit, to say the least. "I won't allow you to quit. I didn't raise a quitter!" General Harding pounds his fists on his desktop.

Chris stands tall and says, "I won't allow you to control my life any longer. I have resigned from the clan, and I'm resigning from you."

"Chris, the security of the nation is in jeopardy, and you're turning your back on everything. How can you live with yourself?"

"Actually, I'll be much happier, believe me." Chris turns to leave without being dismissed.

"Get back here, young man!" General Harding yells. "I could have you hunted down and charged with treason."

"No you can't, *dad*. I never signed up for this. I only went along with this charade to make you happy. Clearly nothing can accomplish that." Chris keeps walking out the door and out of his father's life.

Naturally, Chris doesn't feel safe at all. He travels by foot for several weeks until he feels brave enough to visit his mother in Kansas. She reassures him his father isn't going to come arrest him, so Chris reluctantly settles in and relaxes. He helps his mother with much-needed repairs on the house, and landscaping that has gone downhill since his parents' divorce. His mother also farms him out to some of the other neighbors who need fences repaired, houses painted, and general upkeep. One painting job is for Jo Jo.

The whole time Chris works in Jo Jo's yard, he feels at peace. Whenever he leaves her house, thoughts of me, the journey we'd been on, the vision Maetha had given him, and the intel he had given his father over the years replays disturbingly in his head. Mysteriously, Jo Jo's home is the only place his mind can rest.

One day, Chris's friend Dan stops by as Chris is finishing up mowing Jo Jo's lawn.

"Hey, Chris. What are you doing tonight?"

"Nothing much. Why?"

"Well, a couple of us are going out and I thought you might like to come."

"Are you trying to set me up again?"

Dan chuckles. "What? Why would you think that?"

"Uh, I don't know, because the last three 'hang outs' have included a single girl."

"Come on, what's the harm in me wanting you to have some fun?"

"No harm in wanting to have fun, Dan. But what if I don't want to date anyone?"

"I didn't say date. I said have fun."

"Look, I've got a lot on my mind. I could come and just enjoy the company, but the girl you've lined up for me is just going to be depressed that I don't show interest in her."

Dan smiles and says, "You wouldn't be hurting anyone's feelings."

"Where are you going?"

"Same place as last time: Fat Jack's. They have good buffalo wings."

"All right. I'll meet you there at seven o'clock."

"I can pick you up."

"No, I'll drive."

"You're a picky guy, you know that?"

Chris doesn't respond and watches Dan leave. In Chris's mind, he thinks about his strategic method of avoiding the Shadow Demons. If he arrives at Fat Jack's Wings early enough, he can get a parking spot closest to the building, right under the street lamp, so when he leaves after dark, he'll be properly illuminated.

The memory switches to the dimly lit interior of a sports-bar-type restaurant. The female sitting across from Chris is beautiful and friendly. Dan and his date, along with two other couples, talk about the recent basketball games and debate over which team will take the championships.

Chris makes small talk with the female named Sally, but because her name rhymes with mine, Chris's mind is plagued with memories he'd just as soon forget. The future version of me he'd seen in Maetha's vision no longer surfaces first in his mind. Instead, my recent face enters his mind, as I had hovered above him while I evaporated the extra moisture from his lungs along the river bank. Then comes the image of me walking toward the motel after I'd saved my group from the Hunters. He had watched me approach his door, noting the stress lines on my face, feeling helpless for not being able to comfort me because I might slip through the walls in his mind again and discover his secrets. Finally, his memories recall how he felt while he was held back by other team members while I lay on the stone alter. He relives the moment my voice entered his mind, letting him know I wasn't a person with powers, that I wasn't his Healer. This tore him apart . . . but no more so than when he rushed to my broken bloody body.

He thinks how Sally, although beautiful and kind, won't ever be able to be important in his life. She doesn't have a cosmic ability. She doesn't know about Runners, then again, he thinks, neither does Dan.

Clara had advised Chris to be careful who he chose to marry. In his thoughts, while staring at Sally across the table, Chris decides it is time to return to the Runner's compound. Not to run assignments, but to hopefully gain employment and join the staff. If nothing else, he needs to be involved with the world of powers in the rare event the vision of us might come true. Maybe, he thinks, he'll hear something about me through the grapevine.

His memories launch forward to the point when the amulet wearers begin disappearing one by one. Chris had been employed as head of security for the compound for the last two years, so unsurprisingly, he puts himself in charge of protecting Clara and the amulet. He assigns Beth Hammond and a team of her choosing to go investigate the disappearance of the other amulet wearers.

Beth brings word that Clara has been asked to attend a meeting of the clans to discuss the disappearance of the amulet wearers: Curtis Schultz and Charles Rhondell. Chris, Beth, and Clara figure the meeting might be a trick to lure the Runner's amulet wearer out of the compound. They design a plan which includes Clara relinquishing the amulet to Chris. He'll remain in the safety of the compound while Clara attends the meeting.

Once Chris accepts the powerful piece of diamond, he takes in a deep breath as the strange sensations flood through his body.

Clara says, "Amazing, isn't it?"

Chris nods. "I guess this is what Calli felt like when she carried the stone."

"Use the powers with nature's will in mind, Chris."

"You don't have to remind me. Hurry back and good luck."

As soon as Clara and Beth leave the office, Chris sits down in Clara's chair and tries to look for the future concerning me. Not knowing what he's doing in the slightest, he's not able to pull up anything more than a thick blackness. He looks out the window and tries to read the future of the first person he sees. A thirteen-year-old girl named Sage, new to the clan, will one day become the fastest in the clan. Chris searches Sage's mind for her thoughts. Before he's able to detect anything, an intense flowery smell hits his nose. He is able to discern the scent belongs to Sage. He reads her mind and finds she isn't feeling well. He feels her stomachache and experiences her worry. Chris acts with compassion and sends healing energy to Sage, calming her upset stomach.

Chris turns away from the window, feeling satisfied he helped Sage. *If only I could see the future concerning Calli,* he thinks. As he sits in heavy contemplation, he begins to understand how difficult it must have been for me to detect Jonas's cancer yet not be able to fix him.

Chris carries out the duties of running the clan for the rest of the day. He posts two guards outside the door, positioning more at all exterior doors. He's careful not to leave the safety of the office for any length of time. By the end of the day, he's feeling quite secure in his position, having met with several clan members needing his "diamond" assistance.

The next morning, Chris resumes his tasks in Clara's

office. A phone call from Clara reveals the meeting she attended wasn't suspicious in any way. She recommends he be on high alert.

"Thanks, Clara. I'm on it." He ends his call and hangs up the phone.

The office door opens and a young lady walks into the room. Her dark brown hair is pulled back into a tight ponytail, and she wears a blue jogging suit. Viewing the moment in his memory, I recognized the female as Deus Ex.

"Can I help you?" Chris asks.

Deus raises the gun she's carrying, causing Chris to jump out of his chair. His first instinct is to run, but she blocks his way. Chris assumes she is a Runner because of her quick maneuvers. He tries to get around her one more time, but she blocks him and moves close to him, pressing the end of the barrel into his chest.

She speaks in a sweet, girl-next-door kind of voice. "Chris, if you fight me, Calli will die."

Her words stab into his frozen heart. How does she know his name? The bigger question is how did she know to use Calli as a means of getting him to cooperate? The only person with motives dark enough—and a keen awareness of his weaknesses—is Justin Macintyre. Chris assumes he must be the one working with this girl.

Chris raises his hands to show he will be compliant. He asks, "Where's Calli? Is she safe?"

"You'll just have to come with me and find out for yourself."

"If anything has happened to her, I won't give you this amulet."

Deus Ex's mouth forms a pleasant smile. Her mannerisms seem like she could be a perfect honor student or student-body president . . . well, except for the gun she has pressed against Chris's chest. She doesn't look or act the part of kidnapper. I guess this is how she was able to get past the guards outside.

She takes Chris's arm and pulls him to the door. "Ok, loverboy. Here's how we're going to do this. Down the road about a mile is a parked van. The driver is expecting me in about five minutes. If I don't show up with you, the driver will leave and Calli will be killed. Do you follow?"

"Yes."

"I'm going to put my gun away because I know you understand that fighting me will only result in death for your cutie-pie." Deus lifts her jogging jacket to reveal a holster. She secures her gun and readjusts her clothing. "You will do as I say, move when I move, and you'll keep your mouth shut as we leave the building. Got it?"

Chris nods with a scowl.

Deus opens the door. The two guards are nowhere to be found. Deus says, "Let's go."

Deus performs a series of stop-and-go movements down the hall and out into the foyer. It reminds me of the child's game of Red Light Green Light. She opens the door and efficiently disables the two guards in what appears to be a choreographed brutal dance. Then she takes hold of Chris's hand and says, "Run with me down the road."

Chris does as ordered and they speed across the compound property and into the trees. True to her word, he spots the van about a mile down the road. They stop and she opens the window-less sliding door.

"Get in!"

Chris catches a glimpse of the male driver as he lowers his head and steps up into the empty van, just before he's assaulted by Deus. She slams a crowbar into his right knee, debilitating him instantly. Chris instinctually grabs his knee and howls in pain. He looks up in time to see another swing coming his way, hitting his other leg, cracking his shin.

I feel the horrific pain Chris experiences. In my current state, my stomach flips over and over to the point that I have to pause and use my healing powers on myself before reentering his memories.

Deus says to Chris in her sugary-sweet voice as she slams the sliding door closed and climbs in the front passenger seat, "Can't have you thinking you can run off before I get my payment, now can I?"

The driver turns the wheel and accelerates down the road. Chris, in incredible pain, holds both legs and lies on his side, trying not to move. The winding road and the speed at which the driver takes the curves make it impossible to not be thrown around in the back of the van. Every movement brings fresh waves of pain for Chris.

I pull out of his mind once again. I'm mortified to experience what Chris has gone through. I can't believe the level of brutality he's endured at the hands of Deus. I now fully understand the level of hatred he had toward Deus when I first met her. Yet, I'm even more confused why Chris would side with her to kill Neema after everything she's done to him.

Chris squeezes my hand, bringing my attention back. He says, "Keep going, there's more."

I reenter his memories, but choose to skip past his long painful ride to Justin's compound. The scene opens up as Justin is ordering other guys to strap Chris down on a bed. Justin holds a needle which he injects into Chris's arm.

Before Chris blacks out, he looks around the room and realizes he's in the room from his vision. He's finally in the one place he has dreamed about for years, in excruciating pain, about to pass out, but he's the happiest he's been in three years. He knows I will come walking through the door.

He awakens after hearing some commotion in the hall. The door opens and I enter his room. The beautiful, confident woman of his vision stands before him like a dream. I heal his legs and he notices I wear an amulet around my neck. Finally, everything makes sense in his mind. *Calli has the healing ability because she wears an amulet. Of course!* he thinks. I feel what he experiences, the joy flooding his body, the sweetness of my breath, and the warmth of my cheek against his. He's in heaven.

I remember feeling the same incredible happiness as well.

Later that night as we lay in each other's arms after learning I am an Unaltered with a diamond shard in my heart, he wars with his emotions. He wants to be angry, wants to be happy, and feels like everyone is against him. Hearing Maetha's name again stirs unsavory sentiments within him. She has been the source of so much misery in his life, but he can't ignore the reality that I am lying next to him wrapped in his arms. The vision Maetha had given him had come true after all.

Chris's memories speed through Justin's death, Agent Alpha's entrance into the room, Maetha's appearance out of thin air, our escape by the skin of our teeth, and the lengthy run to Indiana.

After arriving at Maetha's residence, Chris begins to put two and two together. He can see the next logical move concerning the diamond will be to insert the rest of it into my heart. When Maetha orders me to go with her, Chris grabs me. No way is he going to let me go without laying claim to my soul first. He captures my head and kisses me like there's no tomorrow—and in reality, he doesn't know if there will be a tomorrow. He wants me to know, without a doubt, that he loves me. He pulls me into a tight hug. I hear myself whisper in his ear, "It will be all right. I love you, Chris."

He watches me walk toward the door, and when I turn my head back to him and smile, he is overcome with emotion. The door closes, and he plops down on the chair and fights the sobs that want to erupt out of his throat. So much has happened in too short of a time. He finds it difficult to comprehend everything. He's saddened by the deaths of the clan leaders only a few hours before and angry that Justin was involved with Agent Alpha and his father.

Chris recalls the distressing moment when Agent Alpha called me by name. He wonders how Agent Alpha knew me. Plus Agent Alpha also recognized Maetha.

As Chris tries to sort through the mess of information within his head, he also understands I am about to receive the rest of my diamond, and he can't even be there to witness the event.

Hans Lindlbauer tries to comfort Chris by telling the story of how I helped him escape the clutches of the government not too long before. He brings Chris the box of Pulse Emitters showing him what I designed. Chris remembers me and Brand talking about them. He promptly takes one, attaches it to his jacket, and runs out the door after me.

Once out in the night air, he can't bring himself to step into the darkness. The fear of being ripped to shreds holds him back. A voice within his mind reassures him that everything will be fine. He will be safe. He closes his eyes and takes a step away from the light and into what he believes will be his demise. Nothing happens.

I pause and reflect on what Chris felt concerning the Demons. I had no idea how afraid he or any other person of powers was of the dark. Understanding his fear of

Demons prompts me to investigate them further and try to find a way to eliminate them.

As I travel back inside his memory, Chris runs through the trees toward the glowing light ahead, where a crowd encircles Maetha and me. He arrives just in time to watch Maetha slam the diamond into my chest. He waits anxiously with more fear than he thinks he can handle until he can't stand it anymore. He yells, "Help her!" and then watches Maetha reach in and remove the diamond. She attempts to remove the shard, but it won't come out without tearing vital parts of my heart. She leaves it in place and repairs my damaged body.

Chris's reality spins in all directions. This is all new territory for everyone involved, not just him. To find out there are people like Maetha, who, come to find out, isn't a Seer or Spell-caster but an all-powerful Diamond Bearer, really blows his mind. Furthermore, I am going to become a Diamond Bearer as well. Maybe not today, but someday. That one really does a number in his brain.

His memories show that after he helps me inside after the failed diamond-inserting attempt, he continues to hold me after I lose consciousness. He smoothes my long hair out of my eyes, and kisses my temple and forehead while he whispers comforting words.

Viewing this tender moment through his memory almost makes me cry.

Once the decision is made to travel to Miami to find out the black rock's identity, Chris feels like he and I can finally get the alone time he has longed for. While he drives the car and I sleep, he thinks about our futures. He hopes we can get to the bottom of everything soon so we can finally relax and develop a real relationship. He looks forward to sharing his life, his interests, his world with me. He wants to get to know me, wants to learn everything there is to know.

Then we stop at the gas station.

Of all the bad luck in the world, he has led us into a robbery in progress. When Agent Alpha appears, after the watch is closed, it becomes clear to Chris that our situation will get worse before it gets any better. He realizes this journey with me is far from over and that our future is still way out of reach.

Chris's memory jumps to the old warehouse in Miami. When he kisses me, it feels as if time stands still. He can't imagine breathing without me in his life. He's ready to throw in all his chips, jump into whatever situation is required to secure our love.

Chris's memories leap forward by a huge amount. We are on the plane ride back to Colorado from Alaska. He's thinking about his new friend, Kikee, feeling happy that we as a team were able to figure out the identity of the yellow stone of the shaman. Sitting next to Chris is Maetha who comments, "You performed well, Chris." Then his ears plug with an underwater sensation muffling the voices around him. As the pressure in his head normalizes, his clarity returns. He begins to realize what has just happened as the fog of mind-control lifts from his brain. He turns in his seat to locate me. When he sees the downturned expression on my face his recent actions weigh incredibly heavy in his gut. He knows he needs to get to the bathroom pronto before he throws up all over Maetha. But to get to the bathroom, he has to walk past me first.

After visiting the bathroom, and regaining control of his emotions, he sits near me and apologizes for his behavior. The amount of guilt flooding his system is so extreme, that I think: if guilt could be used as electricity, he could have powered Las Vegas for a year! He desperately hopes I can forgive him because he doesn't know if he can ever forgive himself. I comfort him with what he considers to be the most important words I could ever say. I tell him I can see the bigger picture and have had a vision of our grandchildren.

These words prompt Chris to reevaluate everything he learned before. He comes to the conclusion that because the initial vision Maetha gave him came true, even after all the logical aspects didn't make sense, then maybe my vision of our grandchildren might come to be as well. He knows he needs to change the direction of his mind and focus more on helping the mission, not wallowing around feeling sorry for himself.

He grasps the realization that the way he can help the most would be to return to his father. He would be able to fight for our future and the futures of our children and grandchildren from within the government facility.

His memory jumps to the point when he leaves the motel in Denver, heading back to the compound. He isn't sad or depressed: he feels invigorated. Part of his invigoration is because of the amazing kiss he's just shared with me before leaving.

He still feels good about his decision after his long drive to Montana. When he arrives at the Runner's compound to pass along Maetha's instructions to Clara to have the compound's occupants split up and spread out to prevent mass attacks, he finds several Runners are already missing. People are packing up, getting ready to move.

Chris calls his father from Montana, as Maetha had instructed, as a mislead to his whereabouts. Then he begins his trip back to Denver. When he stops for gas, he sees his neighbor Jo Jo. Chris can't believe the coincidence of running into her. *What are the odds of that happening?* he thinks.

"Chris, can I ride with you back to Denver?"

"Did your car break down?"

"No. Don't worry about that. I need to talk to you on the way to Denver."

"How did you know that's where I'm headed? Oh wait, you're a Mind Reader, aren't you?"

Jo Jo climbs in the car and waits for Chris to begin driving before she talks. "Chris, I am not a Mind Reader. I've been following you."

"Why?"

"I've been spying on your father and his studies since before you were born."

Chris's heart begins to race. "Do you work for the government too?"

"No. I knew you would become a Runner and that your power would be a difficult thing for your father to deal with. I've been your friend and confidant throughout the years because I knew you'd need support through your hardships."

"How did you know I'd be a Runner?"

"I have the ability to detect which power any one person will develop."

"What's that called? I'm not familiar with that ability."

"Pull over at the next crossroads and I'll tell you more."

Chris does as instructed and puts the car into park. "Let me guess. You don't want me to crash the car when you tell me what you're about to tell me?"

Jo Jo nods. "Chris, my name is not Jo Jo. My abilities are on a level that you've never heard of before, mainly because no regular person has ever known of these powers. Only one other person on the whole earth knows of my complete set of abilities, and that one person is Maetha. I am the one who designed the Sanguine Diamond and instructed Maetha how to use it."

"How can that be? Crimson was the one . . . holy crap! You're Crimson!" Chris stutters.

Chapter 4 - The Bigger Picture

"Don't forget to breathe, Chris," Crimson gently reminds him. "Like I said, I've been following your father's research and it's progress since before you were born. General Harding's projects have the capacity to throw the balance of nature completely off kilter. When you were born, I viewed you as someone who could be instrumental one day, someone who might be able to shut the program down from the inside. I've learned over my many years that insiders are the best choice of options to keep from drawing unwanted attention.

"Even though I considered you as a possible covert insider, I never knew you would choose to go back to your father to serve as a double agent to help the Diamond Bearers. This means you are ready to do what must be done for the sake of humanity. You've proven yourself in my eyes with this single decision."

Chris is at a loss for words. "I don't know what to say. Calli said she saw a vision of our grandchildren and I just want to make sure I do everything I possibly can to have that vision come true. You do know Calli, right?"

"Yes. Chris, you are making a selfless choice. You were never expected to do this. I didn't befriend you to someday get you to risk your life. Your own loyalties and compassion have brought you to this point, and I couldn't be more proud." She smiles with a twinkle of moisture in the corners of her eyes. "Okay, let's get going. We've got a dire situation ahead of us."

Chris directs the car back onto the road. He says, "I can't believe I've had lemonade and cookies with the oldest woman on the earth! This is so cool!"

"I've been closely involved with many individuals over their lifetimes, none of whom ever learned my secret. Then again, none of them ever made the choice you made: to do whatever it takes to support nature's will."

Crimson continues to talk to Chris about the importance of disabling and dismantling the program that could end life as we know it. She gives him instructions and recommendations of what to say to his father so he will agree to let Chris back inside the compound. The most important instruction she gives him is to maintain his position within the facility at all costs.

The details and the revelations brought to his attention through Crimson open his eyes and help him see the bigger picture in a hi-def, wide-screen format kind of way.

Chris's memory jumps forward. He stands facing his father, trying to convince him he is done with being on the wrong side. Agent Alpha stands beside General Harding. Chris says, "I've learned things in the last three years about the most powerful people with powers that I believe you would be interested in hearing. After spending time with them, I've decided you weren't off your rocker at all, dad, er, sir. They need to be eliminated."

"Good to hear you're seeing the reality of our situation, Chris. I can't ignore the fact you walked out on me, though. How can I trust you?"

"I don't expect you to trust me. I only hope you'll give me a chance to get even with them. One lady in particular, named Maetha, really messed with my mind and I'd love to see her go down."

"Are you still in good standing with their group?"

"Yes. I was asked by Maetha to come and try to gather

information for them."

It's obvious to Chris that Freedom doesn't want him back in the compound. Once he gets Chris alone, he says "I have to wonder what you've been told about me concerning the little mishap with the diamond and your friend, Justin. I also have to wonder if you'll cause me any problems while you're here."

Chris maintains his determined facial expression and says, "I'm sick and tired of Maetha and the games she plays. I want to be on the winning team." His scalp begins to tickle as if a small individual strands of hair are being gently tugged. He resists the urge to itch his head, knowing Freedom is reading his mind. Chris uses his pent-up anger toward Maetha to occupy his thoughts. I recognize his actions as a way to try to fool Freedom's mind read.

"You'll have to prove it. Prove to your father, and to me, where your devotions lie."

Chris is taken to an observation room and shown the horrific experiments being performed on people with powers. In viewing Chris's memories, I have to wonder if Freedom facilitated the horror show in an effort to get Chris to crack. Even though the demonstrations are extremely atrocious, Chris maintains his unwavering guise.

His resolution is put to the test when his father orders him to bring me to the compound. Chris knows it is a test, but he doesn't know if he will have the strength to carry out the order. He wonders if there may be another way, recalling Crimson had said, "There's often more than one correct way to do things. Don't be afraid of being flexible."

By the time Chris arrives at the motel and is back in my presence again, his mind fights against his orders. He doesn't want to take me to the compound and expose me to the danger there. He doesn't want to be forced to watch me die.

When Jonas offers to take my place, Chris is incredibly relieved.

Once it is agreed that Chris will take Jonas instead of me, he has Brand repeat a couple of times so he can kiss me without killing me. Viewing Chris's memory in this way allows me to relive each of his repeats, and that is probably the strangest thing to see. I have no memory of each kiss, only the last one. He kisses me five different times, each kiss slightly different, but all amazingly sensual . . . and each ending with Freedom appearing nearby. Then Chris leaves the room and heads back to his father.

Freedom is livid that Chris brings Jonas back to the compound instead of me. He corners Chris and gives him the shakedown, meaning he literally strips him down look-ing for cameras, microphones, and other surveillance equipment. Finding nothing, he demands that Chris "pass the message along that Jonas will die by six o'clock that evening if Calli doesn't come to the compound." Freedom orders Chris to have Brand and Deus come as well. At this point, he tells Chris he is Brand's and Deus's biological father.

Chris takes the information and mouths it to the hidden camera outside the compound, imagining my face instead of a lens. Inside, he feels apprehensive. He knows Freedom is watching him closely, waiting for him to slip up.

Chris wishes he could see the future to know whether or not it will be a good move to have my group come to the compound. More than anything, he hopes we'll at least be able to secure the release of Jonas, and the four of us will be able to escape unharmed . . . and his position within the compound will remain intact.

Chris's perspective of what he views while watching the showdown between Freedom, me, Brand, Deus, and

Jonas through the observation glass allows me a different angle too. Chris feels helpless. He tries to convince his father to give the order to kill Agent Alpha. At the same time, he tries to act like he doesn't care about me. The course of events concerning what happens to Freedom is similar to when Justin died . . . a quick, well-executed, acrobatic positioning of Freedom's body in front of the bullet General Harding orders his guard, Max Corvus, to shoot. Chris recognizes the signs that indicate Brand repeated with Freedom to get him in that position. Nothing else could bring about the same stupefied expression, Chris thinks. Chris assumes he probably had the same expression when Brand repeated with him the first time, only he almost crashed the car he was driving.

Chris has to act like he doesn't care who lives or dies. His friend Jonas lies bleeding to death on the floor. I stare at him through the glass, speak to his mind, and basically tell him I am about to shove Freedom's diamond into my chest. Chris is terrified and figures I will end up like Jonas.

The blinding light caused by the explosion of the diamond entering my chest makes Chris and his father raise their arms to shield their faces. When Chris lowers his arm, he sees me on my knees, hunched over, with blood covering my body . . . but I'm still alive.

Relief inundates his body as it becomes apparent I am healing.

General Harding freaks out, swears, and shouts all kinds of exclamations because of the unbelievable events he has witnessed. They both watch me heal Jonas's chest.

"I want those . . . whatever they are!" his father says, less a request than a demand.

My own memory fills in the blanks of our escape because Chris's memories end when Brand lands one of his trademark precise kicks to the groin that incapacitates him.

From a girl's perspective, this is a first-hand experience of unparalleled pain, pressure, nausea, and discomfort like I have never felt before—and one I will never forget. The experience leaves me wondering why nature has left the male's most vulnerable parts hanging in the open.

By late evening, Deus Ex arrives at the gate, wanting to be let inside. General Harding accompanies Chris outside to speak with her.

General Harding says, "Why would I want to risk my own neck by allowing you inside this complex after watching you help the enemy today?"

"They lied to me. No one told me about the diamond Calli carried, or that Agent Alpha possessed one inside his body. You'd do yourself a favor by allowing me back into your compound because I know how many other diamonds are out there and I can help you get your hands on them."

General Harding turns and glares at Chris. "What is she talking about, Chris? Are there more than two of those diamonds?"

"He's not going to tell you anything, General. He's working for them."

General Harding's head whips toward Chris. "Is that true?"

"I was, but not anymore. Maetha lied to me too."

General Harding stares at Chris then moves his focus to Deus Ex on the other side of the gate. "I don't think I can believe either one of you."

His father is probably going to kick him out of the compound based on Deus's accusation. Crimson told him to do whatever was necessary to remain in the good graces of his father and keep his position within the facility. He takes a deep breath and says, "Give me a task, sir, and I'll prove where my loyalties lie. Let me demonstrate rather than try to convince you with words."

Deus straightens her spine and says, "Test me as well, General. I want to help you collect diamonds, and you have the weaponry needed to accomplish the mission."

General Harding contemplates for a moment and then says, "All right, the two of you must work as a team and go get me a diamond. Prove yourselves to me. Confirm to me, Chris, that you're not a double agent, and Deus, earn your right to work by my side."

Deus bows her head. "Thank you, General, sir. I have a plan already." She presents the plan, including a back-up plan of a mock kidnapping which, she explains, will give them another opportunity to secure a diamond if the first plan fails.

Chris is shocked that she has already pre-planned to this extent.

I recognize, however, that she must have repeated many times until she found the plan the general would like. If the plan is successful, it will appear that Deus is working on her own, not for the government, and that Chris is just in the wrong place at the wrong time. General Harding approves the plan, provides Deus with the military-grade high-powered rifle she needs to blow out a heart, and sets them to their task.

Once Chris and Deus are on their way, she says to him, "I know you're trying to play both sides of the fence, Chris. You can't fool me."

"Think whatever you want."

"You'd be smart not to get in the way of me completing this mission."

"I won't get in your way," Chris responds. In his mind, he envisions what will happen when Deus Ex tries to pick up a diamond—death. His spirits are lifted slightly with the knowledge Deus will die through this task while he proves himself to his father.

Deus adds, "I want Maetha to be the one. She is the biggest threat to me. Once she's dead, I'll take her diamond and you'll return to your father and tell him I fled with the stone."

"That wasn't the plan. Besides, why would I stand by and watch you take the diamond and have all the power for yourself?"

Deus says, "If you do as I say, I won't kill you. I will use you and your knowledge of both your father's actions and those of the Diamond Bearers to complete my mission."

"Your mission? So now I'm your spy too?"

"No, you are only *my* spy. You no longer work for Maetha or your father. You will give me the intel I desire when I desire it, or I will hunt you down."

Chris banks on the fact that Deus will die in her attempt to secure a diamond, and he believes that if Maetha truly knew the reason for the sacrifice of a Diamond Bearer, she would actually volunteer to help balance nature.

The information Crimson gave Chris helps him prepare for what is about to happen. I am *not* able to access Crimson's information through Chris's memory with my extraction. What I can see is that Chris feels this is nature's will being carried out. This is Chris being able to maintain his important position within his father's compound.

His memory reveals his concentrated efforts to control his mind and actions when he arrives in Indiana and I launch myself at him, pinning him against his car with my kisses. *This is weird to feel from his point of view.* He has to stay on track, and he needs to act quickly before any Bearer picks up on his intentions. He pulls himself away from me to try to take Maetha outside, but she is unavailable. Chris's stress mounts, and he worries the plan will be exposed.

Then Neema offers to talk with him instead.

Chris's memory shows him handing the velvet box to Neema and stepping back while she is gunned down. Even though he knows her death is for a higher purpose, he still struggles to keep the contents of his stomach down. Deus tells him to leave and meet at the rendezvous point, and he doesn't hesitate. He runs for about a minute before he has to stop to vomit. Then he continues to run.

Once he arrives at the parked car Deus had waiting, he lets out a shout of frustration to the sky and drops to the ground in exhaustion. Even though Crimson had basically ordered him to do what he just did, guilt takes over. At least, he figures, he will only have to wait about an hour before returning to the lake. He is anxious to explain to Maetha, and to me, that Crimson had ordered him to remain in his father's good graces and by doing what he just did, he has kept his place and eliminated Deus Ex at the same time. He knows the Diamond Bearers will view Neema's death as a necessary sacrifice, one condoned by Crimson. He hopes I will see it that way as well. He keeps reminding himself that all their futures are dependent on the success of this mission.

A half hour passes, and Deus Ex arrives at the car. Chris is devastated, and inside his head he's cursing, using every word in the book, plus a few more. *Why is she here? Why didn't she die? Was Deus actually able to pick up the diamond?* Chris wonders.

"Where's the diamond?" Chris asks.

Deus is angry. "Give me the keys, Chris!" He tosses them to her, and they get in the car and drive away.

After a few minutes, Deus says, "We're executing Plan B. I couldn't even touch the diamond. Something about being too near it caused my powers to activate and put me into a repeating loop until I withdrew my hand. So now the

Bearers can come rescue you, and this time you will pick up the diamond."

This was all for nothing! Neema's death was for nothing! Chris fears for every Bearer's life, including mine. His biggest fear is that I will be the one to come to his rescue and be killed. He begins preparing himself mentally for that probability.

Deus drives to a pre-planned destination, an old farmhouse in upstate rural Indiana. Chris is tied to a chair in the barn, where he plays the part of having been kidnapped. They will wait for the attempted rescue.

Deus and Chris wait for several hours. Finally, Deus leaves the barn to go use the little girl's room. After she has been gone thirty seconds, Crimson appears beside Chris and unties him.

"I thought she'd never leave," Crimson says.

"When did you get here? I didn't see you come in."

"I've been by your side since Neema's death. I followed your vehicle here and have been inside, sitting over on that workbench all day. Come on," she motions for him to follow her.

"Can you become invisible?"

Run! Crimson speaks to his mind.

Chris and Crimson flee the scene and run to Massachusetts, where Crimson has a car parked. They drive it to the ferry and then to Maetha's home.

Chris's memory slides to an earlier point today before Duncan and I arrived, when he and Crimson arrived at Maetha's home. Maetha told him then that I had witnessed the death of Neema and am taking it rather hard. She told him that eventually he would need to allow me to extract his memories in order to fully understand his motives, but the extraction would drain all my energy for several hours. Chris is completely taken aback to hear I witnessed the murder. He wonders how I will ever be able to see him as a good person again. Even with a mind extraction, will I be able to forgive him?

His final thought, before I pull out of his mind, is of his new conviction. He hopes I will be able to understand his side of the story and in time allow him back into my life. He will continue to fight for the will of nature whether or not I am by his side. Naturally, he hopes I will be with him, but he is prepared to continue the path he has chosen, stand his ground, and see this to the end.

I open my eyes and look at our clasped hands. I mentally let go of his, and he untangles his fingers from mine. An incredible wave of exhaustion washes over my body. Extracting his memories definitely taxes my energy levels, just as Maetha said it would. My eyes travel slowly from his hands up to his face, coming to a halt when I reach his eyes. They are full of tears on the brink of spilling over. His mind tells me he viewed all those memories as I did, so he knows everything I saw.

He speaks in a whisper, with a slight smile. "Calli, if you had read my mind when Neema died, you would have known exactly how I was feeling even though my face didn't show it." The tears overflow and run down his cheeks.

I reach up and place my hands on both sides of his face, pulling him to me. The infusion of energy from our skin-to-skin contact helps revitalize me immensely. I gently kiss his lips. He wraps his arms around me and caresses my head and back while he returns the kiss. The tender moment is one I truly didn't think would ever happen again. But now, being held and kissed by him, with a full realization of the past events, tears run down my cheeks as well. Chris moves back and gently swipes my tears to the side and then pulls me into the most comforting embrace I have ever had.

"I'm sorry I hurt you, Calli. I didn't mean to." He hugs me tighter. "I don't want to let go of you."

"Please, keep holding me." So much is racing through my mind. I'm still processing the events his mind revealed to me. I basically just saw the movie of his life along with all the reasons for his recent choices. I can't hold those choices against him. I don't want to be angry or upset with him anymore.

"I have no secrets now, and it's such a relief," he whispers into my hair. I feel his warm breath on my scalp and it sends shivers throughout my body.

Are you going to let him off the hook or not? Jonas's voice comes into my head.

I bolt upright with a sudden jerk and say, "Yes."

Chris has a surprised expression because of my quick move. "Yes?" he asks.

"Uh," I say as I stand, close my eyes, and shake my head a bit. "Yes, it is a relief." My head begins to swim with dizziness, which causes me to tilt sideways. I shuffle my feet to catch my balance.

Chris jumps up and clutches my upper arms to help me gain my footing. His thoughts wander. *The extraction drained her strength. However, she seems relieved to know the truth. Does she forgive me?*

Jonas's voice says, *Just forgive him already, Calli. Poor guy is beating himself up, and draggin' his heart through the mud isn't helping.*

Chris places his hands on my waist and asks, "What are you thinking?"

I look up into his eyes and move next to his body, placing my hand on his cheek, and whisper, "That I forgive you." He pulls me into another hug. My head fits nicely against his strong chest just under his chin, and he rests his cheek on top of my head. I try to look for our future but can't see long term. I do see we are about to leave and head to Ohio.

Good job, Calli, Jonas says to my mind.

I answer back, *Did you hear and see everything?*

Yes.

You know, it's rude to eavesdrop, Jonas.

It's no different than when you read other people's lips.

Sure it is. What if Chris and I someday . . . you know . . .

What do you mean 'what if?'

Yeah, well, you better excuse yourself from my head if that ever happens.

Mary's here trying to teach me how to control my powers. I told her about our mind link, and she said it's because of our shared diamond. She also said one of us will have to surrender our chunk so the diamond can be whole again. I just don't know when that will be.

I'll ask Maetha.

No, ask Crimson. I'm really jealous that you get to meet her in person. I wish I were there.

"Calli, are you all right?" Chris asks. I hadn't realized he is holding me at arm's length, observing my behavior as I speak to Jonas's mind. "Are you having a vision?"

I open my eyes and look up at him. "Jonas can communicate with me because we share a diamond. I told him to quit eavesdropping." I smile, reach up, and kiss Chris on the cheek. "Come on, we better get going if we're going to get to Ohio before dark."

"What?"

"Isn't that where we're going?"

"Calli, Chris," Maetha calls out. "Come back over here."

We walk hand-in-hand back to the group that has reassembled on the patio. A few other Diamond Bearers have bi-located to us: Mary, Alena, Hasan, and Fabian stand nearby.

Crimson speaks to the group in her soft, authoritative voice. "Continue to avoid the presence of obsidian. Remove yourself if you detect it in your near future. Preserve the lives of people with powers whenever you can and as discreetly as possible. I will accompany Calli and Chris on their journey."

Hasan offers, "I'm not far away, I could join in."

"No, it's not necessary. The deeds that have to be done can only be accomplished by these two. This is what we've been preparing for. This is what they've been prepared for."

What? I wonder.

Jonas speaks to my mind. *Calli, don't you realize? She's been preparing you all this time. Your whole life has been shaped for this moment.*

Why do you know more about me than I do?

Mary told me. Don't worry. Crimson is going to tell you all about it soon enough. What an honor to have met you back when you were unaware, and to see your progress.

The group stands up from their chairs, and the bi-located Bearers disappear. Crimson says to Chris and me, "It's time. Let's go."

Chapter 5 - Primal Stone

Crimson says over her shoulder, "Keep hold of her hand, Chris. She needs to draw from your energy till hers returns. If you let go, she won't make it twenty seconds before she passes out."

"I don't plan on ever letting her go." He wraps his arm behind me and clutches my shoulder, pulling me to his side as we walk to Crimson's car.

I feel my energy levels drop slightly. I tell Chris with my mind, *We have to have skin-to-skin contact, Chris. My shirt prevents me from absorbing all of your energy. Oh, and I can hear all your thoughts, by the way . . . you know, because of the diamond.*

Skin-to-skin, I like that. He slides his hand from my shoulder to the back of my neck under my hair. He rests his hand on my bare skin and gently caresses my skin with his thumb.

Electrically charged energy courses through my body.

I wasn't sure if you were telepathic or not. Thanks for the heads-up. He winks at me.

You realize you winked at me right before leaving with Neema, too. I thought about that later, and it really made my head spin. I couldn't figure out why you would do that, and then . . . well, you know.

I knew nature's will was being carried out. Although I truly thought Deus would die.

Crimson presses the button on her key ring to unlock the doors of her four-door, eco-friendly, hybrid vehicle. I'm not surprised one bit by her choice of automobile. It fits her personality perfectly. "You two sit in the backseat," she says, pointing to the back passenger door.

We climb in and close the door. Chris effortlessly pulls me onto his lap and wraps his arms around me. He rests his lips on my forehead. My body naturally melts into his. For once, I'm free of uncertainty and doubt. I can tell he's feeling the same way, even without reading his mind. It doesn't matter whether or not Duncan is right about us being destined lovers. What I know is what I feel at the moment: peace, love, comfort, happiness, and, of course, a little lust.

Crimson climbs in the car and shuts her door. "All right you two, enough of that for now," she says. "Put on your belts."

I feel my cheeks heat up as I slide off Chris's lap and pull my seatbelt across my chest. The ten seconds it takes for me to do so without Chris's skin contact is almost more than I can handle. My vision blackens and my fingers begin to tingle.

Chris's concern speaks to my mind. *The truth came at a heavy price. Your aura is dimming.* He takes my hand in his and covers it with his other hand, restoring my energy levels. *There, that's better.*

Crimson interrupts us as she drives the car out of Maetha's driveway. "Let's clear the air here. I can hear everything you tell each other with your minds so there's no point in using mind-speak. Plus, Calli, you'll regain your strength sooner if you don't use any powers. Give it a rest."

Chris and I look at each other as if we'd been caught being naughty, and then we both smile. Chris whispers, "When you smile, your aura explodes. I love it."

My mind is on overload. For one thing, I am ecstatic to be with Chris and to know everything will be all right between us. Second, I am in the presence of *Crimson,* for goodness sake! I'm not quite sure how to act, what to say, or how to think.

Crimson responds, having obviously read my mind, "Calli, just be yourself. Think of me as Jo Jo, if that helps. I'm not a rockstar, nor am I a goddess. I'm a human, like you, who is an agent of nature's continuation."

I ask, "Do you have a Sanguine Diamond in your heart too?"

"No, I have a different stone called the Primal Stone. The power of my stone is what created the diamond you have in your heart." Crimson maneuvers her car through the streets of Martha's Vineyard as we absorb and process her words. She answers Chris's apparent thoughts. "And no, Chris, we aren't taking an airplane. If my feet are to leave the ground, it won't be under someone else's control while confined to a tin can."

"You said you've been preparing Chris and me for this mission?" I ask. "For how long?"

"It is not important how long I've been working this out. What you should be asking is: at what point did I decide to use you two, and how many others are aware of my intentions?"

"All right, answer those questions for us then," I say. She sounds just like Jo Jo, or at least the way I always imagined Jo Jo would sound. When I knew her, I couldn't hear anything. Her present matter-of-fact personality and actions are exactly as I remember.

"Calli, I have followed you just as I've followed each of Maetha's descendants who are firstborns, and I will continue to do so. When you experienced your accident in middle school, I had already determined you would be a possible candidate to become a Bearer. What I didn't expect to see at such a young age was your strength and bravery while enduring excruciating pain. The medical professionals had to hurt you to help you, yet you kept your wits and never lost your self-control. I needed a plausible excuse to enter your life officially, so I amplified your injuries, causing your hearing to be disrupted. The months that followed when we spent time together became your qualification period. Each Bearer goes through this, so I can be certain they will be effective agents of nature. I also wanted you to be able to read lips—an ability no other Bearer possesses. I prolonged your recovery until I felt you'd mastered the skill sufficiently.

"I want you to know, Calli, that none of my other Bearers possess the strength, courage, or intelligence you do. That's why you're with me at this moment and not someone else. I'm impressed with your ability to think quickly on your feet, with the fact that you ask questions, the way you have a ready acceptance of constant change, and how you have a desire to stay on top of new knowledge. Your science-oriented mind has served you well, and it will now serve humanity to its fullest."

I feel overwhelmed. I've never thought about myself and what comes naturally to me as being unique, especially in comparison to other Diamond Bearers.

Crimson drives her car onto the ferry. She parks in the only space left on the boat, and then the ferry locks up and begins moving. If I didn't know better, I'd think they had been waiting for her.

"Let's go up on the deck and wait to continue this conversation until we're back inside the car," Crimson says. "Calli, try to avoid using your powers. Instead, focus on absorbing Chris's extra energy."

We follow her instructions without question and out of respect for the possible eavesdroppers on board the ferry. Chris and I hold hands constantly, as per Crimson's orders. We stand by the railing and watch the sailboats off in the distance.

"Calli, I'm going to propose to you someday. I hope you won't be afraid to accept my little velvet box," Chris says with a twinkle in his eye.

"We'll just have to wait and see, won't we?" I tease him, but I know his fears are genuine.

"What do you think of Crimson, or um, Jo Jo?" he asks, changing the subject.

"I'm in awe, honestly. I don't know what to think . . . kind of like how you felt when you found out Jo Jo was Crimson."

"Yeah, that was a bombshell, but no more so than when I learned we've been prepared and positioned for this mission our whole lives."

I realize Duncan must have known this when he tried to convince me predestined love didn't exist. I definitely want to learn more about Duncan's life and the fact that Freedom is responsible for training the evil clan of Healers that included Duncan's wife.

Wow! Bigger picture indeed!

"Hey, where'd you go?" Chris places his hand on my cheek and pulls my gaze up to his.

"Sorry, I—"

Chris leans forward and brushes his lips across mine. A million nerve endings instinctively ignite throughout my body, and I kiss him back, not caring about the dozens of onlookers. I feel an incredible burst of energy surge through my body. Chris breaks the kiss and rests his forehead on mine. Then he pulls me into an embrace, and we both look out over the water.

No one can convince me that I don't know what love is ever again. As far as I'm concerned, Chris and I are the ideal destined lovers, especially considering the Diamond Bearers and Crimson have been working toward a common goal that utilizes Chris and me and our love for one another. Without our emotional connection for each other, the Death Clan wouldn't have crumbled . . . literally. Without our love, and the need to defend and protect it, Chris wouldn't have made the ultimate sacrifice and returned to his father's side. He wouldn't be in the prime location—in the only position possible—to bring about closure and protection for people with powers and Diamond Bearers.

The proverbial freight train slams into me with a force strong enough to take my breath away. I look up at Chris and say, "It's *you!* You are the solution!"

Before he can respond to my outburst, Crimson steps between us, breaking our contact, and says, "Not here, Calli. Wait till we're in the car."

I glance around and find many people watching us. My strength begins to wane once again, and Crimson takes my hand and places it in Chris's and walks a few steps away from us. I had definitely figured it out, or Crimson wouldn't have barged in like that. Chris's eyes find mine again. I figure he's trying to send me his thoughts, but I know better than to read them. Everything I think about in my head is an open book, and Crimson the Librarian is on duty. We'll be back in the car soon enough.

Once we are safely locked inside the car and driving off the ferry at Falmouth, Massachusetts, Crimson speaks before either Chris or I can. "How's your energy level, Calli?"

"It's getting better."

"Good." She directs her next words to Chris. "Our conversation was about when I decided to use you two. Before you were born, Chris, Merlin reported to Maetha that your father was performing experiments through government testing on pregnant women in an effort to create superhuman powers in a controlled setting. I had

Maetha set Merlin to work on using his connections in the Senate Budget Committee to hopefully get the funding pulled on the T19 project. Your father was fast becoming a bigger threat to the world's people than the Death Clan. However, both would need to be dealt with before too long."

Crimson stops the car at a crosswalk to let pedestrians cross.

She continues, "Then you were born, Chris. I detected that you would become a Runner, which would cause many problems because of the intensive work your father was involved in to eradicate people with powers. I formed a friendship and a bond with you in the hope of having increased opportunities to read your mind and determine the types of research and experiments that were being carried out in the facility once your powers emerged and your father began to study you.

"Merlin was successful getting the T19 program shut down about six years after your birth. Six years after that, when the running power emerged in you, my careful planning and preparation fell into place. Your father did exactly what I suspected he would do: study you like a lab rat. Over time, you and I developed a deep friendship, and yes, I tried to give comfort and aid whenever I could. I never liked using you to get information about your father, Chris, but it was the only way to do so without arousing suspicion.

"Maetha was tasked with giving Calli the opportunity to choose to become a Bearer. I had approved Calli already, and Maetha felt all the pieces were in place to set the plan in motion. When she told me the male Runner who would fall in love with Calli would be you, Chris, I was initially troubled, but then things progressed, I couldn't have been more pleased."

Chris interrupts, "Wait, you didn't already know I would fall in love with Calli?"

"No. I don't know everything, Chris. I was still busy observing your father, among other things. I know your life has felt out of control. Understandably so. You've always been a good boy, one that I've admired. Did you know I babysat you several times when you were an infant?"

"No."

"I did. Wonderful memories. I love holding new babies and marveling at nature's incredible ability to move the species forward." Crimson turns off the road at a gas station, parking the car at the pump. She pulls a card out of the glove compartment and hands it to the eager gas attendant, instructing him to fill the tank with premium. She continues, "Once I learned you and Calli would meet at the Runners' compound, I was astounded by the odds of that happening. I didn't arrange that, nor did Maetha."

"We were destined to be together," Chris says with confidence.

"Well, that's a matter of perspective," Crimson responds.

"What do you mean? I saw my own future, and it included Calli."

"You labeled it as destiny. Humans tend to put labels on many things even though the events we think are foreordained would have happened anyway. We are all where we are because of choices made by us, by others around us, or by those who lived before us. Seers are constantly thrown off by individuals acting spontaneously and out of character. It's how you were able to walk into one of the largest Diamond Bearer gatherings and not be detected as a possible threat. Consider this, Chris. Because you dwelled on the vision from Maetha, you made decisions that led you to the fulfillment of the vision. Calli also saw your vision and her future physical appearance. She altered her appearance during the last three years to better fit the image she had seen. But those things would have happened anyway, whether or not you two acted on them. You would have ended up at the Runners' compound in time to take possession of the amulet and be kidnapped. Calli would have grown and her looks would have matured naturally without knowing what she was supposed to look like."

I interject, "But Maetha said I had altered my looks, as if I was ahead of schedule."

"Maetha doesn't know everything, Calli."

Chris shuts his eyes and shakes his head. "This messes with my mind."

Crimson says, "I know. It's why I make it a practice not to look for the future in that way. I won't be tempted to make sure it plays out as witnessed."

"Well, if we were always going to end up together, then I call that destiny," Chris says.

"If you like. Had you not seen the vision of Calli, you wouldn't be referring to meeting her as 'destiny.' Think about that." Crimson accepts the receipt from the gas attendant, starts the car, and pulls out into traffic again. She continues, "Chris, you've always been my pet since you were born and I held you in my arms. Our relationship was one that allowed further insight into the workings of your father's compound. I didn't realize I could use you until you made the decision in your own mind to return to your father and become an informant for the Diamond Bearers. You displayed the will to serve nature *at that moment*. You decided that relieving or preventing the suffering of others was more important than even your own life. That kind of decision can't be forced upon any person, and not many in the history of the world have actually made that kind of monumental choice. When you made that choice, I decided to open your mind further and allow you to make an even bigger choice: whether or not to work with me. When you participated in the removal of Neema's stone, you proved yourself to me fully."

I try to rationalize in my mind exactly what she is saying. It sounds as if she is putting Chris on the same level as the other Diamond Bearers. Also, I can't decide if I like the way she refers to Neema being gunned down as simply "the removal of her stone."

Crimson addresses my thoughts aloud. "Calli, when a Diamond Bearer accepts one of my diamonds, they are accepting my rules."

"I guess I didn't get the memo."

"You accept nature's will, don't you?"

"Yes."

"You've learned the rules and acceptable behaviors of Healers according to the will of nature, and I've watched you exercise the rules with wisdom. You accept my rules."

"Your rules? So what are you? Mother Nature?" I joke.

"Sure, if you want to label me as such. The Primal Stone gave me the ultimate power to shape mankind. I've followed the patterns that occur in the world around us and tailored my rules accordingly. People who use their power against others and cause suffering are done away with, one way or another. The Sanguine Diamond was created to facilitate that purpose, and Neema knowingly went against my rules. She knew her time as a Bearer would be cut short. She just didn't know when I would remove her diamond."

"She went against your rules?"

"Yes. The Sanguine Diamond was created to help humanity progress and to prevent people with extreme power from annihilating the human race. For the most part, we've succeeded. Although there was that hiccup of the Dark Ages."

"What do you mean?" Chris asks.

"My Bearers were put in place to make sure humanity continued onward and upward—not to determine the legitimacy of religions. The Dark Ages represented a time where humanity floundered with little progress. The Crusades brought about many deaths, but they weren't something I felt we should get involved with. Understand that I am all about choices, and people have their right to choose what they believe and have faith in. But the world slipped into a pattern of oppression and an absence of progress, and religion seemed to be the cause. Some of the Bearers began to get involved, but that only brought about the Inquisition and witch-hunts.

"Religious and spiritual beliefs have existed through-out the history of humanity. Long ago, people with extreme power wanted total dominion and, ultimately, control over other people. They formed beliefs and superstitions and used guilt and fear to acquire wealth and power from the people, all with the promise of happiness after death."

Chris interjects, "You really don't like organized religion, do you?"

"On the contrary, everyone should feel hope in life, and if believing a certain way brings hope, then I don't have anything against that. The Dark Ages weren't about bringing hope into others' lives. They were about controlling the masses by restricting critical thinking and questioning. An open mind will use questioning and evaluation to ascertain a new direction of thought. Through inquisitive minds, progress is made.

"Only 380 years ago, Galileo Galilei was sentenced to

house arrest by his religion for heresy because of his research. He expanded on existing research and challenged the idea of a geocentric, rather than heliocentric, solar system. The belief of the day was that our planet was the center of the solar system, with everything revolving around it. Using his telescope, Galileo proved we revolve around the sun. Maetha had the idea to get involved after Galileo was punished for standing by his scientific findings. She brought the case to my attention, pointing out that humanity's growth had stalled. So I gave my permission to the Bearers to help individuals with scientifically-oriented minds.

"I assigned a handful of Diamond Bearers to search the future for advancements and technological break-throughs and then to guard and protect the inventors and scientists and their important family members and friends—anyone who would help bring about those breakthroughs. Whether it was a nephew, a spouse, or a maid, if a person had influence over the inventor, they were guarded. By ensuring survival of those who would bring about advancements to mankind, the Age of En-lightenment was born. This gives you an idea of just how much a forced belief system can cause progress to stagnate, because once the Diamond Bearers began preserving progress, great changes resulted. Especially in the last 200 years."

Chris speaks up. "Doesn't it go against nature . . . er, your rules . . . to keep people from dying? I mean, if your Bearers go around saving important people so some invention can be invented, isn't that controlling nature? Isn't that like playing God?"

"No one is kept alive longer than their natural life span. Also, to imply that I'm playing God is an undefined accusation. Whose god are you talking about, Chris? You don't live as long as I have without understanding that each region of the world has different ideas of what an all-powerful deity or deities means to them. When Bearers get involved with an individual for the sake of humanity's progress and are spotted or detected by others who see us as mysterious or unexplainable, it actually helps religious believers have hope and security. I see no harm in humanity labeling those events as anything else."

I jump in. "Yeah, but some would argue against that kind of thinking by saying organized religions bring about more death and suffering. Basing your beliefs on something unexplainable only furthers your faith in a potentially negative way. Don't you think? Think about all the religious extremists."

Crimson continues her mini-lecture. "Unexplainable incidents are going to happen whether a Diamond Bearer is the cause or not. People cling to the hope of the unknown. It has always been that way. The only thing that truly scares people is the unknown, and death is the biggest unknown of all. When someone comes forward with 'knowledge' or a 'faith-promoting' story of what happens when you die, people come running like moths to a porch light."

Chris asks, "So what *does* happen when you die?"

I look anxiously at the back of Crimson's head for the answer as if she is the brightest light and I am a light-starved moth.

She responds without missing a beat. "I don't know. I haven't died yet." Crimson smiles in the rearview mirror. "The Age of Enlightenment has allowed for—in most parts of the world—the freedom to investigate, explore, and question everything without fear of imprisonment or death. But I digress. I want to get back to Neema and how she disregarded my rules."

"Right," I say.

"Neema told you how she fell in love with Henry and how she persuaded Maetha to make him a Bearer. Well, she already knew I disapproved of him becoming a Bearer, yet she pushed and pressured Maetha anyway. In the end, Maetha accepted and created a new Bearer. I spoke personally to Neema and reminded her that she had gotten my approval to receive a diamond many centuries prior, but this single choice had just stripped her of her rights. I told her that at some point she would be relieved of her diamond and she wouldn't be able to prevent her death. The consequence of her choice with Henry was that she would lose the right to be a Bearer, but not before she witnessed the reason why her choice was against my wishes."

"You knew what Freedom, er, Henry was going to do?"

"No, I only knew that it wouldn't turn out well if Henry wielded the powers of the Sanguine Diamond. His pattern of choices and the trajectory of his life were enough for me to know he wouldn't use his power wisely. I wish I could have seen his future back then because I would have removed his stone immediately."

"Wait. You can remove diamonds? Why did we have to shoot out his heart then? Why didn't you just remove his diamond?" I ask.

"By the time I realized he should be relieved of his diamond, he had discovered the obsidian and was able to hide from me."

"So obsidian is your weakness too?"

"Everything has its opposite. Everything in nature has a foe. Even intelligent, top-of-the-food-chain homo sapiens can be brought down by a microscopic virus. The Primal Stone is countered by the Yellowstone obsidian, but as you know, the obsidian is countered by Imperial topaz. Yes, obsidian affects my powers, and yes, I knew of its existence long before Henry ever did. I actually used it just as I used the Sanguine Diamond. I instructed the early inhabitants of North America to use it against evil uprisings. Of course, that got out of hand quickly, and I then had to introduce its opposite to the Alaskan tribe you met with in order to prevent their extinction.

"Once the area around the outcropping was designated a national park and the military began guarding it, I figured the obsidian would be protected. I had no idea Henry was behind its protection, using their services because he was using obsidian, too. You see, even my own choices have consequences. It's a natural law that can't be avoided."

"I'm confused. I don't understand why you didn't just get rid of the obsidian outcropping. You could have buried it with a landslide or removed it in its entirety and dumped it in the ocean."

"Where in nature does something like that happen? Everything lives and thrives in a symbiotic relationship. I have lived as long as I have, and humans have advanced as far as they have, because I respect nature's way. Now we find ourselves in the interesting predicament of needing to fight to survive. I will fight back as naturally as possible with the understanding that sometimes cataclysmic events push progress back. However, I fully understand that nature always rebounds from calamity."

Crimson slows the car as a large truck merges onto the highway.

"You said Chris helped remove Neema's stone. Did you have a hand in planning her death?"

"Calli, the last thing I want you to do is view me as a cold-hearted killer. Neema made her choice with Henry. Her consequence and redemption came in the form of helping Chris maintain his position with his father.”

"So, you knew she would get her heart shot out?”

“Yes, I knew Deus's plan. I knew which Bearer I wanted to help Chris maintain his position, so I told Maetha through telepathy to finish her conversation with the other Bearers before talking with Chris. Then I put the thought into Neema's mind to offer her assistance to Chris. She didn't know what would happen. She didn't know she would die at that moment. I was saddened as well, but Neema made her choice when she pressured Maetha to make Henry a Bearer and her time to right the wrong had come.”

I don't know what to say. I glance over at Chris, whose eyes hold deep concern.

Chris asks, “Are there other Bearers with bullseyes on their backs?”

“Yes, but not for the same reason as Neema. I won't identify them, but there are a handful of Bearers who are not following the rules. They're not breaking them. They just don't get involved with matters anymore. They don't help humanity progress. Their diamonds would be better suited in new, younger Bearers.”

Chris says, “Well, that's already happened with Jonas. Now there are two young Bearers.”

“Would you remove their diamonds because they aren't doing their job anymore?” I ask.

“I'll give them the opportunity to do better. If they don't, I'll have them hand over their diamonds for rebirth.”

“Rebirth?”

“Rebirth is when a new Diamond Bearer is born. The diamond rebirth process—like what Calli went through—has been done many times over and always follows a certain order of transformation. However, Diamond Bearers are not always born because of a splintering diamond.”

"Shadow Demons are also born when a diamond rebirth is performed, right?" I say.

"Correct. The exploding diamond transforms those trying to harness its powers into new forms."

"It would seem, then, that avoiding an explosion would prevent new Demons from forming."

"Indeed, Calli."

"How else are Bearers created?" Chris asks.

"Sometimes a Bearer is created by carrying the diamond for a time to become accustomed to the muted powers before inserting the whole stone into their hearts." Crimson sighs and says, "Your friend Jonas is the first person to have a diamond introduced into his body without any prior familiarity. He would have died if you hadn't healed him, Calli. I haven't decided what will become of him, whether he'll keep the diamond or not."

What? Ask her why? Jonas yells inside my head, causing me to scrunch my eyes closed and put my hand to my head.

Chris turns his attention to me. "What's wrong?"

Crimson eyes me suspiciously.

"Jonas is always in my mind and thoughts, and I'm in his. He wants to know more."

Crimson says. "What you two are experiencing is what I call quantum entanglement. I have the same kind of connection with Maetha because of the shared Grecian Blue Diamond. The difference is I *gave* her the blue shard so we could have the connection, whereas Jonas was never approved of, never qualified to become a Bearer. Furthermore, he has the bulk and you have the shard. It should at least be the other way around."

I'm thrown for a loop. Maetha and Crimson share the Grecian Blue Diamond?

Tell her I want to be approved of. What do I need to do to keep the diamond?

"Will Jonas be able to qualify?"

Crimson speaks to me but addresses Jonas. "You must exercise restraint, first of all. Inserting your thoughts into Calli's mind right now keeps her from the vital healing she needs. You will have several opportunities to prove yourself, Jonas. Don't try to be someone you're not. I can see right through that behavior. You were assigned to Mary, and Calli was assigned to Duncan because they are the only other Diamond Bearers who understand quantum entanglement enough to help you."

Jonas asks: "One last question. If you remove my diamond, will I die?"

"You're already dead. Your years were extended unnaturally. Not only were you kept alive longer than you should have been, you then became an unnatural Diamond Bearer. But before you jump to any conclusions about where you think I'm going with this, understand that evolution depends on unusual and seemingly unnatural events taking place in a species. Who am I to say it was right or wrong on the grand scale of things that you became a Diamond Bearer? However, you didn't get the opportunity to choose that responsibility like everyone else. It was thrust upon you. What you choose to do with this current situation will determine whether or not you keep the diamond. To answer your question with clarity, yes, you will die if I remove your diamond. Now, exercise your restraint and don't project your thoughts into Calli's head until she's completely healed. Enough said."

Jonas accepts Crimson's instruction.

I ask, "Would you tell us about the Grecian Blue Diamond?"

"I suppose now is as good a time as any. We have several hours of drive time ahead of us."

Chapter 6 - Mother Nature

"Over my lifetime," Crimson continues, "I've experimented with many stones, crystals, and elements in the pursuit of transferring some of my power or capturing cosmic energy rays. The Primal Stone allows me to see energy beams. They appear similar to shooting stars, except in the daylight. The streaks of light actually hit the ground like lightning. Some areas of the planet get hit more often than others, because there is a gravitational or electrical force that pulls them inward. The Egyptian Great Pyramids are one such place. Mount Olympus is another.

"The beliefs and superstitions of the early Greeks in the timeframe now referred to as the Heroic Period helped people with intense powers blend in and also gave them a logical place to live: on Mount Olympus. The powers of Mind-control were new to the world but not to the universe because they existed in the Primal Stone. For some unknown reason, the powers hadn't been hitting the earth yet. Around what would now be referred to as the fifth century BCE, I detected the new powers emerging and could foresee the possible catastrophic results. I decided to capture the powers, the same way the powers were captured and infused into the Sanguine Diamond. I knew I would need more Diamond Bearers with these special abilities to help rein in the rampant formation of these powerful people. I was successful in forming the small Grecian Blue Diamond, dividing it into five pieces, and delegating its responsibilities to five Bearers. One of the

Bearers being Maetha.

"The humans born with the ability to control minds began dying off naturally over the course of a couple hundred years. I noticed a dramatic drop, almost a complete halt, in how many humans developed the mind-control ability. I estimate one or two humans every twenty-five years are born with the mind-control ability. A few are walking the planet today and I keep my eye on them."

Crimson turns the wheel and changes lanes to move around a slow-moving vehicle. "Long story short, all of the Bearers of the Grecian Blue succumbed to its tempting power and misused the abilities. I, along with Maetha, removed the shards from each Bearer. You see, Blue Diamond Bearers can spot other invisible people. Maetha helped me hunt down the remaining four. Once all the shards were collected, I decided to hide them in the most secure place on the face of the planet: inside myself. I let Maetha keep one shard for her own use and because of the quantum entanglement it would give us—like a video phone between us. Because of that connection, I'm always able to be up-to-date on the goings on with my Diamond Bearers without their knowledge of my presence. I am able to pull back and not allow myself to be seen by the others. Most of the Bearers have only seen me twice in their entire life: once for qualification, and once for induction into the Bearers' Clan. They don't know I have the connection to Maetha. They don't know I have the rest of the Blue Diamond. Well, except for Mary and Duncan."

I know Mary is one of the oldest Bearers and Duncan is the newest, except for Jonas and me. I wonder what happened for Duncan to find out that Crimson and Maetha share a Blue Diamond?

I say, "Freedom knew right away that Maetha had a Blue Diamond when she froze everyone in place after

Justin died. Why?"

"Henry had been searching relentlessly for the blue stone all because of some ancient writings he discovered which told of its existence. The writings also told of various sea creatures and land monsters that have never been found. Maetha tried to redirect him from his pointless search connecting the lack of evidence of those creatures and monsters to the lack of evidence of the Blue Diamond. After a while she gave up, knowing he would never find what he was—"

Crimson stops talking. Chris and I exchange perplexed glances. She finally speaks, saying, "I need to communicate with Maetha for a while."

Crimson continues to drive in silence. Chris tightens his grasp on my hand and says, "I can't wait for this to be over so we can start our life together."

"Our life together started almost three years ago, Chris."

"True, but I haven't had a chance to really get to know you yet."

"What if I have habits that are pet peeves to you? What if we're not compatible? Or you don't like me reading your mind all the time? What if you hate my cooking?"

"You cook?"

"Sort of."

"I doubt there's anything about you I won't be able to deal with."

"Okay, what if *you* have habits *I* don't like?"

"Well, perhaps we will be able to see beyond each other's idiosyncrasies."

"My mind isn't in marriage-mode like yours, Chris. That doesn't mean it won't ever be, but for now that part is a little way off in the distance. Besides, how would we provide for ourselves? Where would we live? Do you get paid money to work at the Runners' compound?"

"What are you saying, Calli? Don't you want a future together?"

"Of course I do, but that doesn't mean we have to rush into it, right?"

Before he can answer, I receive a heightened awareness that another Sanguine Diamond no longer has a Bearer. The sensation feels as if a piano tuning fork has twanged inside my chest. I am about to feel for the diamond to try to identify which Bearer has just died when Crimson quickly maneuvers the car onto an off-ramp, almost missing the exit altogether. She turns right at the light and quickly pulls into a parking lot.

"Hold my hand, Calli," she says, reaching over the seat to me. I take her hand after letting go of Chris's.

Maetha's voice enters my mind mid-sentence: . . . *and he's working for General Harding again and must have an open line of communication to give her the exact whereabouts of Hasan. Yet, I can't enter his mind or bi-locate to him.*

Other voices join in on the conference-call-like conversation. Mary says, *It's not surprising that Rolf returned to the only safe place he can go. How safe is he really?*

Kookju, a Bearer I'm not too familiar with, says with an Asian tang to his accent, *If bullet-proof vests aren't going to protects us, as Hasan's heart was still able to be blasted out through the vest, then I feel it's time for another disappearance. I've already chosen my location. Give this two-hundred years and it will resolve itself.*

Amenemhet says, *Let me guess. You, Chuang, Jie Wen, Yeok Choo and Marketa are going to your secret retreat in upper Mongolia? Don't you think Rolf will look there first? He knows all of our preferred hideaways.*

Maetha confirms Amenemhet's thought. *Hiding won't*

work this time. We have to stand up and fight.

Kookju says, *We disagree. What good will it serve nature to seek out our own deaths?*

Fabian asks, *Maetha, is it safe for Mary and Jonas to be on your island if Rolf knows about it?*

Mary jumps in. *We are presently relocating.*

I am relieved to hear her voice and hear that she is looking out for Jonas's safety.

Jie Wen asks, *What does Crimson feel we should do?*

Maetha answers, *She hasn't offered any suggestions. We know the will of nature must be upheld. That is our duty as Diamond Bearers. We will stand up and fight.*

Jie Wen persists, *Of course. But surely Crimson would be able to offer some insight. She has finally surfaced, making her presence known to all. It must be for a reason. She foresees something monumental or she wouldn't have risked everything by coming forward.*

Amenemhet responds with a sarcastic flavor to his words, *I wasn't aware you could read her mind, Jie Wen. Besides, we've always operated independently of Crimson. She works on her own duties. We work on ours.*

I look at Crimson, wondering why she doesn't just speak up and comfort the other Bearers. Maetha's voice says, *Our focus needs to be on retrieving Hasan's diamond before Deus figures out how to pick it up.*

Too late, Merlin says. *Rolf already instructed an Unaltered soldier on how to do so.*

Maetha says, *The diamond has no owner yet, Merlin.*

Yet. The Unaltered is on his way to pick up the diamond. It's being guarded by Deus.

Where is the diamond located?

Pittsburg, Merlin answers.

My heart thuds against my ribs. Pittsburg is just a few hours away from Brand. Is Deus making her way to him?

Maetha says, *I'll alert Calli so she and Chris can be on guard.*

I wonder why she keeps it a secret that Crimson is listening in on the conversation. Crimson lets go of my hand, and I immediately reach for Chris as my energy slides. He takes my hand in his and gives me comfort. I understand he has no idea what is going on, but he exercises patience. I want to speak to his mind, but I don't know what Crimson wants him to know.

Maetha bi-locates to the passenger seat of the car and address Crimson. "I think Calli should disguise her location with obsidian."

"No, not yet." Crimson shakes her head. "She needs to draw strength from Chris so she's fully recharged by the time we reach the Repeater. I'm not worried about Rolf being able to locate her diamond. You work on helping the other Bearers try to remain undetected, and continue helping Merlin with his duties. We will continue on the I-90 to Ohio."

"Understood." With that, Maetha vanishes.

Crimson turns the car around and waits for traffic to clear.

Chris asks, "What's happening?"

"Another Diamond Bearer was killed," Crimson states in what I feel is a rather bland manner.

"Who? When?"

"Hasan, just a few minutes ago in Pittsburg." She crosses the road and turns onto the onramp to the interstate, then accelerates. "We will drive straight through until we get to Ohio, stopping only for food and gasoline."

I can't decide if Crimson is more worried about Rolf zeroing in on my diamond or Deus reaching Brand before we can. Or maybe she's concerned about who will be the first Unaltered to touch Hasan's diamond.

Crimson adds, "You can take that bullet-proof vest

off, Calli. It's not going to save your life, obviously."

We stop in Springfield, Massachusetts for lunch.

I ask Crimson, "Don't you carry a supply of Clara's granola bars?"

"No, they're designed for Runners to rebuild their bodies. I prefer to eat real food. You two stay here. I'll be right back." Crimson reaches under the passenger seat and pulls out a reusable grocery bag and heads into the store.

Chris unlatches his seatbelt and slides closer to me, turning his shoulders square with mine. He has a seductive look in his eyes. "Calli, I still can't believe we're together finally." He leans his head towards mine, and our lips meet delicately, sending tingles all the way down to my toes. He smells so tantalizingly good, I can't help but inhale his scent and relax into the kiss. Our lips meld together at various angles, soft, yet commanding, causing my body to buzz and heat up.

He pulls away slightly and smiles. "I swear you could light up a pitch-black stadium with your aura when we kiss." He moves his mouth to my neck by my ear and whispers as he lightly kisses my skin, "I knew you had died when you were on the stone altar because your glow was gone." He takes my hand in his and kisses my palm and wrist. "And when Maetha tried to insert the diamond, I waited anxiously for your glow to return as she healed you. After that, I noticed how my touch on your skin charged your aura whenever I held you. Just like now." He pushes my sleeve up to my elbow and continues kissing a trail up my arm. I notice his kisses charge my body faster than simply holding hands.

I've never made-out in a backseat before, let alone in

the middle of the day in a crowded parking lot. In fact, I haven't ever made-out at all. Well, unless you count the time in the motel room just before Chris left to return to his father when he had Brand repeat with him while he kissed me over and over. Of course, I had no idea Chris had made out with me until I extracted his memories earlier today. I'm not even sure if this extremely sensual moment counts as making out.

Yeah, you're totally makin' out, Calli, Jonas says in my head.

Dude, come on! The only time you interrupt is when Chris and I are close.

Yeah, 'cause it makes me feel what you're feeling, so I take notice.

Well, you don't have to interrupt us, you know.

"Are you all right?" Chris asks while still holding my arm to his mouth.

"Yeah, it's just . . . there are a lot of people around . . . and Jonas."

"Jonas? Is he eavesdropping again?"

"He can't help himself."

Chris straightens up and lowers my arm, yet still holds my hand. I don't read his mind because I already know what he's thinking. He says, "He's not supposed to be in your head at all."

Jonas responds, *Tell him you have all your strength now.*

"He says I'm back to normal."

I glance around nervously at the other vehicles in the parking lot, looking for someone to test my powers on. People walk to and from the store's main entrance while vehicles circle round and round like lazy vultures, waiting for the best parking spots.

I zero in on a girl no older than me who stands by the driver's side of the car directly in front of us. She balances a crying baby boy on her hip while she fishes through her purse for her car keys. The baby is probably one year old. She has already set two grocery bags on the hood of her car to make it easier to hunt for the keys. The child wails on. I realize with stark clarity that I could be in her situation if I had made different choices somewhere along the way. I am old enough to have a baby. I suddenly don't feel like a teen any more.

Feeling sympathy for the girl, I use my mind-reading power to determine she left her keys inside her locked car. Not good. I know I can't help her with that problem, but I can calm her child to help make the situation a little easier. I heal the irritating rash on the baby's bottom, which is the cause of his discomfort, and he instantly quiets down.

Then I turn to Chris. "Let go of my hand."

He does so and scoots away from me ever so slightly. I notice I don't weaken right away, so I use my powers again. I speak to the mind of the now frantic girl, who is still searching inside her purse for the keys. I suggest, *Are they in the car?*

The girl freezes in place, then bends over and looks inside the car. Her head drops in frustration. One of the bags on the hood of her car tips over, spilling the contents, including several different kinds of diaper rash ointment. The girl pulls her cell phone out and makes a call, holding the phone to her ear with her right shoulder, while pulling the child further up her hip on the left. With her right hand, she picks up the contents of her bag and carries on a conversation on the phone. Talk about multi-tasking! *Now that girl has superpowers!*

I look for her future, the point when she will realize the baby's bottom has healed. I experience her elated relief that her child is no longer in pain, but also her confusion because of the small spots of blood still in the diaper from the rash the baby had been battling for weeks.

I turn to Chris, still feeling my complete powers, and ask, "Is my aura still strong?"

He smiles warmly. "Yes. Completely."

"Your kisses healed me," I say, feeling my cheeks heat as blood rushes to them. "I didn't know you were a Healer," I tease.

"On second thought, I think your aura is dimming. I better play doctor with you again." He moves closer and takes my lips possessively. My heart races in my chest more intensely than before, and I feel the pain of the diamond shard tearing my heart. I wince a little and focus my healing powers on the pain. At some point, I'm going to have to have this thing removed.

The car door opens, and Crimson clears her throat. We pull apart quickly, and Chris repositions himself in his seat. "Take this, Chris," Crimson says. She hands him an overloaded bag filled with vegetables and fruits. Her eyes are on me as she says to Chris, "I see you fulfilled your assignment, Chris."

Chris's gaze shoots to the floor in embarrassment.

"That was an assignment?" I ask Chris, feeling a little hurt, but then the diamond in my heart warms my cold reaction. I read his mind and find he was *more* than willing to do as Crimson asked. In fact, he would have taken the private opportunity to kiss me whether or not Crimson had given him the order.

Crimson climbs in the car and sets her bag in the passenger seat. "Calli, the energy between two people in love is an incredible thing to behold. I could see the glow through the windows by the checkout stands. Don't panic, though. Not many individuals can see your glow. It's part of the color spectrum that regular human eyes cannot see. Perhaps someday love energy will be harnessed and used as a new clean power source."

"Beth saw my aura the first day I arrived at the Runners' compound, and Chris saw it too." I look at him. He nods his head in agreement. Crimson starts the car and pulls into traffic.

Crimson continues, "Beth Hammond's ability to view auras is a gift that I gave her many years ago, and she has yet to use it to its full capacity."

"Does Beth know you too?"

"No. She was unaware of my presence. I also gave Chris the same power, but your aura is the only one he can see."

Chris's eyebrows shoot upward. "You did? When?"

"Just after Maetha gave you the vision of Calli. Auras are like fingerprints. Each one is unique. There's a discernible difference between what Beth sees when looking at Unaltereds in general and what you see when looking at Calli's individual aura."

My mind races a mile a minute. "Wait a second. Maetha and Beth tried to teach me how to see auras. Is that something that can be taught?"

"No. My powers aren't the same as Maetha's, and she is unaware of everything I can do. In order to view an Unaltered's aura, a physical change has to take place within the eye—a change only I can bring about. I've personally altered each Diamond Bearer so they can view auras . . . well, with the exception of you and Jonas.

"I'm telling this to you two, and through Calli I'm also telling Jonas. Certain bits of information I give you will not be able to be extracted from your mind, nor will you be able to share the information in any way: not through speaking or thinking or writing. You'll know which bits I've blocked because you won't be able to discuss them . . . but you'll remember them. Each Bearer is privy to some type of exclusive information. Maetha knows information that you will never know, Calli, but that doesn't mean anything negative. Now you know something Maetha doesn't. In fact, Calli, to answer a question from your past, the Bearers work together as a group because each one understands they know something none of the others know. It's an equalizing feeling, especially for newer Bearers who learn that Maetha, Mary, and Amenemhet have been alive since the ancient Egyptian times. Their age automatically places them higher in rank in the human mind, but it shouldn't be that way. The only leader of a Diamond Bearer is nature's will and, secondarily, me."

Crimson drives the car effortlessly and merges into heavy traffic. She says, "Go ahead and select something to eat out of the bag. Everything is organic, so there are no chemicals on the skins to wash off. I also looked them over carefully for bacteria. They're clean."

I choose a particularly delicious-looking apple. Chris pulls out a yellow pear speckled with brown marks.

Crimson continues talking, addressing Jonas as well. "You three are young and full of ideas. Your traditions are from the present day. Your ideologies are current, yet your minds accept the teachings of old. The older Bearers don't have that luxury. Their thought processes and actions are dictated by outdated traditions. You'll be the same in a thousand years. Who you are will never change. The difference is that you are you in today's day and age. Even Duncan doesn't have the advantage you do. His day and age was not long ago, yet long enough that the technologies of today baffle his mind. Maetha has tried to keep up with the evolving world of science, but her mind is always struggling to accept the changes. Still, of all the Diamond Bearers, she's the only one who could influence the world's governments to make them deal with the nuclear threat of the last century. It's because of her willingness to continue to try that I've allowed her to live after going against nature's will with Henry."

"How many times has Maetha gone against nature?"

"Several, like when she controlled Chris in Alaska. I was particularly unhappy with that one."

"How so?" Chris asks curiously.

"As I told you, the power of two people in love is incredible. At that time, and with the extenuating circumstances of needing to use obsidian to hide from Henry, Maetha's actions of taking your memory and feelings for Calli away was for Calli's survival. Maetha crossed the line when she took it a step further and used your indifference to Calli to allow her to feel pain and suffering. Maetha knew that if Calli became deathly ill, the tribal shaman would step forward and hopefully use the yellow stone, which she did. I have yet to decide what the consequences will be for Maetha."

"Would you remove her diamond?"

Crimson doesn't answer immediately. "I'll know what the appropriate course of action will be when it presents itself to me."

Wow! My mind is blown away by the realization that Maetha could lose her diamond for ordering Chris, while in his mind-controlled state, to befriend Kikee. I almost feel the punishment is a little over the top because everything has worked out in the end. Chris and I are back together, and finding the golden topaz resulted in Freedom's death. I'll just have to wait and see what happens in the end.

The next several hours consist of conversations and naps, especially during the several times Crimson holds private conversations with Maetha. I call my parents from a truck-stop payphone and tell them to remain at the cabin because we don't know what Deus is capable of just yet.

At five o'clock, Maetha bi-locates to the front-seat once again. She speaks reverently. "The diamond Hasan bore is in a safe location now."

Crimson's mind speaks to me. *Maetha's memories are coming into my head through our Blue Diamond connection. I will view them and then send them to you and Chris.*

Chris and I both nod our heads in unison, making it clear she has just spoken to both of us.

While Crimson focuses on the road ahead and Maetha's memories, Maetha turns to me and asks, "Are you recharged yet?"

"Yes."

"Excellent. This whole situation is intensifying, as you will soon see."

I don't like the gloomy tone in Maetha's voice.

Crimson interrupts. "Done. You did well."

Maetha nods and then vanishes. Then Crimson transfers Maetha's memories to our minds.

The sensation racing through my body is like cool, rushing water as a vision fills my head. The scene plays out as Maetha invisibly materializes near Deus Ex. I see what Maetha sees, as if I am the one at that location. Hasan's dead body lies near a tree just a few feet from a deserted parking lot. His heart has been blasted out of his chest and lies in the nearby grass. The edges of his diamond sparkle as occasional rays of sunlight manage to shine through the dense leaves that wave lazily above. Heavy traffic rumbles by in the distance beyond a large field of weeds. Birds chirp and fly from branch to branch, unconcerned with the gruesome scene below.

Maetha's eyes travel over Hasan's body, examining the bulletproof vest and its inability to stop the large caliber bullet that was used by Deus. I wonder to myself what Maetha feels as she views yet another long-time friend's dead body. Her memory doesn't provide that detail.

Deus answers her phone, obviously irritated. "How much longer?" She paces around in a circle as she listens to the voice on the other end. She says, "I already tried—yes, I have one, but it's personal size, not enough to counter the powers." Her fingers travel up to her necklace, grasping the small obsidian. "No! I don't have a bigger one!" Deus dramatically holds the phone at arm's length and looks to the sky, exhaling an exaggerated sigh, then she brings the phone back to her ear. "Listen, . . . no, you listen! I want a Hunter, Seer, and Reader to go with the Runner and Healer Travis is bringing me." She pauses while the other person speaks, then says, "What do you mean he won't allow that? You'd better tell the general that if he won't let me have any of the special crystals, then he'd better supply me with the walking talking version. You of all people should understand what I'm up against here, Rolf!" She ends her call and pockets her phone. Then she begins practicing her karate moves on an imaginary opponent.

The scene jumps forward. I can't tell how much time has passed. A car pulls into the parking lot and comes to a halt near Hasan's body. I recognize the driver. It's Travis from the college party! What's worse is Beth and Anika are in the backseat. They appear scared but otherwise unharmed.

Travis gets out of the car but before he closes his door, he says to Beth and Anika, "Don't even think about running or your parents will die."

Maetha's voice sounds out in a different way. She issues a telepathic order: *Amenemhet, Merlin, Fabian. Anika Evanston and Beth Hammond have been kidnapped. Their families are in danger. Do what you can.*

Deus turns to Travis, "It's over there." She points to the bloody heart. "You better not be thinking of trying anything foolish or I will hunt you down and kill you."

Travis lowers his chin and with angry eyes replies, "Don't threaten me."

Deus remains by the car while Travis walks over to the heart, bends down, and picks it up without so much as a flinch. Then his body slumps over, and he falls to his knees, still clutching the diamond.

I hear Maetha's telepathic voice saying, *Put it in your pocket so it's not touching your skin. The sensations will be easier to deal with.*

Travis looks at Deus and asks, "What did you say?"

"I didn't say anything. Hurry up."

He pauses and then stutters, "Just give me a minute to figure this out. Toss me your water so I can wash this thing off." He points to the bottle of water Deus has in her utility belt.

Deus lets out a huff and pulls out her water and tosses it to Travis. Then she opens the back door and removes a pair of handcuffs from her belt. She says to Beth, "I know you're thinking of running. Let's just put a halt to that right now." She hands Beth the cuffs. "Put those on your ankles."

"What if I don't?"

Deus pulls her hand gun, cocks it and presses the barrel on Beth's temple so fast Maetha almost misses viewing it. "Not doing as I say would be a bad choice."

Maetha looks over at Travis while Beth clamps the cuffs to her ankles. Travis is attempting to separate the diamond from the heart tissue. He has to actually tear the muscle from the stone because it's so firmly attached. The effort reminds me of opening a clam or oyster and having to cut the muscle that's attached to the inside of the shell. Once Travis has removed most of the flesh, he rubs the diamond in the grass and splashes water over the stone.

Maetha speaks to him again. *Put it in your pocket, Travis.*

"How do you know my name?" he asks the voice in his head.

"What?" Deus responds, not realizing he isn't talking to her.

I know everything about you, Travis. Don't worry. I'm trying to help you. Put the diamond in your pocket, now.

He pushes the large stone into the front pocket of his blue jeans.

If you take the diamond back to General Harding, he will kill you. This girl is very powerful, and you need to get away from her, but you only have one shot at it. You have to follow my instructions perfectly. Can you do that Travis?

"Okay."

Deus says, "Let's get out of here before someone calls the cops. I'm driving." She climbs in the driver's seat and starts the car. Travis jumps in the front passenger seat.

Maetha says, *I'll be with you even when you're driving. Try not to speak aloud when you talk to me. Use your mind to communicate so Deus doesn't hear. She is going to kill you once she no longer needs you. I want to help you get away from her.*

Travis says, *I don't understand what's happening. I was only told to pick up the package and bring it back. I feel so much going through my body. What's happening to me?*

Try to ignore these sensations. Focus on your legs and your muscles. When I tell you to run, you need to access the running power that is inside the stone in your pocket.

The what?

No time for answers. Just focus on your legs and muscles and be ready.

"Are you kidding me?" Deus shouts. "You brought me a car that's out of gas? You better have money to fill it up!"

Beth chuckles. "What, are you broke Deus?"

"I have more money than you'll ever have," Deus snips back.

"Left it in your other utility belt, huh?" Beth laughs.

"Shut up!"

Travis interrupts. "I have a debit card. Don't worry."

Maetha exclaims, *That's it, Travis. That's how you'll escape. You'll have to go inside to pay for the gas.*

No I won't. The card works at the pump.

Enter the PIN number wrong so the pump tells you to see the cashier. You need thirty seconds away from Deus to escape without a hitch.

Okay, I guess.

Deus pulls up to the gas pump and orders Travis to fill it up. He gets out and swipes the card and selects debit. Like clockwork, he enters his PIN number wrong and the screen on the pump instructs him to go inside the building. He steps up to Deus's window and tells her he needs to go inside to prepay.

"Fine." Deus rolls her eyes and adds, "Grab some more water for everyone while you're in there."

Travis walks nervously to the doors and enters the convenience store. Maetha stays by his side and issues exact instructions about where to walk. She directs him to the back storage room. He stands in front of a door marked "Emergency Only."

"Hey, you can't be back here!" a male worker says as he walks toward Travis.

"I'm leaving in just a few seconds, sir," Travis replies in a calm voice.

"You're leaving right now or I'll call the cops."

Maetha instructs him: *Once you push that door open, an alarm will sound and Deus will know you've fled, but she won't be able to do anything about it. She won't even be able to drive far because she's almost out of gas. You'll need to run as fast as you can for at least five minutes before you stop. I will find you.*

How?

No questions right now. It's time. Go!

"That's it, young man, we'll let the cops deal—"

Travis pushes the door open, activating the alarm, and runs. Maetha's memory doesn't follow him, only watches him disappear in a flash. The angry employee is slow to stop yelling threats to the empty space where Travis stood moments before. Maetha hurries out the door and around to the front of the building, using her power to stay invisible. Deus appears to have just realized she's been tricked and runs into the store to try to find Travis.

Maetha uses the opportunity to speak to Beth's mind. *It's Maetha. You two need to run!*

"Run, Anika!" Beth encourages her.

"Not without you."

Beth points to her ankles. "I'm cuffed. I won't get far. Go!"

"Where am I supposed to go?"

"Anywhere but here! Go! I'll be fine."

Maetha's view of the girls begins to fade. She speaks to Anika's mind. *Run across the street to those bushes. You should be able to make it. I'll meet you there.*

Anika looks at Beth one last time, not wanting to abandon her friend. Then she takes off running and makes it across the street before Deus comes out of the store.

Don't worry Beth, Maetha says. *We'll get you out of this. I can't help you right now in the state I'm in. I'm about to lose connection.*

Deus comes running out to the car, cursing up a storm. She climbs in the front seat, retrieves her cell phone from her belt, and dials a number. "Where's the next one? This one got away." Deus's face is so red with anger, she looks as though she could literally explode. "Let me talk to the general—I don't care what he's doing. Just get him!" She waits anxiously. She turns in her seat and looks at Beth. Then she leans over the back seat, eyes searching for Anika. Her eyes shoot back to Beth.

Beth shrugs nonchalantly and says, "She took off when you did."

Viewing Deus's meltdown through Maetha's memory is rather gratifying, I have to say. Deus turns her attention to the phone call. She takes a deep breath and speaks in a controlled voice, nothing to indicate her actual level of aggravation. "General Harding, I apologize for interrupting you, but we have a problem. Rolf isn't telling you everything. I don't think you can trust him. Rolf recommended I use Travis to pick up the diamond, which Travis did, but now he just ran away with it. Rolf either planned that or he knew that might happen. He should have warned me." She pauses. "I still have the Runner, but the Healer got away. . . Yes, I'll do that . . . I need the other powers as well, sir. Do you have anyone else? All right, I'll see you then."

Deus ends the call and dials another number. Maetha's memory fades all the way out as Deus says: "The Healer escaped. Kill her family!"

Maetha's memory shifts to a park where she sits across from Travis at a picnic table. "You did well, Travis." Maetha becomes visible, causing him to jump up and step away.

"What . . . who are you?"

"I'm the guardian of the stone you hold, and I want to help keep you alive. You only have a few minutes before the enemy arrives to seize it. They will kill you."

"I don't want to die!"

"Then you need to get rid of it. You see the woman walking on the path over there?" She points to a lady in a green Runners' suit. "Take the stone to her and say, 'I'm giving this stone to you to take care of.' She'll probably ask why, and you say, 'I'm relinquishing it to you.'"

"What?"

Two men in dark suits walk into the clearing nearby and stand still.

"You'd better hurry, Travis. You see those two men?"

Travis jumps up and runs to the woman. I recognize her as Avani, a Diamond Bearer, even though she isn't wearing her bejeweled head scarf and colorful clothing. She has long wavy black hair and light brown skin. The green Runner's suit compliments her expertly lined brown eyes. Travis says the words as Maetha instructed, and Hasan's diamond is relinquished into Avani's possession.

Avani extends her hand to shake Travis's. As she grips his hand firmly, she says, "Do you want to learn more about this stone? Or have you had enough for the day?"

Travis looks at Maetha questioningly. He answers, "I want to know more."

Avani responds, "Then we have to leave now."

Travis glances over to Maetha, who says, "Go with her, Travis. She will help you. I'll meet up with you later."

With Travis's hand still in hers, she leads him away. Maetha turns and faces the black-suited men, whom I now recognize as Merlin and Amenemhet. Merlin looks her in the eye and says, "Anika's family members were already taken three days ago."

Maetha looks at Amenemhet and says, "Go to Anika. She's going to need comforting. Take her to Jonas and Mary."

Chapter 7 - Death by Deus

The vision ends, and I shake my head a little and blink my eyes. The rushing water sensation settles down, and my body begins to feel normal. I instinctively glance at the front seat where Maetha had been only moments before.

Hasan's death has everyone rattled. What's going to happen to his body? How was Deus able to kill him without anyone hearing? How was she able to kill him period? We may never know.

I ask, "Crimson, what is going to happen to Anika's family? Will they be found in time?"

"They're already dead. That's what Merlin was telling Maetha."

"So is Beth's family dead as well?"

"I'm afraid so."

My eyes instantly mist over at the reality of the situation. What if Deus finds my parents? Or Chris's mother? How would I feel if I found out they had been killed ? I wonder how Beth and Anika will handle the news.

Jonas's sympathy and grief for Anika enters my mind. He feels horrible for her and wishes she could be with him before she gets the news of her parents' deaths. That way he could give her healing comfort to help ease the incredible shock wave her body will go through.

Crimson must have read my thoughts because she states, "Calli, death is something that a Diamond Bearer can't avoid. It's unfair and unjust that these girls have to deal with this now, but we have to stay the course and understand that many more will die if we don't find a way to put a halt to Deus and the government. Situations like these make or break people. As a Diamond Bearer, you need to push aside your emotions and clear your mind. In a couple hundred years, when you no longer personally know those who are suffering from loss, it will be easier to stay focused. You will never lose your compassionate side, though."

I ask, "Is there any way to hold off giving Anika the news of her parents' death until she makes it to Jonas?"

"That's a good idea, Calli. I'll tell Maetha."

Jonas thanks me, and I feel his peace, but also his anxiousness. I don't envy being in his position. I respond back, alerting him to the possibility that Anika may blame herself for their deaths because she ran.

A few hours later, we arrive in Brand's neighborhood. Crimson decides to park several blocks away to avoid being seen by Deus, should she arrive.

I get out of the car and run most of the way to Brand's house. As I get close, I slow to a brisk walk up to his front door. Before I can reach the door, Brand opens it.

He says, "No, I don't want to go."

He has repeated, obviously.

"Come on, let me explain."

"You are still the most stubborn girl I know, Calli. Come in." He opens the door wide enough to let me inside. I walk to the nearest couch and sit down. He launches into the conversation, making it clear to me he has repeated several times to gather most of the information from me. "So, if I understand you correctly, Deus is on a rampage shooting out Diamond Bearers' hearts with the aid of General Harding, and you want me to help kill my half-sister? I guess I shouldn't be surprised. I mean, after all, I was tricked into killing my biological father."

"He had to die, and you know it. If you're going to repeat with me, at least take me with you so I know what I've already told you."

"You've told me enough. I don't want to go."

"I'm not going to force you, but let me ask you a question. What *do* you want, Brand?"

"I want a normal life. I want to feel accepted and loved. I wanted to try a relationship with Suz, but I don't think that's going to work."

"Really? Why?"

"I already met with her. She can't get past the idea that I'm a hypnotist. Remember, that was what I told her in the dorm. I think finding out that her mother had an affair messed up her mind, and she's still trying to figure things out. Not only did she prove her dad was not her dad, she lost her father figure because of the divorce. Her mother resents her, her biological dad doesn't want anything to do with her . . . not that I'm surprised to find that out. My dad is a real piece of work, too . . . well, the man who ignored me most of my life, I mean. I thought about repeating with Suz to show her I have a superpower, but decided against it. She needs time to figure herself out."

"Well, Brand, why don't you come with me and help save the world while she figures her life out. She'll still be around when we're done."

"That's just it, Calli. I don't think Suz and I will ever work together. We're both too needy, and our situations are too closely related for either of us to really be able to grow. How could either one of us heal when we're too busy trying to make the other person feel better?"

"Listen, if Deus is able to successfully kill off all the Diamond Bearers, there won't be much of a world for you anyway. Diamond Bearers help ensure that humans continue living. They guard and protect humanity, and right now they're being picked off one by one. Beth and Anika were kidnapped, and their families were killed."

That gets his attention.

"You can stay here and bury your head in the sand, or you can come with us and help set up a better future for us, our children and grandchildren."

"I won't kill anyone."

"What?"

"I'll come, but I won't be used to kill anyone else."

"Okay, I guess."

Brand pauses and slightly tips his head to the side. "What does that mean, Calli?"

"I'm not sure. When you say you won't kill anyone, are you going to leave if we have to take a life?"

"Don't involve me, and I'll stick around."

I can't see the point in bringing him along, knowing in advance that he'll leave . . . probably when we need him most. "You know what? Never mind." I stand and walk to the door, grabbing the door handle.

"Excuse me? Where are you going?" He rushes to my side.

"We'll figure out a different way, so you don't have to be involved." I pull the door open and stand on the threshold. Brand pushes his way out and stands there, blocking my way.

"You can't . . . " he pauses and looks at my chest with a horrified expression. My eyes travel down to see a distinct red bead of light hovering over my heart. Then the ground spins violently around me.

Brand takes me back to the point where I arrive at his

house to ask him if he'll come with us. He opens his front door, wearing a jacket with one of my Pulse Emitters attached to his collar. He says, "All right, I'll do it, but I'm serious when I say I won't kill anyone." He rushes through the doorway and takes my hand. "Now run, before Deus gets here."

I don't hesitate a second. I tighten my grip on his hand and take off running into the night. We dash through his sleepy neighborhood and arrive at Crimson's parked car. I push Brand in the backseat with Chris, and I climb in the front with Crimson and throw her a nervous glance. "Drive!" I order.

She reacts without so much as a word as to why.

Chris turns to Brand. "What happened?"

"Calli was almost shot at my house."

"Already? By Deus?"

"Who else?" Brand asks. He points to Crimson and asks, "Who's this?"

She turns her head briefly and says, "I'm Jo Jo."

"Are you a Diamond Bearer too?"

"Sure."

"Well, get us out of here!"

With her eyes on the road, she smiles pleasantly and increases her speed.

I announce to them, "Brand has agreed to help as long as he's not asked to kill anyone."

Chris huffs as he says, "Yeah, right. What if it's self-defense?"

"I'll just repeat back before the attack. I don't have to kill anyone, and I can make sure I don't die."

Chris turns his body to Brand. "Deus is clever. She is methodical. She'll figure out a way to kill you."

"I highly doubt it, Chris. I can repeat further back than she can."

"Yeah, and that's why your power is the only thing that can kill her."

"Nope. Not gonna happen."

Crimson clears her throat. "You have the right to choose not to be involved, Brand."

"Thank you!" Brand settles back into his seat and eyes Crimson curiously. "So what's your story, Jo Jo? Did you become a Diamond Bearer the same way as Calli?"

"No, my story is a bit different."

Brand's tone of voice changes completely as he replies to Crimson, "I guess when a group of Healers gets it in their heads that they can dominate the world, they go berserk."

"The process always seems to follow the same path."

"So tell me, Crimson, why now? Why step forward now?" Brand asks.

What? Is Brand repeating with Crimson? Has he just held a Q & A with her? I wonder how many questions he has asked and for how long? And why is Crimson playing along?

She answers Brand's question. "Never before in the history of the Sanguine Diamond has a Bearer been killed, but never before has the repeating power been around. The Bearers were established to help prevent the annihilation of the human race, which seems to be bent on destroying itself. Sometimes I wonder if it wouldn't be wrong to allow that to happen so nature could start over again."

"Again?" Brand asks.

"Of course. Many times in the past the world's population has been greatly reduced or wiped out by natural forces like asteroids, mega-tsunamis, or volcanic ash blocking the sun long enough for most plant life to die. Humans are resilient and can live for a long time on sparse diets void of nutrition—just look at what people eat today.

However, a major catastrophe can also be viewed as a fresh start. Progress is set back a few thousand years, or in some cases millions of years, but nature always finds a way to move forward. The same type of extinction threat loomed last century during the Cold War. I don't know how long it would have taken for nature to rebound if the world had been decimated by nuclear weapons. The future was not bright. The crisis was averted . . . for now."

Brand rubs his eyes. "Do you really think the world is headed for the end?"

"Not the end. A new beginning, perhaps. It has taken millions of years for life to evolve to this state, and it would be a shame to have to start over again."

"So you think that by eliminating the government's research on people with powers and preserving Diamond Bearers, this will prevent a total wipeout of the human race? That sounds a little too over the top to me."

"I've been giving this a lot of thought as well, Brand. I've come to the conclusion that if Bearers go into hiding long enough for Deus and you to die of natural causes, then their lives will be preserved. However, if the government research isn't halted or at least slowed, then all people with powers will be eliminated by the time the Bearers emerge from hiding. Who knows, perhaps the government will follow up on Freedom's research and create more Repeaters like you and Deus."

"Deus and I are not the only Repeaters," Brand states confidently.

"You are now. Deus murdered the others."

"What?" I exclaim, jumping into the conversation.

Chris asks, "When did that happen?"

"Right after I rescued you from the barn, Chris. The files she retrieved when she helped Brand escape the compound included the information about where the other

Repeaters were located. Henry had collected the Repeaters and put them in a mental hospital in upstate Indiana." She looks directly at Brand in the mirror and says, "You would have known that if you had looked at the files like she wanted you to." She turns her attention back to Chris and continues. "You said Freedom was trying to capture Brand and Deus as well. I believe he realized he had created the key to his own death. He was too late in realizing that. With the knowledge of their location, Deus swooped in and murdered the other Repeaters in a single move, eliminating the possible threat to her own life." She looks at Brand again. "I would guess Deus wasn't necessarily trying to kill Calli on your doorstep, but *you*, Brand. As long as you are alive, you are a threat to her the same way the Diamond Bearers are."

"She got my address from the files, didn't she?"

"Probably," Crimson answers.

"I don't understand you, Crimson." Brand looks out the window, probably at the passing lights of the countryside. "Do you have more powers than Diamond Bearers do?"

"Yes."

Brand turns his attention back to Crimson's eyes in the rearview mirror. "Then why don't you use them? I mean, you seem like you just stand by and observe, figuring things out after they happen. Why not view the future or read minds to find out for sure?"

"Because that's not how nature works. Nature evolves after an event or mutation. It doesn't try to prevent the event."

Brand folds his arms across his chest. "Well, it doesn't take a rocket scientist to see that you're not following nature completely."

"Go on."

"Why are you trying to stop Deus? Why did you have Calli recruit me? You might as well go running in on your white horse and take the government out on your own. So what if your involvement creates a bigger problem? Just take care of any new problems as well. No, I think the reason you are so concerned with this problem is because Deus knows detailed information about *you* that's contained within those files. *You* are now in a position *you've* never been in before. You can be killed by Deus, and you're trying to prevent your own death. You don't need me to kill Deus. You just want me to save your ass."

"What makes you think that?"

"Because there's nowhere on the face of the earth you can go that government satellites or drones can't find you. This is a new day and age. Technology has advanced exponentially, and along with it came the creation of Deus and me. Suddenly your peaceful little passive existence is threatened. You would go against nature's ways to save your own skin."

I cut him off. "Brand! Knock it off!"

"Or what, Calli? Come on!"

Crimson speaks to my mind: *Let him go, Calli. He needs to feel he is important here.* Then she says to Brand, "Brand, I have one word for you: evolution. Species have survived after genetic mutations because they fought to survive. Their mutations either help or hinder them, and only the strongest survive. Not all are born strong. They have to learn how to be. If one person steps in and saves the lives of many, the saved won't have developed the strength to survive. Am I afraid of Deus? Not personally, but I am worried about your safety and the safety of the general population. I only have to outlive you and Deus, which I can do easily enough because there *are* places I can go that drones and satellites can't find me. I'm fighting for the survival of the human race as you know it."

Brand presses his back into the seat and relaxes his body. "Well, you're up against some pretty difficult odds. The government has files on you and your red spinel."

"The files are all misleading. Red spinel doesn't have the powers they think it does.

I ask, "What does red spinel do?"

"Many years ago, I tried to use the stone to harness powers of healing. It worked somewhat, but it was being used to prolong life unnaturally. Red spinel developed the reputation of being the immortality stone, and people from all over flocked to collect their own pieces of spinel. Royalty would place it in their crowns, believing that they might be able to escape death. Oftentimes, the red stone was referred to as 'ruby' to throw off any thieves who sought the immortality stone. Over many centuries, the lore of the spinel died out, and the red gems kept the name of 'ruby' until not too long ago, when it was determined that the valuable 'rubies' were actually spinel. Then the lore resurfaced, and I suppose that's where Henry and the government got their ideas that spinel could make you immortal. There's nothing to it. Spinel is no more powerful than golden topaz. Both stones will only hold their power for just so long."

I add, "Like a battery. Deus told me she was trying to get her hands on spinel. Maetha and the other Diamond Bearers still believe spinel is important. Haven't you told them?"

"No. I don't see the need to. Besides, if I had updated everyone, Henry would have been updated as well. He spent many years investigating and hunting for the exact spinel. Those were years not spent harassing my Diamond Bearers."

Crimson turns the car into the empty mall parking lot

where Suz and I used to go when we were bored. Memories of my high school days flood my mind. I project my thoughts into Chris's mind. *This is where I used to hang out a lot. Also, it's where I first discovered Brand had a superpower.*

Crimson says, "Let's set a trap and try to rescue Beth from Deus."

Brand grunts at the mention of Deus's name. "If she hurt Beth in any way, I'll . . . "

"Kill her?" Chris prompts.

"No. But she won't like it, whatever I do."

Crimson says, "Calli and Brand, go stand by the side of the building, well away from the doors, in clear view. Chris and I will position ourselves a bit further away. When Deus attempts to shoot either one of you, repeat back with Calli so she can tell me which direction the shot came from. Chris and I will retrieve Beth and meet you across the road over at the pet store. Deus may not even figure out she's been played. She'll only think that Beth got away, and Rolf's intel on where Calli's diamond would be was wrong."

"Sounds good," Brand says.

Crimson drops us off at the sidewalk under a street lamp.

Chris sends me his thoughts. *Be careful, Calli.*

I reply with my mind, *I'll be fine. Don't worry.* I close the door and Crimson drives away.

"Is she always like that?" Brand asks.

"Like what?"

"Never mind."

"Brand, when the laser light was on me back at your house, did Deus ever get her shot off? I mean, did I get shot before you repeated?"

"No."

"Do you think Crimson is right that she was aiming

for you?" I ask.

"Maybe. Or maybe she couldn't decide who to kill first?" I laugh and then Brand's expression changes. "She's about to shoot you."

"What? Did you just repeat?"

"Yes." Brand studies the surrounding area, looking in the direction of the pet store.

"Where is she, Brand? Crimson, are you hearing this?"

Yes. Hold your positions.

Brand turns to me. "The laser bead was on your left front shoulder and slowly moving down and over." He points to the center of my chest. "We have less than two minutes before it appears again."

I say, "Crimson said for us to hold our positions."

"Tell her I think Deus is positioned by the pet store. The bead isn't angled at all. It's dead on square. She's definitely trying to kill you, not me."

Crimson's voice enters my head. *We have her in sight. She's exited the vehicle and has the gun resting on top of another car, aiming.*

I tell Brand what Crimson says.

He asks, "What's the make and model of the car?"

Tan, Pontiac, Grand Am, four doors, Crimson responds.

As soon as I relay the information to Brand, the world spins wildly as he repeats back to when Crimson drops us off at the sidewalk. Brand says to Crimson as we climb out of the car, "You're looking for a tan, four-door Pontiac Grand Am near the end of the parking lot directly across the road by the pet store. Oh, and don't park by the pet store. Park further down by the stoplight. Try to grab Beth the moment Deus exits the car. Don't forget to count to thirty."

Crimson eyes him curiously and nods her head.

Brand turns to me and says, "Maybe we can get this

right this time."

"How many times have you repeated?"

"Four. All the passing traffic is our saving grace here. Deus has to wait a few seconds before she can take the shot, which will hopefully give Chris time to carry Beth away. We'll see."

We stand waiting for the events to unfold. The seconds seemed to click slower and louder than a grand-father clock in a horror show. Then Crimson's voice shouts, "Run, now!"

I grab Brand's hand. "We're running." He doesn't resist as I direct our superfast legs behind the nearest tree and then along the parked cars out of Deus's line of sight. Crimson's voice tells me to run in the other direction toward the fast-food building behind the strip mall. Since Brand has not repeated yet, I figure this escape will be successful.

We reach Crimson's car and quickly jump in, Brand in the front-seat and me in the back with Beth and Chris. Crimson begins to pull forward, but Brand abruptly yells, "Left! Turn left." She does.

I turn to Beth and give her a hug. Her ankles are still cuffed. I ask Chris, "How did it play out on your end?"

"Easy. Brand's description of the car helped us find it right away. Deus got out and I crept up to the other side of the car. Beth opened the door, and I picked her up and ran."

Crimson adds, "I let the air out of the back tire while Chris took Beth, and then counted to thirty and stabbed the front tire with a screwdriver. The sound pulled Deus's attention away from you. That's when I told you to run. Deus realized Beth was gone but couldn't do anything about it, so she tried to complete the shot on you, but you two were gone. Plus, her back tire was flat, and she couldn't repeat back because more than thirty seconds had passed. She'll have to steal another car now."

"Yeah," I say. "I noticed she was driving a different car than the one from Maetha's memory."

Beth says, "She knows how to hotwire a car in a couple of seconds."

Brand chuckles. "Well, now she's driving a red sports car. We just avoided her. Boy, is she upset!"

Beth asks, "Do you think she'll figure out that you've repeated with her?"

"How would she know? I can repeat beyond her."

Beth says, "You don't understand what it feels like to be unable to do what you want to do all because someone like you is preventing it. When that guy, Travis, kidnapped Anika and me, we didn't try to escape because we didn't want our families harmed. After we arrived at the dead Diamond Bearer and saw Deus standing there, all proud of herself, I decided I wasn't going to stick around. But before I could run, she made me put these cuffs on. You see, I think I had already run away, but she repeated me back and prevented it. Well, now think about the fact that she tried to shoot you guys, but ended up losing me, *and* her car was disabled. Don't you think she'll put two and two together and realize you're more powerful than she is?"

"She might, but what's the difference? She'll keep trying to kill me anyway."

"That's true. She was headed to your house to kill you when she got a call sending us to the mall."

Brand says, "That's what you saw, Beth. She actually came to my house to try to shoot Calli, but I repeated back to the point before she arrived."

"That makes more sense now. When we stopped in the parking lot she said something about changing her mind and how she was going to kill Calli.

I ask Beth, "How were you and Anika captured?"

"Is Anika okay? Did anyone go help her?" Beth asks.

"Yes. She was picked up by other Diamond Bearers and taken to a safe location."

Beth lets out a sigh of relief. "Well, after all of us parted in Denver, we were intercepted on our way to Montana by a group of soldiers with human auras. I instantly thought of you, Calli, and your aura, so I was caught off guard, thinking they were friendlies. Once I realized we were in danger, I tried to run but found I had no power. We were put into the back of a military truck along with other prisoners . . . other people with powers. I recognized Seers, Readers, and Hunters alike. Not even the Seers could foresee the soldiers coming. I think it was because of the vests they were wearing."

Crimson adds, "Or more likely, it was because they were all Unaltered humans. No power works on an Unaltered."

"Mine does," Brand states. "I used it on the guards when Calli and I were taken. You know, right after I was poisoned. Calli said they were Unaltered."

"Brand's power works on Diamond Bearers too," I confirm.

"How do you figure that?" Crimson asks.

"Because he's repeated with both me and Maetha."

Brand adds, "And Mary. Don't forget her. That's how we discovered Freedom was using Rolf to spy."

"He's repeated with you too, Crimson." I'm not sure if I need to point this out to her or not.

"I know," Crimson says, "but I'm not an Unaltered. I was originally a Healer."

"What?" A collective question comes simultaneously from our mouths.

Crimson doesn't elaborate on her past. She says, "Stay

focused on the topic here. The military is using the vests on Unaltered soldiers to round up people with intense powers. Seers cannot foresee their arrival. Mind-Readers can't enter their minds to detect danger. What Beth has been through will continue to happen to more people until we find a way to stop the government's progress."

Beth says, "Well, anyway, after we were captured, Deus Ex arrived and had the one guard separate me and Anika from the rest. She said something about keeping us nearby in case she needed to use us as bait."

Crimson announces, "Everyone should have an Imperial topaz charged with running power on their person at all times to avoid capture."

Beth says, "In a perfect world, we would. I think it's easier just to keep an eye out for the auras of Unaltereds. Did you ever figure out how to view them, Calli?"

I tried to tell Beth that isn't something I can just learn to do, but my mouth won't move. My voice box won't form sounds. I realize this bit of information is being blocked by Crimson. Instead, I say, "No, I never did."

"I'll help you later on." Beth turns her head and directs her next question to Crimson. "So are you a Diamond Bearer as well?"

"I'm friends with Maetha." Crimson turns her head to Brand and asks him, "Would you tell her everything I told you?"

Brand nods his head and turns around in his seat to face Beth and says, "So that's why we're heading back to Colorado."

Beth's eyebrows rise as she replies with a long drawn out "Oh." Then she puts her hand to her head. "Don't spin me around anymore."

I don't think I'll ever get tired of Brand's power. In the blink of an eye, he's probably talked to Beth for over an hour.

Still holding her head, Beth asks, "Do you have any water or food? Travis wasn't too concerned with our stomachs or bladders."

I reach down for the bag of food Crimson bought and pull out a bottle of water and an apple.

Brand turns and faces the front. He points to the right and says, "Crimson, turn in that alley."

"Hey," I exclaim. "We're really close to my house. Do you think I'd have time to grab something?"

Brand answers, "Can you do it in two minutes?"

"What is it?" Chris asks.

"My great-grandmother's journals. They're in a box in the basement."

Brand responds, "You can, but it will be a little tricky trying to give Deus the slip after stopping."

Crimson speaks to me. "The information contained in those journals will be helpful in our mission." She turns into my back driveway, as if she has been there a hundred times, and I jump out of the car. Chris follows close behind.

I punch in the code to the house security system and open the door.

"Wait," Brand says as he runs toward me. "It's taking too long. Let's get this done right."

Chris rolls his eyes a little at Brand's overconfidence, and the three of us enter the back porch. It is strange to be arriving to an empty house, knowing my parents are still in Maine. A fleeting thought fills my mind about the possibility of strangers being inside my home, waiting to attack, but the fact that Brand hasn't repeated eases my fears.

I follow Brand as he leads the way to the basement. The box is at the bottom of a pile of boxes. Clearly we have repeated a few times.

"Grab it, Chris," Brand orders with a flick of his finger.

Chris quickly moves the other boxes off and picks up the heavy box underneath.

"We have to go now!" Brand says on his way to the stairs. He takes them two at a time.

Chris mutters some indiscernible words under his breath as he follows me up the stairs.

Crimson has turned the car around for a faster exit, with the trunk hatch open. She waits for us to put the box inside and then shouts, "Get in!"

Brand is already in the front seat. Chris and I pile into the backseat as Crimson drives away. My head is pressed up against Beth's knees, and my rear is in the air in Chris's face. It takes a second to reposition while being tossed around by the motion of the car. Between hitting potholes and turning sharp corners, I'm surprised I don't get a concussion.

"Left, then sharp right!" Brand orders.

"Seatbelts, please," Crimson states sweetly. I look up at her through my hair, which has fallen over my face. The sharp right throws my body into Chris's arms, and he settles me in between Beth and him. I pull my seatbelt and latch it just in time to weather a sharp left.

"Lights off!" Brand demands. Crimson quickly complies. Up ahead, a red sports car blows through the intersection, not seeing us coming from the side direction. Four police cars, in hot pursuit, chase after Deus with their lights flashing and sirens wailing. "Turn right and get us out of this city!"

Crimson turns right, setting us on a course in the opposite direction from Deus.

Beth asks, "Do you think they'll catch her?"

"Not a chance," Brand states confidently. "I was in a car chase like that once. Repeaters have all the advantages."

Beth responds, "Well, do you think she will catch us?"

"No, this gives us a gap she can't close."

"Brand," I ask, leaning forward toward the back of his seat, "why is she letting the cops chase her? I mean, couldn't she have prevented that from happening?"

"She's only got thirty seconds to deal with. I imagine she avoided them at first, but at some point she would either have to allow more time to pass or she would simply lose her edge. The fact that the cops are so close behind her makes me think she's not worried about them. In the end, she'll throw them off by disappearing into thin air, or so it will seem. She'll find a way to run from the car and avoid being detected."

"Oh." I sit back in my seat with less understanding than before. "I still don't completely understand the whole repeating power. Like, for instance, when we were in the Denver motel room, and you and Deus were in the repeating battle that I had to end with obsidian, why was I able to open the pocket watch?"

Brand says, "I lose a fraction of a second every time I repeat. I'm pretty sure the same goes for Deus, but I'm not positive she loses the same amount of time as I do. So if I repeat the same two minutes over and over, the point I repeat back to is always moving forward on your normal timeline."

"Oh, like when Maetha and I watched you fight the gang at Cedar Hills Amusement Park?"

"I guess. I always let stretches of time move forward once I'm satisfied with the outcome."

"How much time do you lose with each repeat?"

"A tenth of a second."

"So in every second, you can repeat about ten times

before you can't undo it?"

"I think the easier way to look at it would be to say I lose a tenth of a second that can't be fixed every time I repeat."

"Do you lose the same tenth of a second if you repeat a full two minutes versus repeating ten seconds?"

"Yep. Activating the repeating power causes a tenth-of-a-second loss."

"Have you ever run out of time?"

"Yeah. It sucks."

"What happened?"

"I ended up getting my nose broken. Luckily for me, the other guy just walked away afterward. That was when my power first surfaced. I figured out pretty quickly that I don't have forever to get something right."

Chapter 8 - Casualties of War

Crimson directs her words to all of us in the backseat. "You can access the box in the trunk by pulling the back of the seat down on either side. I suggest you get several pairs of eyes reading those journals while we have time on our hands. I plan on driving throughout the night. The individual reading lights above your heads should be enough to read by."

"Can't we pull over and just open the trunk?" Chris asks.

"We shouldn't give Deus any opportunity to catch up with us," Crimson replies. "I'm sorry, Beth, but you'll have to wait till we're in a safer position before we can get those cuffs off your ankles."

"No problem at all, Crimson," Beth says.

The three of us figure out the easiest way to get to the box in the back. The task isn't easy, but we accomplish it with greater finesse and style than when we did piling in the car during the fast exit from my house.

Soon we are reading the journals of Anamaria Radu, my mother's great-grandmother, who lived from 1883 to 1981. Anamaria lived long enough to tell my mother some interesting stories that stuck with her. The journals were passed on to her when Anamaria died. My mother was nine years old then.

Beth turns a page in the journal she's holding. "Boy, it sure would have sucked to live before toilets were invented."

"Or toilet paper," Brand adds.

Crimson says, "It's probably hard for you to imagine, Beth, but you need to realize there are still plenty of places in the world that don't have running water and flushing toilets . . . or toilet paper."

"Eww."

I say, "Here's something interesting. Anamaria was ten when she wrote this entry in 1893. She visited her dying grandmother, who told her about the ancient vampires and demons. Anamaria didn't write what her grandmother said, just that the subject was brought up. Maybe her later entries will have more detail."

"Some of these pages are stuck together, or are illegible." Brand struggles to separate two pages.

"Be careful, Brand," I say.

"It's no use. I've tried five times to separate these pages, but they always rip."

Crimson looks over at him. "Move on, Brand."

"Look for anything that refers to Demons and dangers of the dark, Brand," I instruct him.

"Do you think we'll be able to discover a way to get rid of the Shadow Demons altogether?" Chris asks.

"I'm not sure, but I do expect we'll learn more about them in the process of sifting through these journals."

Chris says, "I can't even imagine what it would be like to be able to go out in the dark without a Pulse Emitter and feel safe."

"Well, even without Shadow Demons, there are still dangers in the dark," I say.

"You know what I mean."

Beth says, "Many people with powers are able to be out at night now, thanks to your discovery, Calli."

"Hopefully we'll soon be able to make it possible for everyone to be safe outside. I don't deserve all the credit here. I couldn't have created those devices without Brand's help."

Brand shoots a surprised look my way. Why is he surprised I would give him credit? He quickly brushes off the compliment. "Nah, the idea was all yours, Calli."

"I couldn't have done it without you to help me test the end-product."

"Doesn't change the fact that they were your brainchild, not mine."

Beth laughs. "You two are pathetic. Just accept the compliment that you've done something incredible and move on!"

We continue to read for a few hours more and then one-by-one fall asleep to the mild rumbling of the tires on the road.

Once the sun rises, Crimson pulls off the freeway and stops at a gas station. She pulls up next to a truck that's parked in front of the building. Without speaking, she unlocks the doors and gets out of the car. The driver of the truck rolls his window down and hands something to Crimson, who accepts the item. I can tell the man is a Hunter by his appearance and his scent. Crimson then opens Beth's door and bends down and unlocks Beth's cuffs with the key the Hunter has just given her. After she's finished, she hands the cuffs and the key back to the man in the truck and he drives away.

Crimson gets back in the car and says, "We're in Des Moines. We're going to go meet with Clara Winter." Crimson lets me know that because of her connection to Maetha's mind, she was able to have Maetha make the arrangements with the Hunter ahead of our arrival.

I speak back to her mind. *It must be nice to have access to Maetha's long list of helpers. You probably have a longer list, I'd guess.*

The list of helpers is a shared list. The difference is, the helpers don't know who I am.

Oh.

Crimson drives to one of the hotels along the main street and pulls into the parking lot. Clara stands next to her car, and beside her is a boy about the age of twelve.

"Nate?" Beth nearly shouts once she sees him. "Why is he with Clara?"

None of us speak, which I think is appropriate. Crimson should be the one to tactfully deliver this news.

Crimson parks the car and turns to Beth. "Come with me. Clara has something to tell you." She addresses the rest of us. "The rest of you are to wait in the car."

Chris, Brand, and I sit silently in the car while Beth's life is destroyed behind the closed door. My super-hearing could allow me listen if I wanted to, but I don't. My emotions are hard enough to keep under control.

I sit in the back seat next to Chris. His arm is around me and he pulls me close to his body. I feel safe and comfortable in his arms, and I tell him so with my thoughts.

He replies, *I wish I didn't have to go back to my father's compound and could just stay by your side, but I can't have that wish right now.*

After about a half hour, Crimson comes out and sits in the car with us. She says, "Beth wants to continue traveling with us. She's a strong girl."

Brand asks, "How did she take the news?"

"As well as can be expected."

I ask, "Is her brother a Runner?"

"No, he's a regular boy. Clara found him hiding when she arrived at their parent's house to pick up Beth. Beth had arranged for Clara to meet her there after she left Denver. Clara was the first to discover Beth's parents, but it was too late to help them. She called the police and reported the crime. Nate escaped injury, but he was quite traumatized by the whole thing. The fact Beth was intercepted and seized on her way home, *and* that her parents were killed before we pulled her from Deus's captivity means this is a 'take no hostages' mission. The same probably happened for Anika. Her family was most likely killed before she escaped from Deus Ex, not because of the escape. Good thing she is on her way to be with Jonas."

Chris tenses up. His thoughts reveal the reason: *My father is acting on all the information I've given him over the years. He has names and addresses of people with powers because of me and my spying. I have to end this, Calli.*

Crimson speaks to both our minds. *You'll get your chance, Chris. I have no doubt. But don't waste your energy on berating yourself. What's done is done. You will have the opportunity to clear your conscience.*

Brand lets out a despondent sigh. "How do they get away with it? Why is this kind of thing happening in our country?"

Crimson responds, saying, "People fear what they don't understand. Cosmic powers are frightening to those who don't have any, and this leads to governments taking a defensive stance."

Beth comes out and climbs in the car. She wipes her swollen eyes and clears her throat. "I need to care for my brother now, and the best way to do that is to ensure he has a future. Let's finish this and tie up all the loose ends."

Crimson replies in a smooth, comforting voice that I recognize as a form of her healing power being delivered through her words. "Beth, you are a strong individual with the ability to compartmentalize your pain . . . for a little while. We will press forward and complete our mission one way or another and we'll give you emotional support along the way. Brand will help you." Crimson instructs us to rearrange our seating. Chris will be in the front passenger seat, which will allow Beth to sit next to Brand.

Crimson says, "I gave Clara the order to take care of your brother. Your mother's sister is handling the family's affairs and will be in contact with Clara concerning final arrangements."

Beth nods. "Aunt Steph will handle everything the way my parents would have wanted. Let's get back on the road, please."

I place my hand on Beth's knee and infuse her with emotional support. "I'm so sorry this happened, Beth."

She thanks me for my positive energy and then lays her head on Brand's shoulder. He pulls her close.

Crimson backs out of the parking lot and enters traffic once again, heading toward the I-80 on-ramp.

We have nine or ten hours of driving time ahead of us before we reach Denver. Joking and having fun seems like it would be in bad taste and disrespectful to Beth. So I look over the journals in an effort to keep my mind calm and clear.

Several hours into searching the journals, I find an entry in which Anamaria writes about her grandmother speaking of a Demon hunter who would travel around cleansing the shadows with a bag of rocks. The man was later hanged for being a sorcerer, but her grandmother told her the night air was more peaceful because of him.

I know I need to get my hands on some obsidian. I

speak to Crimson's mind: *Do you have any obsidian? I want to test something with the Shadows.*

Yes, in a lead box in the trunk. When we're in a safer situation, we'll pull it out and let you do your experiments.

She has apparently read my mind.

Brand's demeanor has changed completely. He isn't dropping puns or jokes anymore, and it is obvious he's behaving this way for Beth's sake. The biggest change of all is that he isn't repeating. How do I know this? I can finally read his mind.

Even though he isn't repeating, his mind still doesn't look or feel like anyone else's. It's as if his brain is built differently. Normal mind-reads, like Beth's for example, consist of immediate thoughts and emotions up front and center. Brand's mind contains regrets and wishes that he could have brought about different results with different repeats. I actually have to dig deeper to find out what he's thinking about Beth. I find he is genuinely concerned about her and cares for her. He hopes nature will step up and make sure General Harding pays for what he has done to wreck the lives of so many.

I view some of Brand's memories after I figure out how to do so. His relationship with his father was exactly as he had portrayed: distant and uncaring. So much about Brand's personality makes sense after viewing different altercations he had with his father. Brand's memories about his mother are similar to his memories of his father. She was distant and constantly nervous around Brand.

The memory of the day his mother found Brand and Suz together is strange to view through a mind-read. The scene is an alternate universe kind of thing, because technically nothing ever happened. Brand's mind holds the memory of her words and the revelation concerning Suz, but I know if I could look into his mother's mind I wouldn't find any indication the conversation ever took place.

The whole thing makes me immensely grateful that I have parents who want the best for me and who support me.

I search Brand's mind for the day he caught me looking at him across the high school cafeteria. Several memories line up like tabs in a file cabinet. They are repeats . . . with me! Each one begins with him catching my eye and then walking over to me.

"Hey, it's Calli, right?" he says. "I haven't had the opportunity to get to know you."

My response—which I have no memory of ever saying—is, "What makes you think that will happen now?"

His mind zips back to the beginning, or what I realize was a split second later than the beginning. The next approach is quite lame. He comes to my table and says, "When did they let you out?"

"Huh?"

"Out of heaven, because you are absolutely perfect!"

I stand and throw a nasty glare at him and walk away.

His mind zips again, and this time he says, "Hey, Calli, wanna come sit with us?"

"Why?"

"I don't know. You look kind of lonely all by yourself."

"I don't feel lonely, and besides, I don't think your admirers would approve." I motion over at his table. He looks over to find frowns on the girls' faces.

His mind zips back. "Hey Calli, could I sit with you?"

"Why?"

"You look lonely."

"I don't feel lonely."

His mind zips again. "Hey Calli, mind if I sit here?"

"Why?"

"Because you've got the perfect table. Secluded, private, and perfectly alone . . . just the way I like it."

"I doubt that. I've never seen you sitting all by yourself."

"That's because the girls never leave me alone."

"You don't seem to mind."

"Well, I just want to get to know you a little better."

I roll my eyes and stand. "You can have the table." I walk away with my lunch tray, and he lets out a frustrated grunt.

His mind zips again and again and again. Each time his results are that I brush him off or act disinterested. I note the distinct difference of what Brand feels for me as a person compared to what Chris feels for me. To Brand I am nothing more than a contest. The more he tries to win me, the further away he ends up. Finally, his mind zips back to where our eyes meet across the room, and he lets the time play out without coming in my direction. From his perspective, I quickly look away, embarrassed, and take my tray to dump it. Then I walk to my locker. Brand jumps up and follows me with new ideas of how to win me over.

Knowing that Brand loses a tenth of a second with each repeat, I am now able to see and understand the process firsthand. From my perspective, the small amount of time that our eyes locked across the cafeteria lasted a second and a half. What I actually observed was his many repeats, all causing him to lose a tenth of a second, which made it appear he was stationary in his seat. From Brand's perspective, however, he was trying frantically to figure out how to get me to smile and soften my tough-girl exterior. If I had fallen for his charms, I would now have a different memory. The reality of just how powerful Brand really is hits me hard.

I remember going to my locker after the awkward moment at lunch and getting my books. When I shut the door, Brand surprised me with his presence. He was ready to pick right up where he had left off, but he only tried once, which I shot down effortlessly. That frustrated him to no end. His patience worn thin, he had exclaimed, "Why doesn't it work on you?"

Through it all, though, I was proud of myself for never caving in to his charms. I kept my strong will even though I was being manipulated. I couldn't say the same for the other girls.

Now, here in the present, Brand is no longer manipulating Beth. He shows respect, true concern, and compassion . . . which borders on love. In my matchmaking college escapades, I looked for the futures of couples to determine if they would be good matches. In this case, I decide not to look for Beth's future to see if they will end up together. They are both my friends, and I don't want to be in the position of knowing the future and having to watch them struggle. If I knew they weren't going to make it, I might be inclined to tell Brand to just give up on her, or the other way around with Beth. On the flip side, if they were struggling and I knew they would make it in the end, I might feel inclined to help them through their battles. No, I feel it's best not to look for their future at this time. We all have too much on our plates at the moment.

Beth is trying her hardest to be strong. I feel so sorry for her. I can't imagine how difficult it would be to hear the news she received. Deep down, I know someday I'll be in her shoes dealing with the death of my parents. Hopefully, it won't be the same type of situation and will happen many years down the road after they have lived long, happy lives.

Around noon, Chris informs Crimson, "It's time I called my father."

Crimson pulls the car off the road into the parking lot of an abandoned business. Weeds grow through the cracks in the pavement. "Chris, I'm getting out here. Drive the car up the road to the gas station on the right. When you're finished with the call, drive the car further up the road and pull over. If you're captured on surveillance cameras, you shouldn't be seen with me."

"Okay," Chris responds and opens his door to get out.

Crimson activates her invisibility first, then opens her door.

Brand and Beth let out gasps of amazement. Brand blurts out, "How does *that* power work, and where do I get some? Can you charge a topaz with it?"

Chris hurries around to the driver's side, closes the door, and straps his seatbelt in place. He follows Crimson's instructions, pulls out onto the street, and drives to the next gas station. He parks by the payphone and turns off the car.

He catches my eye in the rearview mirror, and I read his mind. He feels nervous about communicating with his father, afraid he will mess things up and expose the team to danger. I send him my thoughts. *Your feelings are completely normal, Chris. I'm nervous for you too, however you've done a great job maintaining your dual positions. You'll continue to perform well.*

He nods a thank you in my direction and climbs out of the car.

My eyes follow Chris as he walks to the payphone and inserts a credit card before punching in the phone number. I study Chris again. He stands tall and confident, one hand jammed into his pant pocket, the other holding the receiver to his ear. His broad shoulders carry more emotional stress and pressure than any ordinary guy, but he handles it well. His blond hair flies about, ruffled by the gentle breeze that blows in my direction, bringing his scent to my nose. Mmm, he smells really good!

Chris turns his head and meets my eyes with a sultry gaze. *You smell better, Calli. Almost can't help myself,* he thinks, speaking to my mind.

Wow, I really need to work on not projecting my thoughts.

Chris looks away and speaks into the receiver. "Sir, it's me."

I focus my hearing beyond the nearby conversation between Brand and Beth and listen to General Harding's voice. "Where are you now?" Harding asks.

"Kearney, Nebraska. I'm headed back to the compound. We had to execute Plan B because Deus Ex wasn't able to touch the diamond."

"I already know the details, Chris. Deus is on her way back as well. Are you alone?"

"No, I'm traveling with Calli and her friends. I'm alone right now, though. They still believe I was kidnapped by Deus Ex, and they rescued me. Now they're helping me travel back to you to 'spy' for them. I told them I needed to touch base or you might grow suspicious."

"Excellent. Keep up the appearance that you're *their* spy. I told Deus Ex to come back here and help me with my next project. The two of you have demonstrated your loyalties."

"Thank you, sir. Deus Ex is quite determined to collect a diamond for you. She tried to shoot Calli, but the male Repeater prevented a successful hit. Deus won't be able to kill Calli, as long as he is nearby to repeat the situation."

"I'm not concerned with the other Repeater. In fact,

soon neither of them will be a threat to us anymore."

"What do you mean?"

"You know what I'm talking about, Chris. You just bring Calli to me. All you need to do is get her in the vicinity of our snipers and we'll do the rest."

"All right. I'll contact you when we're in Denver."

They end the call, and Chris walks back to the car with a troubled expression. He climbs in the driver seat and maneuvers the car out into traffic and heads west. After a couple of blocks, Chris pulls off the road and waits for Crimson. He surrenders the driver's seat to Crimson after she reappears beside the car.

Once back on the road, Crimson asks, "What was your father talking about? He said, 'You know what I mean.' Does he have a new weapon?"

"I don't know for sure. At least Deus isn't following us anymore."

Crimson turns the wheel and accelerates onto the road. She only drives a short time before slowing down and pulling into a restaurant parking lot. "Let's go in and eat. I need to meet with Maetha."

We climb out of the car and walk to the front door. Crimson instructs the waiter that we need two separate tables. She and I will sit apart from the others. The waiter seats us and hands us menus. Crimson quickly orders tea and a garden salad. I need a bit longer to decide what I want to eat. I am starved, and I want to fill up.

Maetha walks into the restaurant and heads straight to our table. She sits down by me. I know she is bi-located, but I doubt the waiter will be able to tell.

Maetha and Crimson hold a private non-verbal conversation while I peruse the menu. I can't decide between the homestyle pot roast sandwich and the spaghetti platter. I ask Chris's mind what he is going to choose. He replies, *The broiled salmon and house salad.*

Just like at the Runners compound, huh? Did you ask for some nuts too?

Hey, I happen to like fish, thank you very much.

Well, I'm going to have the spaghetti platter. It comes with a side salad, so I'll get my veggies.

The waiter comes over and asks Maetha what she'd like to drink, she tells him she doesn't want anything. He takes my order for the spaghetti platter, then heads to Chris's table to get their orders.

Maetha speaks aloud, bringing me into the conversation. "We've interviewed Travis thoroughly and learned of a new weapon at General Harding's compound, only it's unclear what he intends to use it for."

Crimson asks, "Should we bring Chris over? Perhaps he knows."

"Yes, I believe he may know something about it."

"Calli, ask him to join us," Crimson says.

Chris, would you come over here for a minute?

Beth and Brand, seated beside each other, watch curiously as Chris gets up and comes to our table. He sits in the empty chair across from me, next to Crimson.

Maetha says, "Chris, we've obtained some information about a machine your father has that removes powers from people. Do you know anything about it?"

"I know about it, yes. I wasn't aware it was a threat, though."

"Travis told us something that's given rise to concern. He says the machine creates power-infused crystals."

"Yeah, it does. The machine removes a person's power and stores it in quartz. It doesn't kill anyone, not like when a person is strapped up with quartz and fed to the Demons. I didn't think it was of any significance because it wasn't hurting anyone."

"Travis's information leads us to believe the machine creates Unaltereds," Maetha states.

"I don't know about that. How do you tell if someone's DNA is completely unaltered? Is there a test or diagnosis?"

"They would have an Unaltered's aura," I say, "and the Shadow Demons wouldn't be interested in them anymore."

"I don't understand why you feel the machine is a threat."

"If your father is able to create many Unaltereds at a time, he could then assemble an army even faster than the time it takes to grow them naturally like Freedom was doing. Couple this with the vests, and you have an indestructible soldier with the ability to sneak up on unsuspecting Readers, Seers, Runners, Hunters, and Healers. Add in the fact that General Harding has a Diamond Bearer working for him, and we've got an even bigger dilemma."

I ask, "Do you really think if people were put into a machine that took their powers away and made them Unaltered, they would then go out and kill other people with powers? Would the new soldier be loyal? Or would they need to be threatened and coerced? I don't see how the machine would be used to create a controllable army. The logistics are just not in favor of that happening."

Crimson agrees. "That's a good point, Calli."

I ask Chris, "Do you know how long the machine has been operational?"

"I don't know for sure, but it's been in the compound ever since I can remember. It hasn't always been operational, though. Long stretches of time would go by when the machine was covered with a plastic sheet. I do know it uses an extreme amount of power and has to recharge between uses."

"How much time between uses?"

"I don't know exactly, maybe a day or two. Ask Travis. He might know. I can always find out when I return, though."

My belly sinks with dread at the mention of Chris's return to the compound. I worry about his safety. I don't know how long it will take to hear from him once he enters the facility. With no way to connect to his mind, I will just be waiting blindly like everyone else.

Crimson takes charge of the conversation. "We'll reach Denver tonight. Tomorrow, Chris will re-enter the compound and begin collecting the information we need. Maetha, you will travel to us for the purpose I discussed with you earlier. Merlin is moving forward with his efforts in the Senate Budget Committee. He thinks he can have the whole program shut down in a month and have General Harding charged with several felonies. If nothing else, we need to prevent the progress within the compound so a shutdown will be justified."

"Understood." Maetha bows her head and leaves the building before vanishing.

The waiter arrives with Crimson's tea and our salads. He lets out an unprofessional huff at the sight of Chris sitting at our table. "Will you be eating at this table or that one?" he asks with one of those tones.

Crimson sighs. "Chris, why don't you return to your table? Your presence is stressing out the waiter."

I suppress a smile, and Chris stands, his shoulders nearly bumping those of the waiter's. I watch Chris straighten his spine as much as possible to overemphasize his superior height to the average-sized waiter, who instinctively steps back to let Chris pass.

The waiter leaves our table, and Crimson speaks to my

mind. *I'm with you on the idea that the general isn't trying to create an army, per se. However, he has something up his sleeve.*

No doubt.

Crimson sips on her tea and takes small bites of her salad.

I ask, "Crimson, do you actually *have* to eat, or are you self-sustaining?"

"I have to eat, just like you, only I choose to eat fresh, healthy food whenever possible. I find my energy levels are maintained by the energy of the earth and anything that grows naturally."

I know she isn't talking about the same kind of energy I am thinking of, the kind that when it drains, you have to take a nap. No, she's talking about her energy powers. I realize I'll have to change my dietary habits if I want to be in touch with the earth's energy. For now, though, I will enjoy what might be my last plate of spaghetti.

Chapter 9 - Repeating with Demons

We arrive in Denver at eight o'clock in the evening. Crimson secures a couple of motel rooms close to each other. She invites Chris and me into one room and hands the keycard to Brand for the other. Just as Brand is about to take the card, Crimson pulls it back and eyes him with her "mother knows best" glare.

"Fine, I'll behave," Brand concedes.

I can only figure Brand had either repeated or Crimson had spoken to his mind.

We enter the room, and Crimson instructs Chris and me to sit down on the edge of the bed. She pulls a chair in front of us and says, "Chris, I'm going to alter your vision to include basic auras. We need to know if your father's machine is creating Unaltereds."

"What does an Unaltered's aura look like? Does it look like Calli's?"

"No. You'll see color surrounding an individual, mostly above the head and shoulders." Crimson reaches toward Chris, then pauses. "I might as well alter both of you at the same time. I like all of my Diamond Bearers to be able to see auras."

Shocked and amazed, I look at Crimson. She smiles at me as she places her right hand on my forehead and her left on Chris's. My heart rate increases with excitement as deep piercing warmth from her palm penetrates inside my head. Tingling sensations tickle the back of my eyeballs. I wonder if Chris feels the same sensations.

I simply can't believe my vision is being altered by the oldest woman on the face of the earth. The possessor of the Primal Stone, creator of the Sanguine Diamond, protector of nature's will . . . and now my mentor.

The heated warmth in my head subsides, and my thoughts turn to curiosity. Like Chris, I also wonder what an Unaltered's aura will look like.

Out of the blue, my mind opens up into a vision. I see Chris standing next to his father in a room that looks like the CT scan room in a hospital. Chris and his father both have auras around their bodies, which shocks me right off the bat because that would mean they are Unaltereds. Then, to my horror, Chris extends his hand toward his father and reveals that he's holding a Sanguine Diamond. His father reaches forward to take the diamond!

I shout and jump right out of my chair. As reality slowly sets back in, I turn around to find Crimson eyeing me suspiciously, as well as Chris.

"What is it?" Chris asks.

"I . . . uh, had a vision."

"About what?"

I search Crimson's eyes, hoping she'll speak to me and order me to say nothing. She doesn't. I look over at Chris's inquisitive gaze and say, "It's nothing. I probably misinterpreted it anyway."

"What do you mean? It's not nothing. Do I die again?"

"Actually, no, that's not what it was about . . . I don't think I should talk about it."

Crimson nods. "Calli's right. Dwelling on future visions is not the best use of our time. Come now, we have a lot to do."

We follow her out of the room and down to Brand's room. She inserts the extra keycard into the slot and opens the door. Brand and Beth instantly sit up straight on the bed and put some distance between their bodies. Their faces flush with embarrassment.

Crimson's lips press into a hard, thin line and she shakes her head ever so slightly. She looks at me and says, "I'm going to retrieve the obsidian so you can conduct your experiments." She leaves the room.

Chris puts his arm around my shoulders and pulls me close. "The look in your eyes has me worried," he says. "I'm not asking you to tell me about your vision. I only want you to know that I would never do anything to hurt you. You know that, right?"

"Yes, I know. I'll discuss it with Crimson later. Please don't lose any sleep over it, Chris."

"Are *you* going to lose sleep over it?"

Crimson enters the room carrying a pewter-colored antique box with ornate filigrees covering it. She sets the box in the center of the table, carefully unlatches the old-fashioned clasp, and raises the lid. My powers rush out of my body.

I hate this feeling!

"What are you thinking of doing, Calli?" Crimson asks me as she sits down on one of the chairs. I know she has already read my mind concerning my intentions. She wants me to voice my intentions to the group.

I walk to the box and glance inside at the several pieces of obsidian of varying sizes. I reach in and pull out the largest and hold it up to the light. "I want to use the obsidian on the Demons. Chris told us that General Harding is able to charge quartz crystals with the Demon's healing power by luring them to a person with powers who has quartz on their body. My logic is, if Demons have powers to give, they have powers to take away." I extend my hand with the obsidian toward the group. "According to the journals, a black rock was used to cleanse the shadows. It might have been myth or folklore, but it also might have had substance. I want to know what happens when a Shadow Demon encounters obsidian." I point to Brand, saying, "And you're gonna help me."

"Aw shucks, Calli. I thought you'd never ask. I just love getting eaten alive." Brand says sarcastically.

Beth's expression is hard to read. "What are you talking about?"

Brand says, "It's how Calli developed the Pulse Emitters in the first place. I had to get eaten several times over in order to come up with the final result."

"What?" Beth exclaims, and then a devious smile creeps across her face. "This I've got to see."

I laugh. "No, we're not going to play around with Brand's life this time. The idea is to have him test just once to make sure the Demons are not a threat."

"Thank you, Calli." Brand swipes his hand across his forehead.

Chris asks, *Did he really get attacked? Did you see it?*

Yes. It was the most horrific thing I've ever seen, but then he repeated back as if it had never happened. Only I remembered it vividly. I'll never get the image of Brand being shredded out of my head.

I know what you're talking about. I've seen the same thing. But those kids didn't get to repeat back to life.

I'd forgotten what his father had shown him at the compound. His words are a reminder of just how serious an undertaking this project is. If I can figure out a way to alter or remove the Shadow Demons, I might be able to save the lives of some captured people as well as the rest of us.

I clear my throat and say, "So here's what I'd like to try. Brand, and I will go out and locate the Demons and find a safe viewing area for you two." I point to Chris and

Beth. "Crimson, do you want to come too?"

"No, I need to communicate with Maetha," Crimson says. "You four can do this on your own."

Brand excuses himself to use the bathroom. Chris and Beth move closer together and begin talking quietly. Crimson uses the opportunity to speak to my mind. *It's not a good idea for both of us to be powerless at the same time. This is your discovery. You need to finish it. I might add that you are the first person to make a serious attempt to tackle the problem in the history of Diamond Bearers.*

Well, that's not saying much, Crimson. It required the use of an Mp3 player and batteries. Those kinds of things weren't around fifty or a hundred years ago, let alone a thousand.

Crimson says, *Twenty-one Diamond Bearers have been unconcerned with the problem for the several decades the devices and batteries were around, thinking nothing could be done. Your mind clicked into motion with new and innovative ideas, and you were able to come up with a plan. That's the type of quick thinking that sets you apart from the other Diamond Bearers.*

I nod and try not to look like I am pleased to hear her compliment, but I am *very* pleased. I replace the obsidian in the lead box and close the lid, feeling my powers flood back into my body at once. Holding the box under my arm, I walk to the door.

Brand comes out of the bathroom and says, pointing to the closed box, "Now that's more like it. I can't stand that stuff!"

I motion for him to follow me. Beth throws out a "be careful" just before we walk out of the room.

Brand and I walk down the sidewalk toward the corner of the building. Brand mutters, "Just like old times, huh?"

"Are you nervous?"

"Well, yeah, of course I am. It goes against all common sense to knowingly walk into danger."

"Well, we're going to keep you as safe as possible, believe me."

"Yeah, whatever."

"So, you and Beth, huh?"

"What about it?"

"Nothing. It's great, I guess. If nothing else, you're helping Beth keep her mind off her parents' death. It's just that only yesterday you were going on about Suz." I catch myself and realize I shouldn't have said anything. "Sorry, it's none of my business."

"It was only yesterday to you, Calli. To me, it feels more like last year. You do realize that if I repeat continuously every two minutes for twenty-four hours, my day lasts over three years, don't you?"

"Whoa, are you serious?"

"You're the brainiac. Do the math. Besides, I've been repeating with Beth. We've been getting to know each other." Brand stops walking and says, "Oh, I forgot." He reaches up and turns his Pulse Emitter off just as we reach the corner. "I can sense them. Do you see them?"

"Yes," I say. The hideous skeletal creatures hover right at the edge of the light, trying unsuccessfully to get to Brand. "It's still amazing to me that just the right amount of light eliminates the danger. I don't know where they go or why they can't attack in the light."

"Or enter buildings or cars. Don't forget that."

I walk into the darkness and stand among the rotten-smelling, floating threats. As before, the Demons float gently out of my way. I step toward Brand and back out into the light.

"It still amazes me that you can see them when no one else can."

"All Diamond Bearers can see them."

It's true, Jonas chimes into my mind. *I can see them now that I have a diamond.*

I open the box and expose the obsidian, causing the Demons to slide further back into the darkness. I walk forward into the dark, only to push them deeper into the shadows. Once I walk a good twenty feet away from Brand, I notice the Demons begin to congregate near him again, so I turn in his direction.

"It's certainly a repellant," I say. I close the box before reaching Brand and am instantly swarmed with Demons. I open and close the box quickly, just for fun, and then chuckle to myself at the little bit of control I have over them. It's entertaining to watch them whoosh away from the presence of the obsidian. I step beside Brand once again and call out to Chris with my mind. I tell him where we are and invite him and Beth to come join us. "Chris and Beth will be here in a second," I say to Brand.

"You called him with your mind? That's so cool! Hey, open the box. I want to walk in the dark without a Pulse Emitter."

"You can't activate your repeating power if the obsidian is exposed, idiot. What if something goes horribly wrong?"

"Oh, yeah, you're right. You make it look so inviting. The freedom to go anywhere at any time is something I haven't had for quite a while."

Beth and Chris walk toward us with their Emitters turned on and nervous expressions on their faces.

Brand motions to their Emitters. "You can turn those off. Don't worry. I can repeat us out if anything goes wrong."

Chris's eyes seek out mine, asking for confirmation. I can tell he doesn't want to put his complete faith and trust in Brand. I can't blame him. The Shadow Demons have been in Chris's life more often than not. After extracting his memories and experiencing his fear, along with the added trauma of watching the gruesome deaths at his father's compound, I can't blame him one bit for being hesitant.

"It's all right, Chris. If there was going to be a problem, Brand would already know."

Chris and Beth reach up and turn off their devices.

I look into the shadows to find a growing number of Demons arriving for the potential feast of powers. Apparently, the smell of three powerful people is enormously inviting. I notice a couple of the Demons are slightly more human looking than the rest. I open the box again and watch as they flee from the four of us. I close the box.

Beth says, "I don't see anything."

"Only Diamond Bearers can see them," Brand informs her.

Beth strains her eyes, giving me the impression she feels she might be able to see the Demons if she tries hard enough. She says to me, "I still remember when you ran out of the cave right into the dark on the delivery trip." She laughs a little. "That was wicked awesome! And scary at the same time."

Chris changes the subject. "So they don't like the sound of your heartbeat?" His thoughts, on the other hand, reveal something else: *Awesome, Beth? Like hell! I died a million deaths when she ran out into the dark.*

"That's right. My heartbeat repels them, but it's also the fact that I don't have any powers. I'm of no interest to them. In fact, if you three went back inside, the Demons would leave this location. They sure hate the obsidian, though. It has an effect on them, but I can't figure out what." I walk into the dark with the box closed.

"What are you doing?" Chris asks.

"I want to get a closer look at a couple of these things," I say as I approach two Demons who look less frightening than the others. I try to bump into them, but they float out of my way before I can make contact.

Brand clears his throat and I notice how the Demons seem to become energized. I glance over my shoulder at everyone. "Brand, I want you to inch closer to the line of darkness. Make the Demons think you're about to walk into their midst. I'm going to open the box and then close it quickly, you know, just in case you need to repeat."

"Fine," Brand grumbles. "Here I go." He bends his knee to move his foot forward. The movement causes a spike in the energy emanating from the Demons. I interpret the energy as their excitement about capturing a person with powers, which, if Clara Winter was correct, is what the Demons thrive on. They died attempting to become more powerful, and now in their altered state, they are still trying to consume powers.

I quickly flash the obsidian and watch what happens. I actually see an energy wave. But this wave is coming from the Demons toward me. I witness the nearest Demon's transformation. Its appearance shimmers, and becomes more human looking.

The ground spins wildly, knocking me off balance. Before I can fall, I find myself standing in the same spot, surrounded by the Demons I hadn't altered yet. "What happened, Brand?"

"You told me to inch toward the shadows. You never told me to stop, so I entered and the Demons started attacking me. Sure am glad you closed the box."

"But Brand, it worked!"

"What?" Brand, Chris, and Beth all ask together.

"Before you repeated, I flashed the obsidian and caused some of the Demons to change form. Of course, now they're back to where they were. We need to do it again, but this time don't cross the line into darkness. Just make them think you are going to. Something about that level of energy spike is different than it is at other times with them. Maybe all three of you should edge closer."

Brand says, "Beth, you got too close. Don't go so far this time."

"This time? I didn't move at all—oh, wait, did you repeat?"

"Yep," Brand says, then lowers his voice and adds, "Please don't do that again. I don't like seeing you die."

The ambient lighting is too dark to see color on Beth's cheeks, but her body language tells me she is completely into Brand. She dips her chin, angles her head, and turns her shoulders and hips ever so slightly in his direction.

"All right," Chris says. "Let's do this."

"Okay," I respond. "On the count of three, move toward the dark." I count out loud and then watch the frenzy within the shadows. I flash the obsidian, causing several Demons to lean toward me. I slam the box shut and watch.

Brand asks, "Did it work?"

"I wish you could see this. It's amazing! They're changing back to human form. Not all of them, just the ones closest to me. Let's do it again." I count to three, and we perform the exercise again. Before my very eyes I watch the transformation of the few Demons closest to me. They look like walking dead guys. One is a woman. I shout, "It's working! Again, let's do it again!"

We continue to execute the same procedure over and over again. Brand has to repeat a couple of times, once for Chris, when he got too close, and once for himself. Finally, I tell them to stop.

"I'm surrounded by creepy zombie-looking dead people,"

I say. "They don't have claws or sharp teeth, and they behave differently than the monsters they were. They don't seem to be interested in you guys anymore. They're just wandering around aimlessly. So Brand, why don't you try walking into the dark?"

"Sure," he responds, less than enthusiastically. He reaches his hand out much further than before and holds his position. Then he moves his whole body past the line of light and into the darkness. Nothing happens. He begins jumping up and down and pumping his fist into the air and yelling at the top of his lungs, "You did it! You did it!" He bounds over to Beth and grabs her hands. She's reluctant, but he pulls her into the darkness and spins her around.

"Brand! Stop it!" she shrieks.

Chris and I laugh at the same time and catch each other's eye. I walk to him and take him by the hand and lead him out into the darkness. His grip tightens with fear, but he continues forward with me into the shadows. Then he pulls firmly on my hand and brings my body stumbling back to his, capturing me in his arms.

"Do you know how long I've feared the shadows? More than half my life." He tightens his hold and kisses me assertively and extremely sensually for several long seconds. I relax in his embrace and wrap my arms around his neck, thoroughly enjoying his kiss.

Beth's giggling and high-pitched laughter pulls us out of our intimate moment, and that's when I smell the approaching Demons. "Back into the light! Now!"

Everyone complies without hesitation, and Brand doesn't have to repeat.

"There are more arriving now," I say.

Brand asks, "So what exactly did you do?"

"I think I altered their power with the obsidian. The Demons who are present now are new ones. The Demons in human form are still here too.”

“Then let's do it again on the new ones!” Beth exclaims.

“Okay, get ready.”

We repeat the same steps as before until all the Demons resemble the walking dead. I confirm the results and the safety of the shadows, and everyone walks toward me once again.

Beth asks, “Do you think it's possible to eliminate the Demons worldwide so we won't ever have to worry about entering the shadows?”

“We're sure going to try! But unless you are with Brand, me, or some other Diamond Bearer, you won't be able to know if the shadows are still dangerous. So I'd keep your Pulse Emitter on at all times.”

We return to the room, and I tell Crimson about our successful experiments.

Crimson says, “We'll have a gathering soon, and you can tell everyone about your findings.”

Jonas says: *Man, Calli, this is huge! I am so glad to know you personally.*

What? You're acting like I'm a superstar or something.

Well, you are! You should hear what Mary says about you.

What does she say?

That you are filling the shoes Maetha always said you would.

Okay, now you're freaking me out.

“Calli, what is it?” Chris asks.

I look around to find everyone staring at me.

Chris voices his assumption. “Jonas is speaking to you, correct?”

“Yes.”

Chris lets out a slight sigh. I know he's frustrated with the private conversations Jonas and I share and that they bring on twinges of jealousy, but he doesn't need to be worried. I don't know how to tell him that, though.

Crimson says, "Jonas and Mary will not be part of the gathering because Avani is about to drop off Anika into their care." Crimson speaks to Jonas through my mind: *Jonas, Anika needs to be with strong supporters—you and Mary— when she's told about her parents. Please help her through the emotional turmoil she's about to experience. You'll be able to hear our gathering through your mind connection with Calli, but don't let it distract you from the responsibility I'm giving you now. Take care of Anika.* Crimson speaks out loud to our group: "We will gather in a half hour."

I'm surprised Beth, Brand, and Chris are included in the Diamond Bearers' gathering. Crimson sits in the far corner at the table by the window. The four of us sit on the bed closest to the door, near the bathroom. The Diamond Bearers begin bi-locating to our location a few at a time. Amenemhet, Duncan, and Avani arrive first. They are followed by Yeok Choo, Kookju, Jie Wen, and Chuang. They stand along the wall, in front of the television and dresser, and anywhere else they can crowd in. All assume reverent, submissive positions in the presence of Crimson.

A knock comes on the door, and Brand says without looking, "It's Maetha."

I turn around, excited to see Maetha. Beth lets her in. Maetha smiles at me as she walks across the room to Crimson. In that short amount of time, Alena, Merlin, Ruth, Aernoud, and Fabian materialize. They stand in front of the window. The room is quiet as we wait for the final two Bearers who will be attending to arrive. Amalgada and Marketa appear and sit on the other bed.

Crimson begins the meeting.

"Welcome. We've reached a milestone in the world of powers. A solution to the threat of the Shadow Demons has been discovered by Calli Courtnae. She will now explain the process so it can be replicated worldwide."

Oh, the pressure. I straighten my posture and take a deep breath, then address the group. "The Yellowstone obsidian cancels the Demons' power the same way it affects ours. When used properly, it alters their forms from animal to human—well, more like decomposed humans. Once they are altered, they're no longer drawn to people with powers, and as far as I can tell they don't change back to animal form."

Heads nod and quiet gasps are heard around the room. I continue. "It's not enough to confront Demons with obsidian. You have to catch them by surprise as they're about to attack." I go on to explain exactly how we performed the cleansing of the shadows and add that without a Repeater like Brand, cleansings will need to be performed through doorways or windows for safety. I recommended that they have a person with powers stand by an open window of a house. As long as someone doesn't cross the threshold or reach outside, they will be fine. The Bearer then should wait to spring the obsidian on the Demons just as they are ramping up in energy."

Jie Wen is the first to respond. "I disagree with the idea of altering the Demons. The Demons keep people with powers under control by limiting the amount of time they can use their powers. Imagine if the Death Clan had been able to roam freely after dark, killing more people. If controlling the Shadows was a good thing," he points to Crimson, "she would have done it long ago."

I respond to Jie Wen, "The idea of eliminating the Shadow Demons is to protect peaceful, innocent individuals. The government is already launching attacks on cosmic-power individuals and clans. Those who aren't killed are taken and subjected to horrible experiments. If these people could flee into the night, lives could be saved."

Kookju argues the same line of thinking as Jie Wen. "Who's to say this isn't nature's will in play? Perhaps it's time for people with powers to be eliminated."

I noticed Beth is wiggling anxiously in her spot.

Kookju continues. "It may be time for a reduction of the population again."

Duncan retorts, "Diamond Bearers have no interest in controlling any people or powers. And we're certainly not charged with reducing the population."

"We weren't charged with maintaining it, either," Jie Wen replies back. Kookju, Chuang and Yeok Choo nod their heads in agreement.

Beth can't contain her feelings any longer. She directs her emotion-laced question to Jie Wen: "So what does a Diamond Bearer actually do all day long? Sit and wish that no problem will ever come your way? Blow off everything as 'nature's way?' And then go home and work on your fantasy football team while families are torn apart by forces against nature? I thought you were the protectors! The Death Clan was eliminated because they were using their powers to kill people. Well, now regular humans are using stolen powers from Demons to kill people, *my people, my family,* and you just want to turn your back? If I had a diamond, I would jump at the chance to personally travel the world to eliminate Shadow Demons. You don't deserve your diamond!"

The room is still. I sure don't want to be the first person to speak after that tirade. I glance around at the other Bearers, wondering what they are thinking. Jonas's thoughts ram into mine, sharing his approval of Beth's harangue. Brand's mind is readable again. He's in awe of Beth and her sharp tongue. Chris's thoughts reveal the respect he has always had for Beth and her perspective. Beth's mind is heavily cluttered with everything else she wants to say and wishes she had said.

Jie Wen's voice enters my mind as he telepathically projects his thoughts to the other Bearers. *Why is she allowed to be at this gathering? She's nothing more than a human trying to sound important. Does she not realize who we are?*

I wonder why Crimson isn't contributing to the conversation until Maetha speaks. I figure Crimson and Maetha have been communicating through their quantum entanglement, and now Maetha is about to speak for the both of them.

Maetha says, *The human girl is here at Crimson's request along with her two male companions. Do you wish to question Crimson's thinking, Jie Wen? Kookju?* Maetha then says aloud, "Beth, your feelings are fully understandable. I do believe you would make a perfect Demon hunter under different circumstances." Maetha turns her attention to the rest of the group and says, "Sometimes when one becomes exhausted with the duties and responsibilities of being a Bearer, they must be relieved of their burden. At Crimson's request, I ask that if anyone is feeling tired of their responsibilities to step forward so your diamond may be retrieved and reborn."

Jie Wen sticks his chin in the air, but keeps his eyes on Maetha. His defiant body language is nothing short of confrontational. Other Bearers dip their chins to their chests out of respect for Crimson.

Crimson stands and glances around the room. Her piercing eyes quietly rest momentarily on each Bearer, one at a time. Finally she speaks. "Throughout the history of human beings, certain things have survived the test of time:

the need to congregate and rely on each other for life's basic physiological needs; empathy and compassion to reduce suffering; and the need for love. When an individual feels they are above any of these needs, they are then considered a threat to everyone else. Before any of you became Bearers, you were Unaltered humans, and each of you displayed the proper amount of compassion to qualify for the opportunity to choose this path. Every one of you in this room chose to follow nature's way. Every one of you now has a choice to make. Either continue being an agent of nature or withdraw from your responsibilities and surrender your diamond. I know there are several of you in the group with conflicted thoughts running through your minds. That is why I have selected and approved several new candidates for diamond rebirth. If it is truly impossible for you to continue in the duty you accepted so long ago, I will personally replace you. The choice is yours."

I glance around the room, wondering who in this group Crimson has identified as conflicted.

She continues, "We now know how to eliminate the Shadow Demons. Every Bearer will comply with the cleansing efforts, unless he or she chooses otherwise. I will be delivering obsidian to those of you who do not have any yet. That is all for now."

The bi-located Diamond Bearers vanish, leaving our small group alone in the room. No one speaks for several long seconds.

Crimson extends her hand toward Maetha, who places a leather pouch in Crimson's hand. Crimson makes eye contact with me and breaks the silence. "Calli, come with me."

Chapter 10 - Crimson's Liaison

I stand up and walk over to Crimson. She leads me out of the room and into the night. We walk away from the motel and across the busy street until we reach a vacant city park. Crimson points to a nearby bench, and we take our seats.

I want to ask her questions about what just happened, but decide against it. Instead, I sit quietly and wait for her to speak.

"Calli, would you tell me about the vision you saw concerning Chris?"

Her question catches me off guard. "Oh, um, well, I saw Chris and his father standing in a room. They both had auras of Unaltereds. Chris was holding a diamond in his hand, and he handed it to his father. That's it."

"Hmm. Distressing." She turns away and stares in the direction of the playground equipment.

"I think I'm developing a greater understanding of future visions," I say.

"What do you mean?"

"Well, I've begun considering several different possible reasons why Chris would hand a diamond over to his father. First, I wonder about the diamond. Whose is it? Whose heart will be blown out? Or is the diamond one of the two without owners? Second, I wonder about the machine Travis talked about. I think we'll find that the machine does indeed create Unaltereds . . . and it will be used on Chris and his father. As for the reason why Chris would hand over a diamond to his father, I haven't come up with anything plausible."

Crimson looks at me again. "Yes, I think you're getting the idea of how to interpret visions. Your young mind isn't cluttered with age-old wisdom. It's still operating with youthful questions and curiosity."

"What? I thought wisdom was a good thing."

"Wisdom isn't a curse, but it tends to slow down a person when they take on a 'been there, done that' attitude. I've observed that the older someone becomes, the less likely they are to ask questions or get themselves in precarious situations. Not that it's a bad thing to protect one's life, but to protect one's routine or way of life by figuring they've seen and done it all . . . well, I think you understand what I mean. Jie Wen doesn't want to upset his routine. He doesn't like change. But being a Diamond Bearer comes with a heavy responsibility."

"I was wondering about him . . . but you already knew that, didn't you?"

Crimson smiles and sets the leather pouch Maetha gave her on my lap. "Maetha charged a topaz with the invisibility power you used to view Neema's death. Where is that topaz?"

"In the vial in my pocket."

"Does it still contain any power?"

"Yes."

The dim lighting from the street lamps is enough that I can see a warm smile on Crimson's face. "My dear, that's all I need to know. Please open the pouch."

Bewildered, I untie the strings that secure whatever is in the pouch. I expect to find another topaz inside. Instead, a brilliant blue glow meets my eyes. I tip the pouch enough for the small stone to tumble out into my hand—the Grecian Blue Diamond!

"Is this Maetha's?" I whisper in awe.

"Yes."

Crimson takes my elbow and helps me stand. With one hand, she clasps my hand—the one that holds the Blue Diamond—and places her other hand on my back between my shoulder blades, just like Maetha did when she was about to shove the Sanguine Diamond into my heart.

"What are you doing?" I ask, as nervous excitement races through my body.

"Calli, I'm asking you to take Maetha's position as my liaison with the Diamond Bearers. You've already proven yourself by not misusing the invisibility topaz, and before that by not imposing your will on others. With this stone, you'll have the ability to control others' actions and speech. You'll be able to alter other people's perceptions and memories of events, like when Maetha helped your hometown forget you had broken the world record. Of course, you'll have the ability to become invisible because that power is included in the power of altering perceptions. Maetha didn't actually become invisible. She only altered people's perceptions of her."

"Wait. Is that how she altered her appearance when she met with my parents?"

"Yes. The Blue Diamond takes the same power a step further and allows you to create the effect of being invisible."

"So basically, the Blue Diamond is the ultimate mind-control stone?"

"Correct. Now, Calli, will you serve as my liaison?"

"What about Maetha? How does Maetha feel about having to surrender her Grecian Blue?"

"She's pleased her fate isn't the same as Neema's."

I glance down at the blue stone, feeling less guilty about taking possession of Maetha's property. "Will I be able to control the powers right away, or will I need to be trained? I mean, I don't want to accidently make someone run out in front of a bus or something."

"You'll be able to use the powers immediately. Your own mind and the intentions that lie inside are what power the stone. You've always had good intentions and a good heart."

"Then, yes, I'll accept the Blue Diamond."

With that declaration, Crimson gently presses my hand to my chest. I uncurl my fingers from around the stone and feel it heat up against my clothing. Yet the diamond doesn't blast into my heart. Crimson controls my movements, causing my hand to rise up toward my face, and my mouth opens. It seems I am about to swallow the stone.

"Relax, Calli. This diamond will not choke you. Once it reaches your stomach, it will travel through the stomach wall and enter your heart. Your pain will be significantly less than what you've experienced before."

I place the glowing diamond in my mouth and swallow. She's right. Even though the size is larger than any pill I have ever taken, it slips down my throat with ease. I double over clutch my chest when a sharp jab in my stomach, followed by intense sting in my heart takes my breath away. I instinctively heal my pain, which *is* much less than I've experienced, and turn my head toward Crimson.

Her mind speaks to me, almost the same way Jonas's does, except I have more liberties within Jonas's mind. Crimson's mind is barricaded off. I can't read her mind, only hear her thoughts, and her thoughts tell me a changing of the guard is taking place.

"Calli, I've decided that when Chris returns to his father's compound tomorrow, you and I will accompany him invisibly. Tonight, I want you to wear your invisibility topaz so it can be completely charged. We need to be prepared for any obsidian when we approach the building."

"Will Chris know we're going with him, or will we be invisible?"

"Chris will know. You can tell him privately that you are the Grecian Blue Bearer. Jonas knows, naturally, due to your quantum entanglement." Crimson pauses and then says, speaking to Jonas through me, "If you'll keep this information secret, I'll remember that when I'm making my final decision on whether or not you get to keep a diamond."

Jonas responds in my head, *I understand completely.*

"I'm still deciding who else will be privy to this change," she says, looking beyond me. "We're going to go test your invisibility and mind-control." She points down the road to an illuminated business sign. "Come on."

We begin walking toward the lighted sign. Crimson says, "Become invisible, Calli."

"How?"

"Well, how did you do it when Maetha gave you the topaz?"

"I'm not sure. I knew the stone was charged with the power, so I just held the stone and hoped no one could see me."

"Your instincts were right and it worked. This will come natural to you. Simply think about any possible person in the near vicinity not seeing you."

"Okay." I close my eyes and imagine being invisible.

"Good job, Calli. You're invisible to others. Now, keep that in mind. If we were walking on a busy street, it would look as though I'm walking alone. People walking in my direction wouldn't know they need to avoid walking into you. You'll need to remember that when you're invisible."

We near the sign, which reads "Finer Diner" in big,

bold red letters. The building is well illuminated, revealing several customers inside. A large man in overalls approaches the door from inside as we near the entrance from the outside. I can tell he's going to hold the door open for Crimson, like a gentleman.

Crimson speaks to my mind. *Remain invisible and see if you can get by him without being detected.*

How hard can it be? I think.

The man, still inside the Finer Diner, pushes the door open and holds it by stretching his arm against the door, his body turned sideways. Crimson smiles and thanks him as she walks by. As soon as she enters, I follow, only to run head first into the man in overalls, who moves to leave as soon as Crimson is through the doorway. The man stumbles, confused and puzzled, trying to figure out what happened.

Crimson says, *It's not as easy as you'd think, Calli. Here's a hint: run through the door as if you're trying not to be caught on camera, like at the convenience store the night before Justin reunited the shards.*

Why didn't you tell me that before I got steam-rolled by the farmer?

Let's sit. Remain invisible.

The waitress, Edie, comes and stands by the table. "What can I get for you, ma'am?"

"A cup of tea, please."

"Certainly." Edie twirls away and heads to fill the order.

I ask, *She didn't see me, right?*

Correct.

You can, right? You said earlier, when you told us about the Grecian Blue, that only other Blue Bearers can see one another.

Yes. In fact, at your track meet, both Maetha and I were there. We were able to speak mind- to-mind, like you and I are right now.

Chris had already received his vision of you, and Harold Bates had the imposter diamond already, so the only remaining piece of the puzzle was you. Your running time had to be just right. Fast enough to be considered a Runner, slow enough to be placed on the delivery team.

So, how exactly did Maetha make me run fast?

She had placed an additive in your drinking water a couple days earlier that had saturated your body sufficiently. She was able to control the substance within your cells using her spell-casting abilities.

But she said magic doesn't work on me.

She controlled the substance, not you. It was the easiest way to make your run believable and it worked.

I think for a second, then say, *Maetha made my parents agree to let me go to Montana, didn't she?*

Yes. The Blue Diamond's power of mind-control works on everyone, unless obsidian is present.

I remember she said magic doesn't work on me when she explained everything after the Death Clan died. It wasn't magic at all. She used the power within the Grecian Blue. *Has she ever misused her power on me, like the way she misused it on Chris?*

No. Let this be a lesson for you, Calli. Controlling your parents' minds didn't hurt them and didn't hurt you. When Maetha controlled Chris's mind, her actions definitely hurt him and almost brought about your death. The events that transpired in Alaska were a turning point for me. I learned Maetha had left the path of nature's way. Maetha knew better than to rush the discovery of the yellow stone. Her lack of patience—or more likely her lack of powers because of the obsidian—caused her to act irresponsibly. You, on the other hand, have had more years of your life without the diamond. You are used to having to wait for results, used to using common sense to figure things out. If the situation were reversed, you wouldn't have made the same decisions. Am I right?"

Edie arrives with the tray of tea and places it in front of Crimson.

"Thank you," Crimson says politely.

"Sure you don't want some biscuits or pie to go with the tea?"

"I'm sure. Thanks."

Edie walks away to service another table.

I wouldn't have made the same decisions as Maetha, I say, as if we were never interrupted.

Crimson selects an herbal variety of tea and opens the packet to remove the teabag. *The lesson is, when you're deciding who to control, consider the outcome. Will it harm the individual or anyone directly associated with the individual? Save your usage of Mind-control for the purpose of protecting others from harm and for maintaining invisibility. In saying that, I will tell you there are some minds out there you cannot control.* She places the teabag in her cup and adds the hot water.

Really?

Other minds that can't be manipulated are those of infants and children up to the age of about two. Usually they can't speak well enough to identify you to others in the room. They may point or smile at what looks like empty space, though. You won't be able to control mentally challenged individuals. As with infants, these individuals aren't usually able to identify you either. Something else to keep in mind is that animals will still see you. You must be very careful around pets. They can give away your location faster than you'd think.

Interesting. I imagine a cat rubbing up against my ankle and intertwining itself between my feet, or a dog jumping up on me. Something like that would look extremely strange.

Calli, a customer is about to leave. I want you to slip out of the diner through the open door. Walk out of sight and then cease being invisible before walking back to the building. I want everything to look as though you are just arriving to meet with me.

Got it.

I follow her instructions and slip quickly out of the door, following closely behind the customer. I wait until no one is around and then abandon my invisible state . . . or should I say, I stop radiating Mind-control. Then I reenter the diner and walk over to Crimson.

"Good to see you, Calli," she says sweetly.

I take my seat again and ask Edie to bring me some tea as well.

Crimson says, "We need to discuss tomorrow's plan. I like to go into a situation knowing what the goal is. This way I can determine whether a decision will result in helping us reach the goal or not. We may be around some obsidian and may need to evacuate if our charged topaz wears off too quickly. The goal is to determine the effectiveness of the machine Chris and Travis spoke of."

Edie brings me a cup, a spoon, and a fresh pot of hot water. I select a packet of chamomile tea and place the bag in my cup. "What if they aren't using the machine tomorrow?"

Crimson pours hot water in my cup. "Well, that's a possibility. We'll need to return another day. Calli, you should prepare yourself emotionally. We may witness cruel acts, violence, or traitorous behavior by Chris. If you gasp or cough, you may be heard. I want you to understand completely that if you are detected, I will remain invisible."

"I understand. I will do the same if you are discovered," I half joke, half mean it.

"Good."

I can tell she's not joking at all.

As we return to the motel, Crimson speaks to my mind, letting me know Chris and Brand have been moved to one room and that Beth and I will be in another. Maetha and Crimson apparently won't sleep, but will remain in our room.

I wonder if I can at least say goodnight to Chris. Crimson's thoughts merge with mine, and she lets me know he already understands he won't be able to see me till morning. She tells me that with my new mind-control power, my potential behavior around Chris might be too overbearing, and we simply don't have time for any intimacy.

Maetha smiles at me when I enter the room and projects her thoughts. *Of all the Bearers to receive the Blue Diamond, you are the one I would have chosen as well.*

I feel extremely humbled, and respond respectfully, *Thank you. If you don't mind me asking, how did you remove the shard?*

The same way it went in. She points to her chest.

I wonder why Crimson had me swallow the stone. My thoughts are answered by Maetha. She says, *We suspected the diamond would enter the heart through the stomach wall, but we were not sure. If it didn't, you'd still have the diamond inside you for a day or so, at which time Crimson would insert it into your heart the old-fashioned way.*

Well, I'm glad it worked the first time. I smile at Maetha, then ask, *Maetha, remember when I said I'd find a way to get rid of the Shadow Demons, and you said you didn't see that in my future? What did you see?*

I saw exactly what you accomplished; I just didn't understand what you were using at that point. What I determined was that you didn't kill the Demons, which is in fact true. You only altered them to a non-threatening state. While you and Crimson were gone, the four of us went back out and altered more Demons. Now they are simply dead Healers, and I might add, I recognize many of them. Plus, I noticed some are so transparent they are almost non-existent.

Crimson's thoughts merge with mine. *Future visions are tricky things, wouldn't you agree, Calli? We'll need to keep that in mind concerning the vision you saw of Chris and his father. I know he wouldn't betray us. He'd only give a diamond to his father if he had a damn good reason.*

I agree.

The next morning, I pull my hair back into a ponytail and fasten hair clips at my temples to hold the loose tendrils out of my eyes. I change into a fresh running suit. I tell Beth, as per Crimson's instructions, I'm going to ride with Crimson to take Chris to his father's compound.

Chris and I climb into the backseat of Crimson's car. She puts it in gear and leaves the motel parking lot.

Sitting next to Chris, I lean my head over and rest it on his shoulder. I read his mind.

I can't wait for this to be over, Calli. Can you talk about the vision you had?

I answer back, *You don't die. Just do and say the things that come naturally.*

I don't suppose you can tell me what you and Crimson did last night?

It's a secret, so don't say anything to Brand or Beth. Crimson had Maetha remove the Grecian Blue shard, and Crimson gave it to me. Crimson and I are going to follow you inside the compound invisibly and observe.

What? Chris turns to face me. *But . . . the obsidian . . . do you have an invisibility topaz?*

Of course.

A quarter mile from the compound, Crimson stops the car and everyone gets out. Chris takes his position behind the wheel, and Crimson and I maintain our invisibility as we run behind his car, all the way to the compound. He parks in the parking lot, and we wait for him to climb out and close the door.

All right, let's do this, he thinks.

Crimson and I walk two paces behind Chris, in time with his footsteps. He halts at the gate and waits to be buzzed in. The large iron gate sluggishly opens just wide enough for Chris and then begins to close. We are able to get through quickly enough.

We are now within range of the obsidian on the outside of the building, and I access my topaz for further invisibility. My heart pounds mercilessly in my chest, which in turn causes it to hurt because of the shard. Yet I don't want to take any energy away from maintaining my disguise in order to heal my heart. Hopefully, I'll be inside the building soon enough and can use my full powers once again.

"Hey Chris," a male voice sounds from the left. A young man wearing a military uniform hurries to catch up with Chris.

"Hey Max. Have you held things together here while I was away?"

"Barely, Chris, just barely," he chuckles. "Your dad will be happy to see you."

"I bet." Chris punches the security code into the number pad, and the door unlocks.

Max grabs the handle and pulls the metal door open. "After you," he says as he waves his hand.

Chris hesitates for a microsecond. Crimson rushes in front of Chris, and I follow her.

I'm glad to be wearing a Runner's suit because of its moisture-wicking properties. Surely I've lost a gallon of sweat out of pure nervousness.

Not nearly enough time has passed since I was in the compound. The tension and heightened security has definitely increased. Once the door closes, my powers rush back into my body because of the lack of obsidian. I switch back to using my diamond powers for invisibility and also to heal my heart pain. The back-and-forth maneuver reminds me of the backup generators at my father's office during a power outage, only I need to make sure I don't accidentally materialize in front of anyone.

Crimson speaks to my mind. *I didn't foresee the complications with your shard and being in the presence of obsidian. I was about to abort this mission out of fear you might die.*

I would be lying if I said I wasn't worried. I'm good now, though.

Chris speaks to Max. "Looks like my father is taking precautions." He points to the security checkpoint directly in front of us. Chris's thoughts enter my mind. *Do you see Max's aura, Calli?*

Yes, I answer silently. *He's the same guy Justin was feeding information to, right?*

Right.

Max says, "Yeah, your dad is a bit on the paranoid side, but you didn't hear that from me." Max turns his attention to a different guard who is standing behind a table. "Hey, Ethan," he says, while emptying his pockets into a gray tub. Max then passes through the archway. Ethan pushes the tub through a small X-ray machine.

How are you two going to get through? Chris worries in his mind.

Crimson glances at me with concern. Our shared minds quickly assess the situation. We come to the conclusion there isn't enough room to squeeze around the guard without touching him. We'll have to go through the arch.

I say to Chris, *We'll walk through with you. If the alarm goes off, they'll think it's you and they'll run you through again.*

"Hello, Mr. Harding," Ethan says, greeting Chris.

"Hello, Ethan. This is new," Chris says, motioning to the detector.

"Yes sir, it is. Please empty your pockets and take off your necklace."

Chris asks, "Why do I have to take off my necklace? It doesn't have any metal."

General Harding has instructed us not to allow any form of rock, crystal, or jewelry into the compound without his approval. Would you like me to call him for approval?"

"No, that's all right." Chris unties his necklace and lays it in the bin. Then he empties his pockets.

"Wait to step through the X-ray machine until I direct you," Ethan says.

"It's an X-ray? Not a metal detector?"

"It's both, sir."

Crap, crap, crap! I mentally exclaim.

Just stick close to him, Calli.

Chris stands at the ready, waiting for the guard to motion him to pass through the arch. We stand close together and take slow deliberate steps forward.

As anticipated, the alarm sounds and a bright blue light flashes on top of the arch. A different guard, who's been standing by the wall, approaches Chris. Crimson and I quickly get out of the way.

"Sir, stop right there," he orders.

Ethan views the screen with a puzzled expression. I look into his mind and view what he sees—a blurred mess. Ethan slams his palm to the side of the monitor. "Darn thing is still going haywire. Sorry, Mr. Harding, would you please step through again?"

"No problem."

Chris complies and is given an all-clear. He scoops his

belongings out of the tub and replaces them in his pockets.

We walk down the hall, straight to General Harding's office. Chris knocks on the doorframe and waits to be invited in.

Chapter 11 - The General from Hell

General Harding stands next to a file cabinet with an open file in his hands. He wears green fatigues and laced-up ankle boots. His short hair shows his age, with silver dominating the brown. He looks up and motions for Chris to enter the room. The hardened creases on his face seem to stiffen a little more at the sight of his son.

I share my thoughts with Crimson as we stand behind Chris, observing the scene. *Chris has such a strong ability to maintain his composure.*

Yes, his life has been tough. Growing up with an army general for a father wasn't easy for him, but it's made him who he is today.

Chris stands straight and tall and waits for his father to invite him to sit down.

"Sit down, Chris," General Harding orders, and Chris complies. "Why didn't you bring the Diamond Bearer girl with you?"

"They think I'm collecting information today which I'll take back to them tonight."

"Who are you talking about?"

"The Diamond Bearer, the Repeater, and a Runner."

"Where are they staying?"

"I don't know for sure. They hadn't selected a place to stay yet."

"Then how will you know where to go?"

"They'll be waiting for me down the road later tonight."

"All right, I'll get my snipers positioned. Tell me where

they'll be."

"They didn't give me exact coordinates. I'm supposed to drive down the road until I find them."

General Harding lets out a disappointed grunt. "I want that diamond."

"Did Deus Ex return?"

"Yes, she's in the lab. You'll work with her today. She's sorting crystals and gemstones. We have a truckload of prisoners arriving in the next few hours. You and Deus will process them."

"Yes, sir." Chris stands and waits to be excused.

General Harding nods and then refocuses on the file in his hand.

We follow Chris out the door. He puts his thoughts on the edge of his mind. *More clan members have been captured. We have to stop this!*

That's what we're trying to do, Chris. You're doing a phenomenal job. Keep in character, Crimson responds.

Chris pushes the door to the lab open and holds it as another lab worker exits. Crimson and I quickly enter the large room filled with tables, gemstones, and microscopes. Several floor-to-ceiling glass cabinets contain jars of colored liquids and stacks of Petri dishes. Four workers wearing white lab coats are hunched over, busily working, one of whom is Deus Ex.

She looks up from a table of assorted stones and crystals. She adjusts her oversized glasses and tucks a loose strand of hair behind her ear. "About time you arrived. Your daddy said you'll be working with me."

"Shut up," Chris mutters.

I know Deus doesn't need to wear glasses. Crimson shares my observation and adds, *She always seems to play her role with a one-hundred percent conviction. She's the ultimate actor.*

The closer I examine Deus, the more I realize I can

view her mind . . . well, the mess that is her mind. My eyes search for her necklace but find nothing. She must have had to take hers off too. Interesting.

Good eye, Calli, compliments Crimson.

Deus unconsciously reaches up and scratches her head. I guess no one's ever told her an itchy head is a sign her mind is being read. She says to Chris, "I trust you put on a good show for which ever Diamond Bearer came and 'saved' you."

"That was the plan." His response is cold and without feeling.

She perks up and her eyes brighten. "Well, I had some more fun on my way back here. I got another chance to get a diamond."

"You failed, though. How do you classify that as fun?"

"Being able to kill *another* unkillable person brings a certain level of satisfaction." She inhales deeply with a pleased expression.

I don't think I can stay calm with her, Chris thinks.

She's testing you, Crimson says with her mind.

I better change the subject. Chris asks Deus, "So what are you working on?"

"Where's Brand?"

"In Denver somewhere. Why?"

"He has something I want."

"Ah, you figured out his power is stronger than yours." Chris smiles, having second-guessed Deus.

"Did you know?"

"No, but I figured it out quickly enough when they were able to take Beth and lose your tail back in Ohio. Obviously, Brand must be more powerful than you."

"Yeah, well not for long. Grab a lab coat and come help me. We're looking for clear stones or pale-colored stones bordering on clear. It's just easier to remove the dark stones. Put the clear stones in this bin for Dr. Condi." Deus points to a grey-haired man on the other side of the room who is bent over a microscope.

While I sit and watch, Deus and Chris take turns insulting each other and trying to outperform each other.

Crimson decides there's nothing we need to do here, so she leaves the room. I follow her as she wanders around the facility. Our minds share information like two computers saving data to the same hard drive. I learn what she learns, and vice versa. We are able to get into the room containing the machine Travis talked about. It looks like a regular CT machine, with nothing special setting it apart from any other medical scanner. The room next to the machine stores many crystals labeled with different powers. Crimson tells me she will try to get inside and investigate.

I head back to keep an eye on Deus just as Deus takes the bin of crystals to Dr. Condi. I figure I'd better see what he's researching so intently.

A female assistant enters the lab carrying a medium-sized metal box.

"Here's the archived material, Dr. Condi."

"Thank you," he says, rather absentmindedly, accepting the box.

The assistant sits beside him, observing his work. Dr. Condi lifts the lid of the box she brought and exposes several gemstones of varying colors. He pushes them around with his finger until he locates the one he wants. He carefully picks up a clear white stone and places it under the lighted magnifying glass. After examining it thoroughly, he says, "Excellent. Let the general know we've found a match."

I step away, not a moment too soon, as the female pushes her chair back and hurries over to the phone. I follow her and listen to the voice on the other end of the phone.

"Sir, Dr. Condi says we have a match."

"Any flaws?" General Harding asks.

"I'm not . . . I'm not sure, sir."

I don't need to use my powers to hear him yell, ordering her to go find out.

"Dr. Condi," she says, raising her shaking voice to be heard across the large lab. "Are there any flaws?"

"No. It's a perfect match."

"Sir, there are no flaws . . . sir?" The assistant pulls the phone away from her ear and hangs up the receiver. I read her mind. *I hate this job! I hate this job!*

Chris and Deus Ex bicker back and forth as the assistant crosses the lab back to Dr. Condi. I remain by Chris and speak to his mind.

Your father is coming.

The door to the lab opens and slams against the wall. General Harding marches in and orders, "Bring it to me!"

Dr. Condi brings the clear stone to the general.

"You're certain?" Harding asks.

"One hundred percent. It's an identical match to the other, just as you thought it would be."

Crimson's voice says to my mind, *What kind of stone are they talking about, Calli?*

I read Dr. Condi's mind. The crystal is quartz, but not just any quartz. This particular quartz came from the same area as their strongest samples . . . samples that now hold all the known powers except for the repeating power.

General Harding hands the quartz back to Dr. Condi and says, "Take it to the crystal room." Then he addresses Chris. "I want you to bring the Repeater in tomorrow."

"I thought you wanted the Diamond Bearer?" Chris says.

"I do, but bring the boy first so I can be better prepared to handle the girl."

Deus addresses General Harding. "Might I suggest you forget about the girl and just harvest the diamond you have right here in your building? Rolf held back information that would have been useful to know. Besides, he's of no use to us now."

General Harding doesn't respond. The entire room falls silent for several long seconds. Then he says, "Young lady, when I want your opinion, I'll ask for it. Until then, just do as you're ordered." He turns and leaves the room.

Chris asks, "What was that all about, Deus?"

"He's *your* father. What are you asking me for?" Deus turns her head and looks up at the clock on the wall. "We need to go meet the truck with our new candidates."

"Right. How could I forget?"

I follow Deus and Chris down a different hallway and into a room with an outside exit and a loading bay. Along the opposite wall, I notice a large cage built out of chain-link fencing. Obviously the cage is meant to house the prisoners.

Deus peers through the peephole on the door and then sits down on a folding chair.

"They're not here yet," she says.

Chris unfolds a chair and sits across from her.

The room falls completely silent—so quiet I worry my breathing might be detected. Chris thinks the same thing. He clears his throat and asks, "So, Deus, what's your plan?"

"My plan? My plan is to outlive everyone else."

"Oh, nothing short of grandiose, huh?

"Why would I settle for anything less?"

A low rumbling outside the door, followed by the high-pitched squeal of brakes halting a vehicle, indicates the truck has arrived. Deus jumps up and peeks out the hole, then she climbs on the elevated loading-bay platform and raises the large garage door. As the door curves up and around on the tracks, the back end of a dark green military truck becomes visible. Deus reaches forward and opens the flaps. Two Unaltered soldiers get out of the truck and join her.

The prisoners are all chained to the inside of the truck and need to be released one at a time and escorted to the cage. As each person marches by, I detect their individual power. Each of the five powers is represented. Then Deus walks out of the back of the truck with Clara Winter.

I clamp my hand over my mouth to trap any sounds of horror that might escape.

Chris doesn't flinch or even acknowledge her. He seems to stare right through her.

I read his mind and find he is near tears, especially when he sees the next prisoner ushered out of the truck—Beth's little brother, Nate.

My heart almost stops when my eyes catch sight of Nate. How were Clara and Nate captured? The fact they were captured is a horrible reminder that Unaltered soldiers are formidable foes. These prisoners are going to be outfitted with crystals and fed to the Shadow Demons to create more healing stones. Nate isn't a person with powers. He's just a regular human, so the Shadow Demons won't be interested in him. General Harding will probably have him shot.

Oh, how I hope we did a good enough job of eliminating the Demons. The sun needs to set in order for me to know.

Chris and Deus return to the lab after the prisoners are processed. I follow close behind. I seek out Crimson with my mind. *Crimson, did you see that Clara and Nate were captured?*

Yes. Remember to stay focused, Calli. I warned you we might see disturbing and horrible situations today.

Where are you?

I'm in General Harding's office.

She allows me to see through her eyes. She's sifting through files in the file cabinet. One particular file catches her eye and she pulls it out of the drawer. Inside are blueprints and schematics.

Calli, look at the walls in the lab. Do you see any seams? Perhaps trim pieces you don't normally see on walls?

I glance around the room at the walls. Most of them are covered with shelving units. I answer Crimson. *No, I don't think so.*

I see the blueprint she's studying. Apparently General Harding has installed some sort of back-up security device inside the walls. Not every wall, but definitely inside his office.

Crimson hears voices out in the hall. She quickly replaces the file and closes the drawer just in time as General Harding enters his office, followed by Rolf and two guards. The general closes the door and then sits at his desk. Crimson moves away to the corner behind the desk and watches. The guards stand along the wall near the door next to Rolf.

I think I'm more panicked for Crimson than she is for herself. I'm not sure, as I can't read her mind. I watch the scene play out through her eyes.

General Harding asks Rolf, "Why didn't you alert Deus to the possibilities of what might happen when the soldier went to retrieve the diamond from the Bearer?"

"Sir, there are so many possibilities. It's hard to predict what a Diamond Bearer will do."

"If it's so hard to predict, then what use are you?"

"I know information about the Bearers that you'll never be able to discover."

"So you're holding your information back until you feel I need it?"

"Sir, I assure you I'm not being deceptive. For instance, I've detected the Bearer Calli nearby. I can feel her diamond."

"That's it? Chris already alerted me to her presence, and he doesn't *have* a diamond. Your usefulness has run its course."

Rolf's expression is one of extreme shock. "Chris knows she's here?"

General Harding nods to his guards, who step forward, seize Rolf by his arms, and pull him back to the wall.

"What are you doing?" Rolf asks in alarm.

Harding slams his hand onto a red button protruding from the side of his desk. A large panel on the wall behind the desk moves sideways at lightning speed, exposing several large pieces of obsidian.

Because Crimson read the General's mind moments before, she is ready for the obsidian. She activates her topaz power just in time to prevent being exposed. Our mind link should have ceased as a result of the obsidian, but it didn't. I can only assume she has other topaz with other powers on her body.

"I'm going to make myself into a Diamond Bearer, Rolf. What's the matter? Can't you see the future?" General Harding pulls a .44 Magnum pistol from under his desk, stands, and grips the gun firmly with both hands. He fires two shots into Rolf's chest.

I witness the gruesome scene through Crimson's mind and feel her shock.

In the lab, the echo of gunfire startles everyone. Guards run by the open doorway, and terrified workers huddle together in the hallway Voices are heard, asking, "Is the compound under attack? Is there a lone gunman or are there several?"

I tell Chris's mind, *Rolf was in your father's office and your father just shot and killed him.*

Chris runs out the door, and Deus follows him.

I stay in the lab, as Crimson instructs, and watch the scene play out through her eyes. I'm also able to view a second perspective through Chris's mind. He and Deus, along with several guards, stand outside the office in the hallway, peering through the partially-closed blinds in the windows along the wall. The guards are shouting and trying to break the door down. Chris hears cursing and expressions of disgust at the gruesome sight of Rolf's body. Words like "bullet-proof" and "secured from the inside" hit Chris's ears. Chris sees his father sitting at his desk with a gun in his hands.

Inside the office, the guards let Rolf's body slide to the floor in a heap.

Harding puts his gun back in the holder under his desk. Then he reaches inside the wall where the pieces of obsidian rest and picks up a chunk the size of a deck of cards. He walks over to the quivering bloody mess that lies beside what is left of Rolf's body.

I speak to Crimson's mind. *He's going to pick up the heart and diamond. Should you stop him?*

No. Just watch.

General Harding extends his hand, pauses, and then grabs the heart and holds it in one hand, with the obsidian in the other.

General Harding looks at his obedient guards and laughs manically. "I'm holding a diamond and I'm still alive. So much for assigning this task to anyone else."

The commotion from outside the door pulls General Harding's attention to the gathered crowd of onlookers in the hallway. Unsuccessful attempts to open the door prompt the general to instruct one of the guards to press the red button on the desk to deactivate the security system. Once it's pressed, the door is quickly opened. Guards pour into the room, guns drawn.

"Holster your weapons. Everything is under control," General Harding says.

Through Chris's eyes, the scene of Rolf's demise is horrific. Others standing around Chris utter words and sounds of disgust at the sight. Chris sends me his thoughts. *I don't want this to happen to you, Calli.*

General Harding walks toward the door, the black rock and bloody heart held out in front of him. Everyone in the hall moves out of his way.

Crimson loses eye contact with him and says to my mind, *Stay where you are. I think he might be headed in your direction. Get ready to use your topaz, and don't let anyone bump into you.*

Okay, I respond.

Crimson remains in the general's office, watching the panel on the wall, behind the general's desk, slowly slide closed. Crimson tells my mind, *The blueprints showed a hair-trigger system for this panel in the wall. As we've just witnessed, once activated, the panel instantly opens, giving the general immediate protection from exposed obsidian. We must be extremely careful, Calli. I'm sure there are more of these security panels throughout the compound.*

I don't hesitate to focus on my topaz power. Moments later, when General Harding enters the lab, the large piece of obsidian in his hand instantly removes my diamond powers.

The general walks slowly to the double sink, where he deposits the two objects. Several guards and curious employees enter the lab, but remain at a distance. Chris and

Deus are among the group. They watch in amazement as Harding turns the water on and scrubs the heart muscle off the diamond. When he finishes, he dries the diamond and obsidian and turns toward the door. He seems shocked so many people are standing around observing him—almost as if he has been inside his own little world for the last few minutes, unaware of the crowd.

General Harding places the diamond in a small glass case he removes from a nearby shelf. He locks the container and walks slowly toward the door with both the case and the large obsidian. Everyone moves out of his way again.

As soon as the obsidian is out of the room, my powers rush back into my body. I focus on refilling my topaz with invisibility power because I sense its level is low. Crimson's mind reveals she's in the hall and will follow him to see where he places the box. I am to remain in the lab.

Through Crimson's eyes, General Harding enters the room containing the crystals and places the box down on the table next to a metal pyramid-shaped object. He hands the large piece of obsidian to a nearby guard and instructs him to return it to his office.

Once the obsidian is on its way down the hall, I receive the strumming awareness that the diamond no longer has an owner.

I send my thoughts to Crimson, *Look on top of the metal pyramid. Is that the clear quartz Dr. Condi found today?*

I believe so. I don't detect any power residing within it.

Crimson reads the general's thoughts briefly, which reveal that he's excited and nervous about completing the biggest accomplishment humanity had ever achieved. He will become an all-powerful, all-knowing Repeater. The lackeys in Washington will never disrespect his research again. In fact, he has several creative deaths planned for his biggest critics. Faces of senators and other people flash through his mind, including Merlin's face. Crimson pulls out of General Harding's mind. He scratches the top of his head, turns, scans the empty room, then leaves. Crimson hurries out before she's locked inside.

After sunset, a full moon shines down on the shackled captives as military guards lead them outside to the far end of the property where spotlights and video cameras are set up. Each person has been outfitted with several crystals in the hope of capturing more of the Demons' healing power.

Crimson and I follow close by, using our topazes to remain invisible. Our mind connection is sustained through the use of the topaz. I speak to her mind. *I can't tell if there are any Demons nearby. We're too close to the obsidian on the exterior of the building.*

I don't know if there are, either. You must resist the urge to help, Calli.

I know. I pray the Demons are gone. I don't know if I'll be able to stand by and watch so many innocent lives perish.

I take a few more steps away from the building, putting enough distance between my body and the obsidian on the exterior of the building so that my powers rush back into my body. I instantly look for Demons but find nothing. The night air smells fresh and safe. Even though I feel relieved, the captives all believe they are about to die. I empathize with their fear, as I have felt it before.

The guards step back and wait.

Several of the younger prisoners cry, and Clara tries to comfort them with calming words. Even though I know they will all be okay, Clara does not. She displays true selflessness.

The lights turn off, all at once. Everyone flinches and braces for attack.

Nothing happens.

Yells and shrieks of happiness fill the air as the captives realize they are safe. This continues for several seconds before the lights turn back on and a voice sounds over the outdoor sound system.

"Bring them back inside."

Crimson and I, both relieved, suddenly come to the next horrific conclusion together—these people are going to be killed inside the compound. No way will General Harding allow them to leave and risk that they will go and expose what is going on in his facility.

We follow the line of ecstatic people inside the building. They are placed in the same observation room where Freedom died. We don't go in the room. Instead, Crimson tells me to go find Chris.

He's easy to locate. I just follow the yelling.

General Harding and Chris are in the lab. A computer monitor behind them displays the outdoor scene of illuminated grass where the prisoners were supposed to die. Deus stands several paces to the side watching Chris get cussed out. I conclude they must have watched the botched attempt on the monitor.

The general demands information. "Yes you do! I know you know why they didn't die. I saw it on your face when the spotlights came back on."

"I don't know what you're talking about. I was confused, just like you," Chris responds.

"No, you were relieved. Deus was confused." General Harding makes an exaggerated face to mimic Deus. "You were relieved! Tell me what you know."

"Fine! I was relieved . . . you caught me. I haven't been

able to feel safe in the dark since I was twelve. I've wished the Shadow Demons would go away for good . . . and when the lights came back on, I guess I imagined myself out there and what I'd be feeling."

"What? You're useless, Chris. They will die, like they should have already." General Harding stalks toward the door.

"You're not even going to harvest their power?" Chris asks.

His father stops and turns to look at Chris.

"What are you proposing?"

"Run them through the machine, remove their power, create another crystal, and then set them free. What's the worst thing that would happen? They go running to the police station and report they were captured and their cosmic power has been removed by the government? How much of that do you think anyone would believe? If you have them killed, their bodies have to be dealt with, like Rolf's. A much bigger headache for you."

"It would take a month to run all of them through the machine, unless I could get a transportable generator to boost the recharge time. Besides, we don't have enough quartz to store their powers. Logistics direct the decision here, Chris. We don't have space enough to house them or enough food to feed them. A bullet to the head is both inexpensive and easy."

"Did you know Diamond Bearers have the power to make people forget things?" Chris asks quietly. "You could make them forget they were ever here."

"What? How do you know?"

"I've seen Maetha erase other people's minds."

"She has that kind of power?"

"They all do," Chris lies.

"Hmm. I guess I'll keep the prisoners around . . . at

least for a while. I'll need subjects to practice my powers on when I become a Bearer."

"Yes, you will." Chris smiles.

"It's late. You should return to your 'friends' and give them an update. Tomorrow, bring the Repeater."

"What about Deus? You could run her through the machine."

Deus's jaw falls open, and a slight squeaking sound comes out of her mouth.

The general says, "Agent Alpha seemed to think the male Repeater was more powerful. If I'm going to waste quartz and all the power it takes to run the machine, I'd better make it worth my time."

"I thought you could use any quartz to contain the power removed from whoever went through the machine."

"Only a specific kind will store the power indefinitely. The piece that was confirmed earlier today is one of those. Bring the boy with you tomorrow. Alive. If you can accomplish that, you'll have earned my complete trust." General Harding hands an obsidian-laced cuff to Chris.

Chris stands, takes the cuff and watches his father leave the room, thinking, *I thought I had already earned your trust, but I guess I should have known you'd keep changing the game.* Chris then sends his thoughts to me. *Calli, are you here? Can you hear me?*

Before I can answer, Deus launches heated words at Chris. "How dare you suggest I be run through the machine!"

Yes, I'm behind you, I say.

"Come on, Deus. I was only keeping the pretense up that I'm loyal to my father, not you. Besides, he didn't want your power anyway." Chris walks toward the door and directs his thoughts to me. *Alert Crimson. We're leaving. You two should remain invisible all the way back to Denver. I think my father might put a tail on me.*

Crimson confirms that she overheard Chris and tells me she will meet us outside the main gate.

Deus blocks Chris at the door. She hisses, "What if he actually had wanted my power? Did you think about that? Don't screw up like that again, do you hear me?"

"I hear you." He steps around Deus and says, "See you tomorrow," over his shoulder as he walks out of the lab.

I let Chris know what Crimson said and then follow him as he leaves the building. We don't have any trouble getting past the security checkpoint. Fortunately, they don't scan people as they leave. Ethan has been replaced by another guard named Juan. Chris asks for his necklace back, and Juan reluctantly obliges. Outside the building, we hustle to the gate so my powers can return as quickly as possible. My topaz is nearly drained.

Crimson speaks to both our minds. *Chris, drive your car toward Denver. Stop at the first gas station. We'll run behind you and watch for followers.*

Chris pulls into the gas station parking lot and waits. Crimson has me exercise my Bearer telepathy, first with Maetha, to find out where she is located, then second to communicate with Chris—all while maintaining my invisibility.

I haven't communicated from a distance with another Diamond Bearer before, at least not on purpose. I feel for the other diamonds as Duncan taught me to do. Several diamonds surface in my mind. I haven't associated the names of each Bearer to all the individual diamonds yet, but Maetha's is one I've identified. Jonas's is another. I carried the one Jonas has for so long I know its signature on a personal level. Plus, I still have a piece of it in my heart.

Maetha congratulates me on reaching her and tells me the address where she and the others can be found. I relay the information to Chris as he sits in the idling car, waiting patiently.

After double-checking to make sure we haven't been followed, Crimson and I climb in the backseat and become visible to Chris. Chris catches my eye in the rearview mirror and begins the drive to the motel. His thoughts tell me he's relieved I'm alive and that we are all out of the compound.

Crimson speaks to both our minds. *I'm relieved as well, Chris. You handled yourself well today. I don't want anything said to the others about Beth's brother or Clara Winter. Nate has a high chance of survival. Beth has had a rough enough day already and doesn't need something else weighing her down right now.*

Chris and I agree.

We enter the motel room and find Maetha, Brand, and Beth waiting for us. I sit down on the side of the bed across from Brand and Beth. Crimson walks straight to Maetha and takes a seat at the table with her.

Maetha asks, "What information did you gather concerning the machine? Is it producing Unaltereds?"

"Yes." Crimson pulls some folded papers from her pocket. "I found these records. They identify everyone who has gone through the machine. Several of them were working today, and yes, they had Unaltered auras."

Chris says, "Well, with Rolf dead now—"

"What?" Maetha exclaims. "I never felt anything."

Crimson says, "The obsidian on the outside of the building creates a barrier, keeping the events happening inside private. Take my hand and review what happened today."

Maetha grasps Crimson's hand in what I figure is the first time in several centuries that Maetha has needed to be filled in on the details of an event surrounding another Diamond Bearer. I can't help but feel guilty.

Crimson's voice says to my mind, *That's a natural feeling, Calli, but don't think Maetha's lost privilege is your fault.*

I guess I don't feel as qualified as Maetha to carry the Grecian Blue.

No one is more qualified than you.

Maetha lets go of Crimson's hand and asks, "So General Harding wants to become a Diamond Bearer? Does he have enough information to actually accomplish that?"

Crimson nods her head.

Chris says, "He wants me to take Brand in tomorrow."

"What? No," says Beth, clearly disturbed.

Brand, apparently having repeated already, says to Chris, "I'll do it. I don't care if he takes my ability away . . . but remember I'm not going to kill anyone."

"What if he kills you?" Beth asks, looking even more worried.

I ask, "Is it a good idea to risk Brand's life in this way? I mean, is there some other solution?"

Brand chuckles. "Aw, you just like having me around to bail you out."

"That, and the fact that you're my friend, Brand."

Brand looks to the floor for a moment and then says, "I have a shot at convincing Deus to rethink her actions. I'm going to try at least. Like I said, I really don't care if I lose my repeating ability."

"She *is* actually helping our cause," Chris says.

Brand adds, "Maybe she can be convinced to come back to our side."

Crimson says, "No, her mind was shaped long ago. She's a survivor and a fighter. She'll never feel secure until everyone she perceives as a threat is taken care of. She's simply getting rid of the government threat, and then she'll continue removing the Bearers."

"But if we could convince her to stop trying to kill off Diamond Bearers, then she wouldn't be going against nature," says Brand. "She helped balance nature when she killed Neema, and she's trying to eliminate the research and prototype weapons that would help the government hunt and kill people with powers and Diamond Bearers. So, technically, she's still on the good side even if she has an attitude about it."

"She killed Hasan," Crimson says. "Hasan was one of the Bearers who actually performed his job."

"Everyone deserves a second chance," Brand states flatly.

Chris says, "I have to take you, Brand. I don't want to, but to keep my position inside the compound I have to comply."

"I'll be sure to put on a good act for you, Chris."

Chapter 12
The Power-Removing Machine

Brand says his goodbyes to Maetha and Beth—Beth's goodbye is an intimate kiss—and then we leave for the compound before the sun peeks over the horizon.

Crimson and I sit in the backseat. Crimson says, "Calli, activate your invisibility."

Brand turns around instantly. "What? You can go invisible? How come you never told me that?"

Before I disappear from his view, I say, "I like to remain a little mysterious, Brand."

Brand turns to Chris. "Did you know?"

Chris doesn't answer. He continues driving toward his father's facility.

About a quarter mile from the compound, Chris pulls over and pretends to retrieve a water bottle from the backseat, leaving the door open while he takes a drink. We slip out. Even though we're invisible, our combined weight climbing out of the car causes it to wobble. If someone is watching closely, they'll certainly wonder why the car moved.

We follow the car to the compound. Chris attaches the obsidian cuff to Brand's wrist, removing his repeating power.

"Sorry, Brand."

"Don't worry about it, Chris." Brand smiles, dimples sinking in.

Crimson says to my mind, *Use your topaz for invisibility until you're away from Brand. If he accidentally bumps into you while wearing that cuff, you'll become visible.*

I do as she says.

Once in the building, Brand is sent through the security arch first, then Chris. We accompany him, causing the X-ray machine to go off again when we walk through. Ethan, who's back on duty, bangs on the monitor for a second time, convinced it's experiencing a momentary glitch.

I spot General Harding just beyond the security checkpoint, waiting for Brand. I find it depressing, and quite rude, that General Harding isn't as happy to see his own son as he is to see Brand. Chris doesn't seem bothered. Being ignored by his father is so commonplace, it rarely affects him anymore.

I ask Chris's mind, *Do you feel like he trusts you any more today than he did yesterday?*

Nope.

General Harding has two guards take Brand directly to the room with the power-removing machine. Chris follows, and Crimson and I follow Chris. On the way, we pass the lab where Deus Ex catches sight of the procession. She quickly drops what she's working on and runs to the door.

Crimson tells my mind to step aside to make room for Deus. I do so.

The guards push open the heavy door to the room with the CT-looking machine. I notice a twelve-inch square, lead-lined window set at eye level on the door, indicating the machine produces harmful rays. The general and Deus follow the guards and we manage to squeeze inside before the door closes.

The machine is positioned in the center of the large room. Along the same wall as the door, a tall narrow glass window reveals the room that contains the power-charged crystals. Next to the narrow window is another security-enabled door that opens into the crystal room. Along the far wall, at the other end of the machine, a safe viewing area is set up behind a partition with a lead-lined observation window which allows a clear view of both the machine, and the crystal room on the opposite wall.

A male technician with an Unaltered's aura stands by the machine. He's holding a clipboard.

"Secure the young man to the table," General Harding orders his guards.

My heart races inside my chest. I resist the urge to look to the future concerning Brand, and instead focus on Crimson's admonishment to remain calm and not give away my location.

The two guards usher Brand forward and force him to sit and then lie down on the table. They remove his shoes and use heavy Velcro straps to secure his wrists and ankles. Then they remove his obsidian cuff.

Crimson says, *Okay, Calli, use the Blue Diamond's invisibility power.*

Brand turns his head to the side and makes eye contact with Deus.

"You don't have to let this become your life, Deus. You can stop everything."

"Why would I?" she asks.

Brand says, "He'll do the same thing to you when he's done with me."

Deus throws a suspicious glance at General Harding. Then she changes her tone of voice to the familiar innocent, sweet girl. "No he won't. My power is nothing compared to yours, Brand."

General Harding speaks to Chris and Deus. "Go behind the wall. Only Unaltereds can stay out here."

Deus and Chris follow the instructions and move behind the wall. Deus asks Chris, "How exactly did you catch him?”

“It was easy. Why? You doubt my abilities?”

“He just seems a bit too willing to throw away something that could be used to rule the world.”

“Maybe he doesn’t want to rule the world.”

Deus pauses, scrunching her eyebrows together, then shouts, “Wait a minute! General Harding, something’s wrong here.”

The general raises an eyebrow. “What makes you say that?”

She points at Brand. “He’s not fighting you. He’s too willing.

General Harding halts what he’s doing. He looks at Brand and says, “Are you up to something, boy?”

“No. I’m just tired of the burden of repeating. So get on with it.”

General Harding says to Deus, “If he’s up to something, he’ll be shot once his power is removed.” The general walks to the wall and stands behind it with Chris and Deus.

I can tell Deus isn’t satisfied with the situation. I don’t dare try to read her mind for fear of revealing my presence. Even though Deus doesn’t seem to understand when her mind is being read, General Harding may. If he sees her scratch her head, he might put the place on lockdown.

Crimson confirms my thoughts. *When I read his mind earlier and he scratched his head, he had the thought that maybe his mind was being read. He dismissed the idea because no one else was around. If he saw Deus, or anyone else, scratching their scalp, he’d probably panic.*

The technician continues to run through his checklist in preparation for the procedure.

Chris asks his father, “How does this machine work anyway?”

General Harding replies, "I don't know. It just does."

"It just does?" Chris repeats, utterly flabbergasted.

"Yes, Chris, it just does! How do tiny microchips hold entire libraries of books and movies? How do phone conversations travel through the air? Do I need to understand how any of that works to know it works? No. The world has eggheads who figure out logistics and technology. Agent Alpha was an egghead with much more knowledge about the subject than I . . . of course, now I know why . . . but that's not the point. He built the machine, perfected it, and used it many times over before he died. I'm going to complete his studies by performing the final experiments. Let's not waste any more time. One moment delayed is one more moment before we're done."

The technician standing next to the control box on the side of the machine presses the final button, after General Harding instructs him to do so. The table holding Brand slowly slides all the way through the center of the humming machine. Then the machine revs up in strength, causing the lights overhead to dim. The table slowly moves back through the core of the machine. A bright white line of light seems to travel up Brand's body as he moves through. The lights in the facility dim even more, while the quartz in the crystal room begins to glow brightly. The white band of light reaches Brand's neck and slowly climbs his face, causing him to shut his eyes. Finally, the process is complete, and the machine powers down. The lights in the hallway regain power, as well as the lights in the room. I hadn't even noticed the darkness because of the brilliant glow coming from the quartz sitting atop the metal pyramid in the crystal room—presumably containing Brand's repeating power.

The table comes to a halt, and the technician releases Brand's bonds.

Brand sits up slowly and smiles at Deus. "You should try it," he says. "It didn't hurt at all."

A bright aura appears above his head and shoulders and I know his power is gone.

"You're a fool!" Deus scolds.

General Harding walks to the glass and peers inside at the quartz, which begins to dim. "It's too hot to handle for now, but that's all right. There are still a few more technicalities to take care of."

Deus eyes the quartz jealously.

"You haven't gone too far, Deus. You can still save yourself."

She spins around and shouts, "What? Save myself? From what?"

"Nature's wrath. You haven't pissed off nature yet. If you leave now, you'll have a chance to survive."

"Take him to the lockup and put him with the others," General Harding orders Chris.

"Yes, sir."

"Oh, wait. Bring a girl back with you. I want to double check the powers of the diamond."

"Yes, sir." As Chris walks out the door, Crimson sends him a message of comfort. She knows as well as Chris does that he will be choosing someone to die. She tells him, *Don't over-think it, Chris. Just take the first female you see.*

The cold-hearted calculation of General Harding unnerves me. Can he really be this cruel? I look into his mind and see a man who operates like a machine. He doesn't see people around him. He sees subjects. He completely lacks empathy or sympathy. The only thing on his mind is the need to become the most powerful person on the face of the earth. I figure it's a good thing he doesn't know about the Grecian Blue.

Deus asks the general, "When do you expect the

transportable generator will arrive?"

"By ten a.m."

My heart pounds anxiously with the news a generator is on the way. Crimson's thoughts merge with mine.

I wasn't aware he'd gone ahead and ordered one. This is not good news, she says.

"What are my orders, sir?" Deus asks politely.

"Return to the lab and do something productive instead of trying to stir up trouble."

"Yes, sir." Deus doesn't show any irritation in her response, but I know otherwise. She leaves the room.

General Harding, two guards, the technician, Crimson, and I remain, waiting for Chris to return. Crimson's thoughts mix with mine. *Did you notice the panels on the wall? One button press and we're on a countdown until our charged topazes run out of power. We need to let this situation play out as naturally as possible in order to achieve a successful dismantling of this facility. People are going to die. That fact cannot be helped. But more will die if this facility doesn't shut down.*

Chris enters the room with a girl who's about eighteen-years-old. Her frightened and trembling body pulls at my heart. I ask Crimson if it is all right to give her healing comfort. Crimson says no. Her reasoning is that if General Harding doesn't see consistent, typical behavior from everyone around him, he might put the place in lockdown—which would uncover the obsidian and potentially expose us.

General Harding enters the security code on the keypad to open the door to the crystal room. Then he says, "Bring her over here, Chris."

Chris walks the girl over to his father.

"Young lady, walk in there and bring me that glass box with the white rock inside."

Scared to death, she steps carefully into the small

room and reaches her hands out to place them on either side of the box. When her hands connect with the box, she begins trembling even more. She lifts the box an inch off the table, then drops it and falls to the ground. Dead.

I'm horrified and livid. How can anyone be so ruthless?

Crimson tells my mind that because the diamond was touching the case, as it had touched the pouch when I carried it in my pocket, the person who came into contact with the case or pouch couldn't handle the intense powers emanating from the stone and the container that held it.

"Well," General Harding says, as if nothing more than a number has just popped up on a computer screen, not caring one bit that a human life has just ended, "I gather the diamond is every bit as powerful as it should be. Remove the body," he says to his guards. The guards pull out the girl's limp form. General Harding closes the door and enters the lock code.

I feel Chris's heated aggravation toward his father. He's about to snap. I also feel Crimson issue him more calming comfort.

General Harding says to Chris, "Only an Unaltered can hold the diamond without dying. The only problem is, who can I trust?"

"What do you mean?"

"I need to know I'll be able to hold the diamond if I go through that machine. Since you displayed your ability to be trusted by bringing in the Repeater, I'm going to send you through the machine and have you pick up the diamond to see if it works."

"What? What if it doesn't work? The diamond will kill me, *Dad*."

"Then I'll know it won't work on me, won't I?"

Chris stares slack-jawed at his father. "You'd experiment with my life? You have all these Unaltered guards running around here. Why use me?"

"I can't trust them. If the procedure works, they might run off with the diamond like the other soldier did."

"How do you know *I* won't?"

"Come on, Chris. You would never do that, would you? Not when you have the proper motivation to comply."

"Motivation? What are you talking about?"

"You'll go through that machine and touch that diamond, or I'll have your mother brought in and make her do it!"

"You wouldn't!"

"Try me."

"You've sunk to an all-new low, General Harding." Chris uses his father's formal title.

"Don't wander off, *son*."

Chris storms out of the lab. Crimson tells me to follow him and try to calm him. I race out the door as it closes and step in time with Chris.

Chris, I'm behind you.

I'm going outside.

I can't go with you. I don't have much power left in my topaz.

I have to get out of here and cool off.

Chris, let me help you.

He stops abruptly and veers off to the left, entering an empty room. *We can stay here for a bit.* He closes the door and locks it.

Are there cameras?

Yes, but I highly doubt anyone will be watching. It's not like the prisoners are in here. Can you believe him? Bringing Brand in didn't gain me any more trust. Now Brand is powerless. Not only is my father going to risk my life, he would bring my mother here and use her as a guinea pig too! He's unbelievable. If Crimson wasn't infusing me with her energy, I'd probably have . . . he pauses.

Chris, I place my hand on his shoulder, *I feel for you. You have to deal with so much crap with your father.*

He reaches up and puts his hand on my invisible hand.

Sensing his concern, I say, *You'll never be like him. Don't worry about that.*

I can feel you, but I can't see you. Can't you allow me to see you but block everyone else?

I don't know. I don't think I should experiment with my power right now.

Crimson confirms my hesitation in my mind.

Chris traces my hand to my wrist and then up along my arm. With his other hand, he reaches forward and finds my other shoulder. He pulls me toward him and embraces me in a firm hug. "I could use some of that healing power right now," he says, his voice box rumbling against my head. His hands move up my body to my neck. He pulls my head away from his chest and holds it steady as his lips descend down to mine in a heated fury. His mouth ravages mine, seeking the comfort only I can give him.

My arms wrap around his neck as I kiss him back. I feel the diamond in my heart heat up as I infuse healing vibes into his mind. I desperately want to help him relax, to lighten his load, or to share in his burden. His hands still cradle my face.

My hands wander. I need to feel him like I haven't felt him before. I trace his broad shoulders down to his chest, then slip my hands around him and explore every inch of his muscular back with my fingertips, all the way down to the top of his pants. He pulls away from my mouth and says on an intake of air, "Calli, I need to be healed, not given a new problem."

Well, I thought your kissing would be causing you problems enough.

"No, it's the opposite. Kissing you is like drinking an antidote for all the wrongs in the world. Your roaming hands, on the other hand . . . "

"So that's how it's going to be," I tease in a playful whisper. "It's the girl's fault when things go too far?"

"Not a chance." He twists me around, pinning me against the door, and kisses me again. This time his hands explore my body, yet in a reserved, under-control way. He runs his hands down my sides. He feels his way up to the zipper on my jacket and unzips it, then slips his hands inside over my tank top and across my belly, then around to my back. He moves his mouth down the side of my neck, kissing as he goes.

I can't help but arch my back and point my chin to the ceiling, giving him access to more kissable skin under my chin. Instead of taking the bait, he lowers his head and kisses my collarbones and the hollow of my neck. He brings his mouth back up to mine and kisses me hungrily. Then he pulls away and steps back.

"*Now* my problem is my own fault," he replies in a husky voice, breathing heavily. He winks in the direction of where he figures my face is. "But wasn't that fun? We need to do that again—soon!"

I agree, I say to his mind.

"Before I go through the machine."

You won't die, Chris.

"I won't? Well, that's a relief."

It's the vision I saw. You'll become an Unaltered and won't die when you touch the diamond.

Crimson's voice interrupts me. *Stop there, Calli.*

"Well, that's good news. Then what?"

We'll just have to find out together, Chris.

The glass box containing the diamond is brought out into the machine room on a rolling table with the use of a large piece of obsidian. The obsidian is sent back to the general's office—thank goodness. My topaz is running low on power.

"Lie on the table, son. It's time for the moment of truth." General Harding excitedly rubs his hands together like a little boy with a pocket full of quarters in a candy store.

I can't believe the amount of disconnect the man has for his own flesh and blood.

Crimson agrees with my observation.

Chris sits down and swings his legs up onto the table. Before lying down, he stares into the glass window at the pyramid-shaped holder. "Is that a piece of special quartz? Will my power be held permanently?"

"Why would I want to preserve your power? I already have more crystals than I know what to do with that contain abilities like yours. That's just a piece of junk quartz necessary to fill the slot so the machine will work."

"Nice to know I'm loved," he mutters as he lies back on the table.

The technician activates the machine, and the table begins moving through the opening. Once the table reaches the end, the motor revs up, the power dims, and the bright light begins its scan as Chris's body slowly moves through the machine. The quartz on top of the pyramid glows as bright as the sun, lighting the room even more so than when the lights were on.

The table completes its journey and Chris sits up. The lights regain strength as the machine powers down. The quartz in the window has already lost its glow. Chris stands from the table with an aura above his head and shoulders.

"Excellent! Now touch the diamond," his father

orders.

Chris glares at his father for several seconds. Then he extends his thoughts to me, saying, *I love you, Calli.*

Chris walks over to the case, reaches inside, and pulls out the diamond.

"Wow! That wasn't so hard, was it?" General Harding declares. "Now you're part of the normal population again."

If you slammed it into your chest, you'd become a Bearer, I tell him.

Yeah, and then I'd be killed like Rolf.

General Harding orders: "Put it back in the case, Chris."

Chris doesn't hesitate and immediately parts with the diamond.

Crimson says to my mind, *Chris is now the owner of that diamond. I think I figured out your vision, Calli. Chris will kill his father by not relinquishing the diamond properly.*

With an estimated four hours to kill until General Harding can use the machine again, the diamond is locked away in the crystal room, which also houses Brand's two-minute repeating stone. If the information in the files Crimson had glanced through is true, the quartz holds the power indefinitely. The idea of anyone other than a real diamond Bearer having a crystal that would give them Brand's repeating power, along with a Sanguine Diamond's powers, is truly scary.

Chris pulls up several files on the lab computer regarding the military vests containing the several different stones. We look over his shoulder as he navigates around the information. He determines the information is backed up in only one other location besides the mainframe computer—General Harding's office.

Chris leads us to the control room, which houses the mainframe computer. He says with his mind, *This computer holds all the information in its hard drive. To my knowledge, my father hasn't sent this information to anyone within the government. The only backup is on his own computer in his office.*

Well, it won't be that hard to seize all the information in one sweep, will it? I respond.

Crimson says, *That won't work. The compound has to implode naturally. If the hard drives disappear during that time, then fine. If they were to disappear today without the logical breakdown of the workings of the compound, the research will be intensified and reproduced.*

We leave the control room, and Chris takes us to a small, round room. He says with his mind, *This room is called the donut-hole.*

I glance around the empty windowless room. The walls are made of the same bricks as those on the exterior of the building. The only door is the one we used. I take note of the change in atmosphere. I begin to feel some of the other diamonds of the group of twenty-one.

Jonas connects with my mind. *Hey, Calli, how's everything going?*

It's difficult to say . . . wait, how you are able to connect with me?

Crimson merges with my mind. *Tell him to leave you to your job. You don't need any interference right now.*

Sorry, Jonas, got to go.

Chris says, *Freedom was able to find Calli whenever her diamond surfaced because Rolf would stay in this room most of the time and then alert Freedom when he detected Calli's diamond. This room is in the direct center of the building. I studied the blueprints and computer files after Freedom died to figure out how this room works.*

Apparently, there's obsidian in these walls. Chris points to the circular wall. *The 3-D rendition showed how the obsidian creates an energy-blocking field that protects the interior of the compound. Obsidian was also built into the underside of the compound and across the roof, well, except above this room, creating a complete donut-shaped torus of energy protection from the outside world. Right here, in the center—in the donut-hole—the protection is gone.*

Maetha's mind connects with mine. *Calli, let Crimson know this was the reason I wasn't able to detect Rolf's involvement with Henry. I would bi-locate to Rolf only to see the brick walls and nothing else to indicate he was with Henry or in a government facility. I ruled him out as a turncoat. Also, tell Crimson that Merlin thinks he's making headway with the Senate Budget Committee to reduce or cut funding to General Harding's compound. Merlin argued that the research was too outdated to be spending tax-payers dollars.*

All right, she heard.

We leave the donut-hole room and walk toward the lab. Standing in the doorway of the lab is General Harding.

"Where have you been? The machine is charged and ready to go, and you're off gallivanting around."

"Sorry. When Mother Nature calls, I have to listen."

I almost laugh out loud at the double meaning to his words.

"Come on, let's get this done." General Harding marches past Chris, motioning him to follow. Two guards fall in step as well.

I try to access my topaz for invisibility, in case obsidian is exposed, only to discover the power is depleted. *Crimson, my topaz is empty!*

Mine is empty also.

Should we go somewhere and charge our stones?

Not now. The general is going to go through the machine.

Chapter 13 - The Newest Diamond Bearer

When we reach the door to the machine room, the general orders two men to stand guard outside. He and Chris enter the room, and Crimson and I slip inside carefully before the door closes.

The technician has already powered up the machine in preparation for General Harding. I realize that even though Chris's father isn't a person with intense powers, he isn't an Unaltered either. He, like almost everyone else on the planet, was exposed to cosmic energy while in the womb. I feel inside his body to try to determine which power affected him. I determine he has increased reasoning and detective skills. Had he been at the center of the cosmic energy ray, he would be a Hunter. It only makes sense that his interests would fall with the military.

The door to the crystal room stands open, and General Harding walks to the entrance.

"Chris, come and wheel the diamond out here."

Chris follows orders and moves the table holding the glass box with the diamond out of the crystal room. His father hands him a key to unlock the small door, and Chris opens it.

General Harding closes the door to the crystal room, which locks automatically.

I notice that the metal pyramid is holding a small cloudy stone, probably another piece of junk quartz. I also notice that Brand's quartz has been moved and is resting on top of the table in front of the pyramid. It still has a strong glow.

General Harding sits down on the edge of the table, unlaces his boots, and removes them one at a time.

A guard opens the door. "Excuse me, sir. This woman would like to join you." Deus stands behind the guard on her tiptoes peeking over the guard's shoulder.

Deus asks, "General, may I please observe this great moment?"

"Of course. Let her in."

The guard steps aside, and Deus enters.

General Harding announces, "Soon we will be an unstoppable team, Deus."

She smiles a self-serving smile. Her mind is unreadable.

The general's use of the word "team" makes me shudder and confuses me at the same time. So far I've only witnessed him berating her. Why would he want to work together with her? One things for sure, the two of them will be a lethal combination if General Harding is able to become a Bearer.

After setting his boots on the floor side-by-side in perfect position, with the laces tucked neatly inside, the general lies back on the table. He turns his head and says to Deus, "Stand behind the barrier to protect your power."

Deus follows his order.

General Harding nods to the technician to begin the procedure.

The table moves through the center of the machine and then starts its return. The lights dim once again as the bright beam of light crawls along the general's body.

I glance over at Crimson, wondering what she's thinking about, hoping she'll let me know. She doesn't. I for one am beginning to panic. I realize the vision I had

had is about to play out before my eyes. Will General Harding actually become a Diamond Bearer, or will Chris kill his own father by not relinquishing the stone to him?

The table finishes traveling through the machine and comes to a halt. The lights regain their brightness, and the weak quartz on top of the pyramid loses its glow quickly.

General Harding sits up and shakes his head. "I feel different . . . better." An aura forms above his shoulder and head. He stands and motions for the technician to leave the room. "Chris, lock the door."

Chris turns the lock, securing the door from the inside after the technician leaves, then walks back to the glass box.

"All right, son, bring me the diamond."

Chris reaches inside the box and wraps his fingers around the Sanguine Diamond. I hear his thoughts about the fact his father just called him "son" without sarcasm or anger. How many years has Chris waited to hear his father call him that? He pulls the diamond out and extends his hand with the diamond in it to his father, just like in my vision. Chris is about to act in a way that will bring about the death of his father.

I'm not sure how I feel about his actions.

General Harding reaches his hand out to take the diamond, but at the last second, Chris pulls his hand back slightly and says, "I relinquish this diamond to you."

What?

The diamond passes between owners without a hitch. General Harding is now a Diamond Bearer. His face lights up with excitement. He examines the diamond closely and then raises both hands, cupping the diamond, and slams it into his chest like he'd witnessed me doing following Freedom's death.

Crimson can't believe what's happened. Her thoughts

are my thoughts. *Chris actually relinquished the diamond to his father.* I feel her incredible disappointment.

General Harding falls to his knees as blood pours out of his chest. "Help me heal," he gasps and reaches for Chris.

Chris steps back and says with a waver in his voice, "I'm not a Healer, Dad. What about the healing crystals from the Shadow Demons? How do I get into the crystal room?"

General Harding shakes his head and falls over onto his side, his bloody chest facing me.

"What's the code, Dad?"

Still no answer. His body stops moving for a moment, and then his heart muscle begins to heal over the diamond. Bone starts to re-grow and knit together. Soon the general begins to move his arms. He pushes himself upright and sits on the floor with his head hanging down, his chest cavity still largely exposed.

Crimson cautions me, *Block your mind, Calli. He might figure out how to access it. New Diamond Bearers access powers in different ways. I never know which power will come naturally to a Bearer.*

Apparently he figured out how to heal himself.

"Watch out!" Chris yells and waves his arm.

I turn and see Deus Ex walking toward General Harding, pointing the same .44 Magnum Harding used on Rolf.

"If it's good enough for Rolf, it's good enough for you. So glad you took my advice and killed him. You showed me exactly how to do it, and where you kept your gun."

General Harding raises his head with an expression of terror on his face. He extends his hand out in front of him as if it might stop Deus.

She pulls the trigger only once.

The bullet hits his hand first and completely amputates it. The hollow point then opens and spreads out before it strikes the general's still-healing chest. The impact almost rips him in half.

The diamond, which hasn't been inside his body long enough for the heart muscle to attach, ricochets against the wall, over to the machine, back to the wall, and then slides across the floor and stops near Chris's feet.

General Stanley Harding's body slumps sideways to the floor, dead.

The twanging sensation settles into my body, letting me know the diamond has no owner.

The guards pound on the door, ordering Chris to open it. Max's face fills the small window on the door.

Deus turns her gun on Chris. "Don't even think about it, Chris."

Chris raises his hands. "I'm not going to open the door, Deus."

She smiles but doesn't lower the gun. "Good. Thank you for giving your father the diamond, like I hinted you should do."

"You said you wouldn't kill me, Deus."

"Are you going to try to stop me from taking the diamond?"

"Nope. I don't want it."

"That's good. I may have use for you, if you want to work with me."

"I'm powerless, Deus."

She lowers the gun and points to the crystal room behind the glass wall. "Not for long. You could take one of each power—not Brand's stone; that one's for me—you could be just as powerful as a Diamond Bearer. You and I could start a new group. With Brand's repeating power and that diamond, I'll be unstoppable. Soon I'll have all the diamonds and then we can go after the red spinel. Think about it, Chris. Immortality."

Crimson begins to move forward, toward the diamond. She's careful not to step in the several pools of blood on the floor, which would give away her location if she left bloody footprints behind. She extends her hand to pick up the diamond.

Without warning, panels on three walls spring open, revealing obsidian.

The rushing sensation of my powers leaving my body makes my stomach lurch. I try to use my invisibility topaz, even though I know it has lost its charge. No luck. Out of the corner of my eye I see Crimson has also become visible. Deus sees me first and reacts quickly by firing off a shot, but she misses me entirely. I roll out of the way and hide behind the large machine. Apparently she isn't such a good shot without her repeating power.

In the meantime, Chris scoops up the diamond, and Crimson runs toward me.

"You knew they were here the whole time?" Deus yells at Chris.

Chris shrugs his shoulders.

"Who's the other Diamond Bearer? Never mind. Give me the diamond!" she insists.

"Okay." He tosses the bloody diamond, and she clumsily catches it with one hand. She shakes it to try to remove some of the remaining blood.

The obsidian prevents us from using telepathy. Crimson whispers to me, "Look for a panel box. Maybe a red button. We need to close these doors."

I know what she's thinking, even though I can't read her mind. The exposed obsidian prevents the diamond from killing Deus, but once the panels are closed, Deus will die.

Max and the other guards continue to pound on the door, demanding to be let in.

Chris yells, "Take us off lockdown, Max. The door is blocked."

Deus fires a shot at Chris. The bullet hits high and wide—a warning shot. "Don't open that door!"

Chris shouts back, "You're crazy!"

I'm not sure what comes over me, but I decide to try to knock the gun out of Deus's hand before she shoots Chris. She isn't at the top of her game. She can't repeat, so somewhere in my garbled thinking, I think I may have a chance. I rush her from the side, and my body collides with hers. The arm that's holding the gun swings in my direction. Her other hand maintains a firm hold on the diamond. We fall to the floor, and she fires a shot, hitting the far wall.

I faintly hear Chris give further instructions to Max to take us off lockdown.

I scramble to wrestle down Deus's arm while she lies sprawled out on her back. Deus swings the fist that's holding the diamond and punches my back, causing me to lunge forward. Then she points the gun at me and fires another shot. I let out a shriek as the bullet rips through the edge of my right thigh like a white-hot serrated knife.

I instinctually try to heal my leg, only to realize I can't . . . not as long as the panels are still open. I glance over to the nearest panel and am relieved to see the panel door slowly sliding along its track. The main door is still locked from our side, preventing the guards from entering. I look down to find a growing puddle of blood around my leg. I press my hands on the wound to try to stop the bleeding. To say it hurts is an understatement.

Deus stands and attempts to enter a code into the

keypad to open the door to the crystal room. Her gun is pointed in Chris's direction as a warning to stay away from both her and the door. She uses her knuckle to press the numbers, as if she doesn't want to loosen the hold on the diamond for a second.

The all-too-familiar "denied" tone from the keypad sounds through the room.

"Come on!" Deus shouts.

"Deus, drop the diamond," I plead with her. "When those panels close, you'll die if you're holding it." *Why am I trying to save her?* Why? Because she fulfilled nature's will by preventing General Harding from becoming a Diamond Bearer. She at least deserves a chance to change her ways.

"I don't think so." She aims the gun at the glass barrier standing between her and Brand's repeating stone. "I know Brand has a longer stretch of time than I do." She fires her remaining shots into the bullet-proof glass, aiming above the quartz crystal. The bullets blast through the window and tear through the metal pyramid but don't shatter the glass window. Deus uses the butt of the gun to pound on the glass. She's able to break small pieces off around the bullet holes.

The panels continue their sluggish pace on their way to closing. Not there yet.

I look over at Crimson, who's still crouched behind the machine. She mouths a message: "Keep trying to convince her to drop the diamond."

"Deus, you don't have to die. Drop the diamond."

Her pounding efforts with the gun became more frantic. She's creating a bigger opening in the thick glass. I begin to worry that she may actually succeed in getting her hand on Brand's stone . . . and yet, what will she accomplish exactly? I wonder how long the obsidian has been exposed. She'll only be able to repeat back two minutes, assuming the power in the quartz is exactly like it was with Brand. Will she repeat back to a point before the obsidian was exposed?

How much time does she have left? At some point she will run out of time.

Chris yells at her, "Deus, drop the diamond! You don't need to die this way."

"Shut up, both of you! I'm not going to die. Nothing can kill me!"

She pounds harder. The hole becomes big enough that she can finally reach her arm inside and wrap her fingers around the quartz. "Oh shit!" she exclaims, as the panels click into place, hiding the obsidian and its power-canceling effects.

My powers rush back into my body at the same time Deus's legs give out. I scan her body and find the diamond has activated and caused her heart to explode within her. Her arm is caught in the glass, preventing her body from falling all the way to the floor. The diamond tumbles out of her left hand, and the quartz falls out of her right on the other side of the glass wall.

I let out my pent-up breath and focus my mind on my bullet wound, willing it to heal. I have lost a fair amount of blood. Crimson's mind melds with mine again as she sends me healing energy.

Guards rush in as soon as Chris unlocks the door. The general is lying in a puddle of inky blood, obviously dead. Deus is hanging oddly by her trapped arm, without any blood to indicate an injury, but she's clearly dead as well.

Max asks Chris, "Sir, are you all right? What happened?"

"Deus shot my father, and then I think she was electrocuted when she touched the stand in the crystal room." Chris points in her direction, and the guards look over at Deus.

Max glares at me and asks, "What is she doing here?"

I quickly glanced over at Crimson and discover she has activated her invisibility. I speak to Chris's mind: *Tell him to seize me and lock me in with the other prisoners. You'll be able to maintain your position and authority over the guards.*

"She sneaked into the facility. Seize her and lock her up with the others. Be careful. This is a crime scene."

Max hands the orders down and glances around the room. I read his mind: *There was another female. I know I saw two females.*

Two other guards come over to me and pick me up by my arms and then haul me out of the room and down the hall. I read their minds to discover they are suppressing their morbid joy that the general is dead.

The guards deposit me in the observation room where everyone else is held and close the door. Gasps and cries are uttered as everyone takes in my appearance. I must look pretty bad with my blood-covered hands and leg.

Brand and Clara Winter rush to my side.

"Calli, you're hurt!" Clara grabs hold of my arm.

"I'm fine. I've already been healed."

Brand asks, "Who shot you?"

"It doesn't matter. We can talk about that later. Right now, we need to get everyone out of here." I notice their shackles have been removed. "You're not cuffed?"

Brand replies, "No, the guards came in, walking like zombies, and removed our restraints a little while ago. Calli, you didn't tell me Beth's brother was here. Why not?"

"Later, Brand." I suspect Crimson had a hand in the guards' decision to release the prisoners from their bonds.

I sense Crimson is about to open the door. I watch through her eyes. I see that she followed the guards down the hall when they dumped me in the room. Crimson viewed the key code in the mind of the guard and she's waiting for both of them to leave.

Before the door opens, I feel that Chris has picked up the diamond from the floor and has placed it in his pocket. He is its owner once again. He sends his thoughts to me. *Calli, can you hear me?*

Yes, Chris, I respond.

I think we can clean this compound out before the 'big boys' get here. If I'm viewing the future correctly, we have about twenty minutes. Crimson is going to help free the prisoners.

The door opens, and Crimson enters the room. Understanding that no one knows who she is and that they will be naturally hesitant to do as she says, she tells my mind to tell everyone to follow her if they want to escape.

"Clara, this lady can help all of you escape," I say. "Go with her. And hurry, there's not much time."

Chris's thoughts enter mine. *Keep Brand. We need him.*

As Clara and Crimson lead the group out the door, I reach out and hold onto Brand's elbow. "Please stay, Brand. We need your help."

"I don't know what I can do to help you now."

"You can hold the quartz that contains your Repeater power and help us make the most out of the small amount of time we have to clear the compound of all the research."

"You could do that as well, Calli."

"You're the one with experience using the power."

"All right, but I'm not going to kill anyone."

"There's no one left to kill."

I think about the fact that Brand's charged quartz is what killed Deus. Not the quartz itself, but her desire to have Brand's power. If he hadn't willingly given it up, she might still be alive. I decide not to share my thoughts with Brand that nature used him to eliminate Deus. Chris had been right when he said Brand's power was the only thing that could kill Deus.

My mind's eye pictures what Crimson is both doing and seeing as she leads the prisoners toward the building's exit. She uses her Mind-control a couple of times to make the guards turn and walk in the opposite direction, allowing the group to escape through the main door. I lose connection with her mind as she enters the obsidian field outside the building but reconnect when she reaches the front gate and causes the guard stationed there to forget he ever saw the group of people leave the compound. Of course, no one in the prisoner group knows what she's doing.

With most of the guards and workers huddled in the hallway near the machine room, I am able to sneak Brand into the lab. "Hide in here," I say as I push him into a supply closet, "until I get back." I don't wait for him to agree before closing the door.

Voices in the hall catch my attention. I hide behind a cabinet and listen. Chris issues commands in the same manner as his father, and with the same authority. "Max, take everyone into the observation room until the authorities arrive."

"Sir, the prisoners are in there," Max reminds Chris.

"I know. Everyone needs to be kept together, away from the crime scene, in order to preserve the evidence."

"Yes, sir," Max says, then issues orders to the crowd.

The sound of shuffling feet and tense whispers filter into the lab as people walk past the door toward the observation room. I know things will become interesting when it's discovered the prisoners are gone.

"Sir, you'd better come see this!" I hear Max shout from down the hall.

"What is it?"

"The prisoners are gone. They've escaped!"

Chris acts as though the news is the last thing he wants to hear at that moment. "Didn't you lock the door after taking the girl to the room? This is the worst time to have a breakout. Max, you and Ethan come with me and we'll perform a search. Everyone else, go in the observation room."

Chris sends a message to my mind. *Calli, take Brand to the control room and remove the hard drive from the computer. It contains the surveillance recordings. All the guards are either with me or are locked up.*

I grab Brand from the closet and we run to the control room.

"What are we doing, Calli?"

"We're pulling the hard drive."

"I thought you were going to give me my repeating stone."

"I will." I push open the door to the computer room. Within seconds, we have removed the vital guts of the mainframe. I send a message to Chris. *Done.*

Good. We're heading to the security room to view the recordings, which of course we won't be able to view because the files are stored on the hard drive that you just pulled. After that, I'll lock the guards with the others and meet you in my father's office. Crimson is already there.

"Come on, Brand." I take Brand by the hand, open the door and peak out. The hallway is empty and quiet. I pull Brand out and we hurry to the office.

I spot Crimson in her invisible state going through the file cabinet. *We have the hard drive,* I say.

Yes, I know. Brand's Repeater stone is right there. She points to the clear crystal on the desk.

"Brand, pick up the quartz on the desk. It's yours," I say.

Brand does so and wraps his fingers around it firmly.

"There's no power in this stone."

Crimson instantly stops what she's doing, and together we ask, "What?"

"Just kidding," he laughs. "Sheez, you're so jumpy."

Chris enters the office. He lets me know telepathically that he, Max, and Ethan performed a quick search for the missing prisoners and then he escorted Max and Ethan to the observation room. "Is Crimson in here?" he asks aloud.

"Yes, I'm here."

"Good. I need to get to my dad's hard drive. Would you throw his computer against the wall to break it open? If I touch it I'll leave fingerprints."

"Certainly, Chris."

Even though I can see Crimson, I know the guys can't. It must look pretty cool to see the computer have its cords ripped out of the back and then fly across the room to the far wall. The shell cracks and the insides are exposed.

Brand asks, "Crimson doesn't have fingerprints?"

"Sure I do. They belong to a deceased woman from Arizona, according to the police database."

"Oh, yeah, that will stump 'em," Brand laughs.

Crimson says, "Brand, help Chris. You two need to go to the lab and search each computer for any files saved to individual computers. Brand's repeating ability will help you do this quickly. Calli, go box up the crystals from the crystal room. Move as fast as you can."

"Got it."

I run out of the room using my running power and enter the machine room. A wave of nausea washes over me when I see the two dead people again. Why did they both have to be so greedy? Their deaths were inevitable.

I communicate with Chris. *What's the code for the crystal room?*

5432, he responds.

How unoriginal, I muse. *Wait! Why did you ask your father for the code if you already knew it?*

He didn't know I knew it.

Why didn't the code work for Deus?

All codes are invalid for a few minutes following a lockdown.

I enter the room and use my quick reflexes to speedily remove the individual crystals from the organizational wall units and place them in a box I find on the floor. I pause for a moment and realize I have the hardest job of everyone. Regardless of where I stand, I can still see Deus Ex out of the corner of my eye, hanging like a rag doll from the window. I try to focus on my task instead of dwelling on Deus's decision to not relent. Once I've cleaned out the crystal room, I take the box to the general's office.

The others have finished their tasks as well. Crimson instructs us to place everything we have collected into a larger box on the floor.

Crimson says, "We don't have much time. Chris, for now, I want you to relinquish the diamond to Calli. Experiencing the diamond's pure strength is hard enough on its own, let alone while needing to keep your mind straight and focused."

"I was actually thinking about that myself, Crimson." Chris turns to me, removes the diamond from his pocket, and assigns it to me. I place it in my pocket.

Crimson announces, "I'll take this material to the gathering. You two need to stay here for the investigation and to tie up any loose ends that will bring any unwanted attention your way." She reaches her hand toward me and reveals her topaz. "Take this, Calli. Start charging it to help you remain invisible, just in case. Come on, Brand, let's go."

"But you'll be exposed when you leave the building," I

protest.

"The guards are gone and the surveillance cameras aren't filming anymore," she says.

Brand asks, "Then why are you still invisible, Crimson? It's weird talking to the air."

"I haven't lived this long by being careless with my powers, Brand. While I can be invisible, I will be." She turns to me and says, "You and Chris need to disable the machine before they get here. Hurry."

Crimson and Brand leave the building, and Chris and I race down the hall to the machine room.

Chris cringes upon seeing his father's dead body. "He got what he was after . . . momentarily, anyway. You gotta hand it to him," Chris says, sadly. He clears his throat and hurries over to the machine. "All we have to do is remove the power source and computer chip." He opens the control box panel and peers inside.

I examine the center ring and the mechanics of what I can see through the channel opening. It looks just like any CT scanner I've ever seen.

"Here," Chris announces. He is down on his knees, reaching under the unit, struggling to grab something.

I join him from the other side of the machine, and together we remove twelve long, clear crystals with points on each end, about four-inches in length and a quarter inch in diameter. I can't tell if they're quartz or not. They are clearly important to the functionality of the machine.

Chris says, "I knew this had to be powered by something out of the ordinary. Only someone with the knowledge, like Freedom, would think of such a thing. My dad called him an egghead. He had no idea what was really going on in Freedom's head."

"Did you get the computer chip?"

"Yes. Let's get out of here." He stands, brushes

himself off, and then freezes as he looks down at the floor.

I follow his gaze down to his father's perfectly positioned boots.

"I'm sorry, Chris."

He glances over in the direction of my voice and says, "Why? It wasn't your fault he was so screwed up in the head." Chris hands me the crystals in his hand to add to the ones I'm holding. "Take care of these. I need to go wait by the gate to approve the entrance of the convoy. It's what would be expected."

I scoop the crystals from his hand. "Where do you want me to stay while the investigation takes place?"

"Please stay invisibly by my side, Calli. I may need you to use your Mind-control. For now, wait by the security checkpoint at the front door."

Chris sits across the table from the lead investigator. The identification hanging around the man's neck identifies him as Criminal Investigations' Special Agent David Whitman. Agent Whitman, a middle-aged man with an expansive mid-section and deep brow lines, looks up from the files spread out in front of him. "Mr. Harding, you witnessed the female shooter's attack on General Harding?"

"Yes, sir."

"To your knowledge, did she shoot anyone else?"

"Not to my knowledge. I just returned from an assignment yesterday."

"You didn't know what you were walking into, right?"

"Exactly."

"We're investigating your father's home in Denver. Perhaps some information will be found that points to a motive. I have a team there now."

I say to Chris, *Ask if he thinks your father and Deus were in a romantic relationship.*

Chris suggests, "What do you think you'll find? Something pointing to a personal relationship between my father and Deus Ex?"

"I can't say, son. Tell me, why did the girl go by that name?"

"Why does anyone change their name, sir? I don't understand it either. Her real name was Samantha Juarez."

Agent Whitman wraps up his interview with Chris and tells him to go wait in what is the same recovery room where Chris and I had kissed earlier. A soldier stands outside the door.

I read Chris's mind. *I'm a material witness, and they're protecting me, or more like guarding me from leaving.*

Well, I'm ready to jump into action and start controlling minds. Just say the word, I reply.

I keep thinking about Crimson and wondering what she would do in this situation. She is so right about the fact that everything needs to come apart as naturally as possible. Let's just sit tight for a while longer. I'm sure we're under surveillance right now, even though they can't record anything. Too bad. I sure could use some of your healing.

I'll send you some. I focus on his mind and heart and send my energy his way.

I gotta tell you, Calli, Crimson fed me energy almost continuously throughout that whole ordeal. She knew how hard it was for me to be around my father and witness his atrocities, but your kisses infused me with more healing than she ever could.

I think she knew that, too. She encouraged me to comfort you . . . not that I needed encouraging.

Chapter 14 - What Does the Future Hold?

Agent Whitman meets with Chris again before sending him home.

I take a moment to look into the agent's mind to find out what he's learned in his investigation. His mind reveals the four bodies were transported to the morgue, and he's had evidence collected throughout the compound.

Well, the little evidence that remains.

I feel his thoughts. The bullets in General Harding's office wall, along with the two guards' testimonies about the shooting, clearly link the general to Rolf's death, Whitman believes. The claims of a clear stone or rock having been inside Rolf's heart are disturbing. If it wasn't for the fact that several people offered the same comment, Whitman realizes he'd have to dismiss the ridiculous claim. He thinks about the two guards also describing how the female prisoner died after she tried to pick up the glass box containing the stone that had been inside Rolf. Her death, they told him, was similar in nature to Deus's in that there were no visible wounds. Whitman realizes he'll have to wait for the autopsy reports to get further information. The whole fiasco feels interconnected in some way. Whitman hopes the staff and guards fully understand the consequences if they reveal any classified information. Especially the one guard who keeps insisting he saw some pretty bizarre things.

Max Corvus.

Agent Whitman is still struggling with his decision to dismiss Max Corvus with the rest of the guards. Corvus seems borderline insane, insisting magical powers really exist, and that some people have diamonds inside their bodies. Max told Agent Whitman that he had dealings with something called the Death Clan several years ago—men over 200-years-old who can kill others with their minds.

Agent Whitman finally decided to just tell Max that everything associated with his work in the compound is now classified and he should just forget what he's seen. Max's reply was: "Just because we seal up and classify everything in this building doesn't mean the magical people out there in the real world cease to exist. They're real! You don't have to believe me, but I've seen them with my own eyes."

Agent Whitman's thoughts at the moment show he is going to have Max Corvus put under surveillance. He writes a sentence on his pad of paper and then circles it in one swift movement.

I think it's a good idea to watch Max closely, too.

Agent Whitman scratches the top of his head and looks up from his pad of paper at Chris.

"I'm sorry for your loss, Chris. Your father had a will filed with the military. You're listed as his sole beneficiary. Here's a number you can call to get more information."

"Thank you." Chris takes the card and puts it in his pocket. His thoughts reveal he doesn't want anything that belonged to his father.

"We'll be in contact with you, Mr. Harding, if we have any more questions. Again, please accept my deepest condolences."

I take one last look into Agent Whitman's mind while he shakes Chris's hand. He figures this investigation will go down in the books as an unexplainable situation, one that will bring great embarrassment to the Department of Defense if the media ever gets hold of the information. General Harding had run an operation independent of the D.O.D, yet he had managed to receive government funding for his secretive, unapproved research. Each employee or guard, with the exception of Max Corvus, has such limited knowledge about the compound's operations that it is hard to piece together a complete picture of what research was actually conducted in the facility. Much of what Max talked about, such as the crystals and "super-powered prisoners", are absent from the compound. The only physical evidence they can find is an inoperable CT scanner. The hard drive from the main computer is missing, and the surveillance recordings are gone as well. Evidence from the general's home only shows a man obsessed with what Harding considers supernatural, metaphysical hooey. In addition, no records or evidence of birth have been found yet for the victims, Rolf, Samantha "Deus Ex" Juarez, or the unidentified girl.

Whitman's conclusion is that something strange happened at the compound, resulting in the deaths of four individuals, but whatever happened will forever remain a mystery. Agent Whitman already classifies the case as unsolvable, due to lack of evidence. The case will most likely be shelved and re-opened only if new evidence or testimony surfaces.

I pull out of his mind, wondering if anyone will ever know how many people with powers lost their lives to Shadow Demons due to General Harding. Those names will never be known by the government.

Chris thanks Agent Whitman, then leaves the room. *I hope I never have to return to this building again!* he thinks, as he fishes his keys out of his pocket.

I activate my topaz to remain invisible while leaving

the compound. Good thing, too. Reporters and cameras line the outside of the gate at least five people deep.

"Uh oh, this should be interesting," Chris says under his breath.

Don't worry. I'll be able to use my Mind-control to part the crowd once we're far enough away from the obsidian. At least I think I will.

Sure enough, when we reach the gate, I feel the rush of my powers returning to my body. The media onslaught begins.

"Mr. Harding, what happened?"

"Mr. Harding, can you explain what kind of research this facility conducted?"

"Is it true a gunman opened fire and killed your father?"

Chris glances over at the guard in the control booth and nods his head. The guard opens the gate far enough for Chris to exit. He pauses before stepping through the opening, allowing me to proceed.

I issue the mental command for everyone to take two steps backward and part down the middle so Chris can leave. I'm unsure if my Mind-Control powers will work on so many people at once. The crowd does exactly what I command them to do. *Oh yeah, I can tell I'm going to like this power.*

Chris says just what he and Agent Whitman agreed: "No comment."

The swarm follows him to his car, but never gets any closer than two steps away. Chris walks to the passenger side and opens it. He continues to say, "No comment," while I slip inside the car, then he leans in and sets his briefcase down on the floor by my feet. He closes the door and walks around to the driver's side door and climbs in.

"That was fun," he mumbles.

We drive away from the compound, and I can't help feeling sorry for Chris. I wonder if he feels emotional about the loss of his father. I know what a healthy grieving process involves, and I understand the loss hasn't had time to really sink into Chris's mind yet.

I'll be there for him when the tidal wave hits.

I communicate with Crimson, who tells me to direct Chris to the regional airport, where Maetha's plane waits for us.

Captain Rutherfield welcomes us on board and offers his sympathies.

Beth and Brand are on the plane already and let us know that Maetha and Crimson left for Indiana. Brand's and Beth's excited chatter is overwhelming, especially for Chris, but he makes an effort to be sociable, even while his mind reveals that all he wants to do is curl up in a dark corner with me.

Soon we are airborne, headed for Indiana, for Patoka Lake.

I use Beth's cellphone and call my parents when the pilot gives the thumbs up. Chris and the others continue to discuss the dramatic events that happened at the compound.

"Mom, it's Calli."

"Hello, dear. How is everything going? I've been so worried. Are you eating anything? Are you feeling all right? When will I see you next?"

"Whoa, Mom, slow down," I laugh a little, but deep down I feel incredibly grateful to have a mother and father who care so much about me. "I'm just fine. Everything is just fine. You and Dad can return home now. The dangers have been eliminated."

"What do you mean eliminated? Did some people go to jail?"

"Don't worry about it, Mom. I'm safe, you're safe, Dad's safe. Right now I'm headed east and expect to be home maybe in a week or so. You can reach me at this number, but I'll keep you updated on my plans."

We say our goodbyes, and I end the call.

I turn to Chris. "Do you want to call your mother?"

"Yes." He takes the phone and dials the number.

I listen as Chris explains in vague, glossed-over language that his father had died. He could have chosen to say just about anything, but he doesn't elaborate. I understand the relationship Chris has with his mother better. He loves her deeply and doesn't want her to worry about him. He finishes his call by promising to visit her soon.

Chris gives the phone back to Beth. "Does anyone want something from the fridge?" he asks.

"I'll take one of Clara's magical juices," I chime in. Hearing Clara's name sparks a realization in my mind. Clara, and Beth's brother, Nate, would have died if I hadn't figured out how to eliminate the Shadow Demons. A sense of pride warms my heart, then a wave of despair fills my mind. I can't help but think of the faceless individuals who died before the Demons were eliminated.

Chris walks back to the small kitchen space, squats down, and opens the fridge.

I watch him with concern. I feel he needs me and the healing energy only I can give him. He has yet to retrieve anything from the fridge. I read his mind and find he is completely zoned out, reliving the horrifying events.

I excuse myself from Beth and Brand and walk back to him. He isn't even aware I have arrived by his side. I place my hand on his shoulder and send him positive energy. He reaches in and pulls out two drinks and hands me one. He stands and closes the fridge door.

"Thank you, Calli. You're the only one who will ever understand what I've been through. Let's sit back here." He leads me to a more secluded area with dual reclining chairs. We seat ourselves and open our drinks.

We sip for a few minutes in silence. I resist the urge to read his mind, figuring I already know the kind of images racing through it.

I set my drink in the cupholder and scoot forward in my seat. I turn to Chris and gently ease the juice out of his hand, set it inside another cupholder, and say, "I don't think we'll ever forget what happened in the final dramatic hours, Chris. I don't think we should. Our memories and experiences are what shape our futures. Let me give you some much-needed healing."

I move into his space and bring my lips to his. I kiss him gently and respectfully, infusing him with my healing power.

He wraps his arms around my body and pulls me onto his lap. One of his hands slides up into my hair, and he angles my head so he can kiss me more intently with his warm lips.

As the healing power is delivered through our intimate moment, I remember the first time his lips touched mine. Well, I sort of remember it. I viewed it through his memory on the banks of the river when he gave me mouth-to-mouth resuscitation and saved my life. Along with viewing what he'd done, I experienced the emotions he felt for me at that time. I remember feeling blown away to discover the depth of his affection. He kissed me while I was unconscious, after the destruction of the Death Clan. That kiss was a sad "good-bye" gesture on his part. He didn't have my same optimism that we'd see each other again.

The next noteworthy kiss I remember came when I

rescued Chris from Justin Macintyre's hold. Finding him, instead of Clara Winter, behind the locked door caught me off guard, and the emotion behind the kiss I gave him came from an incredibly relieved place deep within my heart. Further intimacy followed later in the evening . . . well, as much as was possible because of the amulets we were wearing. The kiss Chris gave me before Maetha ushered me out to receive the diamond after Justin Macintyre's death left a lasting impression. He delivered such passion and possessiveness at that moment . . . just thinking about it makes butterflies swarm within my belly. Then there was the sensual kiss in the warehouse before meeting with the Diamond Bearers and Freedom. I recall how my heart raced with excitement. I think the reason the shard began causing life-threatening injuries to my heart was because of my anticipation of being as close as possible to Chris. I hadn't had a physical relationship with a guy before. Still haven't. I already had the knowledge that Chris and I would eventually become intimate because of the vision I had of our grandchildren. Knowing that eventually he and I would create one or more babies together ignited a thrilling sensation within my body that intoxicated my mind and soul, making my heart become my enemy. Then, within hours, Chris's mind was taken over by Maetha because of his effect on my well-being.

The kiss I gave him on the plane ride back from Alaska was similar to the kiss we are currently sharing. I had wanted to heal his emotions, wanted to calm his mind and help him know the bigger picture. Just as he kept me from dying on the banks of the river by giving me mouth-to-mouth resuscitation, my kisses keep him from sinking into a deep emotional pit. Chris will need many such kisses, I think. The thought of performing "healing sessions" with Chris causes every cell in my body to buzz.

Chris's kiss shifts in intensity. He's no longer drinking in my healing power, he's delivering his own type of medicine—or drug—to my body, causing my heart to race like never before. The pain of the shard tearing apart my vital organ brings my elated brain back to the present. I heal the pain, only to have it come right back when Chris's fingertips move across my body. I let out a frustrated sigh against his lips. I can't wait to explore every inch of his body, but that will obviously have to wait.

He breaks the kiss, looks me in the eye and asks, "How does our future look now, Calli?"

Crimson's voice enters my mind. *Give him back his diamond, Calli. He's earned it.*

Yes, he has.

I scoot back from him, unzip my pocket and remove the diamond, being careful not to let any of the twelve crystals from the machine fall out. I face Chris and say, "I relinquish this diamond to you, Chris Harding. Let's find out together what our future holds."

His eyes widen in shock. He protests, "Crimson told me to give it to you. I don't think—"

"She just now instructed me to give it back to you. I was only holding it temporarily. You've earned the title of Diamond Bearer."

"She told you to give it back to me?"

"Yes, it's yours."

Chris reaches forward with both hands and accepts the diamond. He pulls it close to his body and stares in reverent awe, much like I did when I received the diamond in Harold Bates's office.

I reach forward and cup my hands around his, and together we see the vision I had seen while lying on the stone altar. I stand in a cemetery by a headstone that has Chris's name carved on the front. Several children run toward me. This time I recognize them as our great-grandchildren. Chris's death and burial had come after a long life of happiness and productivity . . . but his life is not over yet! The vision switches to show Chris resting peacefully under a giant palm tree on a white sandy beach. I walk toward him along the beach. He stands, runs to me, and hugs me tightly, then swings my body around. He apologizes for not making it to my funeral.

The vision ends, but further understanding fills my mind. In the vision, we had faked our deaths at the ripe old ages of eighty-six for Chris and eighty for me. The procedure isn't anything new to Diamond Bearers. Completing the lifespan cycle is necessary for our re-maining relatives to have closure. Our loved ones will marvel at our deep love and at the fact that we died within a couple of months of each other. They will remember us as "so in love they couldn't stand to be apart." Our next stage of life as Diamond Bearers will be spent on Maetha's island in Bermuda and on other continents where no one will recognize us. We will be forbidden from contacting or communicating with our descendants. In fact, we won't see any of our descendants for a hundred years. By that time, we won't know them on a personal level. We will always recognize them as our bloodline, but the intimate connection will be gone. But not our compassion.

I look up at Chris and ask, "Did you see that?"

"Yes, I did!" He places the diamond inside his pocket, then pulls me close once again. "I guess I don't need to propose to you at all then."

"Ah, yes you do. The future is not set in stone, sir."

"One step at a time, Calli. I think we need to focus on getting to know each other a little better. For instance," he says as he nuzzles my neck, "I don't think I'm that familiar with this patch of skin."

Chapter 15
The Younger Generation Task Force

We arrive at the resort in Indiana and are met with hugs, tears, and congratulations from several Diamond Bearers. Jonas and Anika come toward us. I'm relieved to see Jonas is doing well. He's learned how to control the diamond's powers enough to not need Mary by him every second.

Yeah, Jonas says to my mind, *she taught me how to heal myself. I think she was getting tired of having to do it for me.*

You're doing a great job, Jonas. How's Anika holding up?

She blames herself for her parent's deaths, even though Avani said her parents were already dead before she escaped from Deus Ex. She wishes she could have been there to heal them.

Yeah, I know how difficult it is to want to heal someone but not be able to.

Jonas smiles at me, acknowledging my attempts to save his life.

I give Anika a hug. "I'm sorry about your parents."

"Thank you," she whispers.

Jonas says, "I'd give you a hug, Calli, but Crimson told me not to."

"Maybe later, Jonas," I say.

Jonas puts his arm around Anika's shoulders and pulls her close. I sense he's giving her healing energy. I also feel their growing attachment.

Amenemhet and Mary welcome us with hugs and tears. I'm stunned to see them display emotions. I guess I thought Diamond Bearers were icy cold, with eyes incapable of tearing up, or so it seems. Then I realize they are still sad about the loss of Neema and Hasan.

Marketa, Avani, Fabian, and Aernoud shake our hands and welcome us to the group.

Duncan approaches me and hugs me tightly. "I'm impressed, Calli. You two really did a great job. Chris, I'm sorry about your loss."

"Thank you, Duncan."

Merlin steps forward and shakes Chris's hand. "Son, you handled everything perfectly. To my knowledge, there will be no further investigation into the events at the compound. Once the current investigation is wrapped up, the compound will be dismantled and shut down. You and Calli accomplished what no one else could do."

I try to tell him Crimson had been an integral part of the mission too, but my mouth won't allow the words to form.

Chris's thoughts enter my head. *I can't say anything about Crimson, either. I think we aren't allowed . . . and that's okay.*

Crimson speaks to my mind. *I only want a select few to know I was at the compound with you.*

Amalgada, Yeok Choo, Kookju, Jie Wen, Chuang, Ruth, and Alena each send telepathic messages of congratulations and support . . . even Jie Wen congratulates us.

Maetha brings the meeting to order.

I notice Crimson is walking around the perimeter of our group, her lips moving. I remember watching Maetha do the same thing in the tent right after the Death Clan died. Maetha had said she was protecting our conversation from eavesdroppers. I now know what actually happened. Maetha used her Grecian Blue Diamond to alter the perceptions of any would-be eavesdroppers, and Crimson is doing the same thing as she circles the group.

Crimson's words sound in my head—a simple chant

of words repeated over and over as she walks, "No one will be able to hear. No one will be able to hear."

"We welcome Chris Harding as our newest Diamond Bearer," Maetha says as she congratulates him openly. "In a short time, we've had some major changes to our group. In all my lifetime, I've never seen so much activity. With the death of Henry, the unforeseen addition of Jonas, followed by the untimely death of Hasan, and Roth's consequence for turning against nature, I guess I shouldn't be surprised with what happened to Chris. But I am. Welcome, Chris."

Most Bearers respond with applause and a verbal welcome.

Maetha continues. "We also welcome Brand Safferson, Beth Hammond, and Anika Evanston as future Bearers."

Chris and I both look at each other, then turn to Brand, Beth, and Anika, whose mouths hang open.

My mind is filled with thoughts from other Diamond Bearers. Many are as surprised as we are. Some have displeased feelings, and a couple of them are downright angry. I'm taken aback with some of the "displeased" Bearers.

"Come up here." Maetha motions for Brand, Beth, and Anika to join her. They slowly pick their way through the group. "As many individuals in the past have been given the title of future Bearer, these two have qualified in Crimson's eyes to carry diamonds—if they so choose, and if the need arises. Brand displayed ultimate selflessness while following nature's will. Beth has, over several years, displayed the integrity and conviction necessary to be a Bearer. Even though she is a Runner, if she so chooses, she can become a Bearer. Anika Evanston was hand-selected by Beth for her dependability and honesty. I've observed her as she came upon mind-bending information and how she processed the information. Not many times in the past has someone been pulled in off the street and entrusted with vital information concerning Diamond Bearers. I'm impressed with how maturely Anika has handled everything—and not much impresses me."

Maetha hugs the three of them and motions for them to return to their seats. Maetha says, "Jonas Flemming. Come forward."

Jonas's mind merges with mine in a panicked flurry as he walks toward Maetha. He thinks, *Oh, man, is this where the diamond is removed from my heart?*

Relax, Jonas, I tell him.

Crimson steps forward and Maetha dips her head in respect, then steps back. Crimson says, "This young man was never approved of beforehand to become a Bearer, as all of you were." Jonas's mind freaks out. Crimson places her hand on his shoulder to calm him. "However, when Maetha witnessed him turn down the opportunity to be healed of cancer, he left an impression. He demonstrated an absolute respect for nature's will and didn't act selfishly, even though it wouldn't have been wrong for him to accept Maetha's offer of healing. She made the decision to include him in her DNA experiments. Then he volunteered himself for sacrifice to prevent Henry from capturing the diamond from Calli. This young man—a boy in the eyes of most Bearers—wasn't afraid to do what was necessary, even if it meant his death. This is true friendship, complete dedication, and nature's will being carried out. Sometimes good people die while nature balances itself. Many good people have died." Crimson nods her head in Beth and Anika's direction. "Jonas has my approval to remain a Diamond Bearer, if he so chooses, and if he stays true to nature's will."

"Yes, I choose yes," he stutters, almost unable to contain himself.

Crimson smiles and gives him a hug. Then she asks him to sit down. She continues. "Only a handful of years ago, this group of Bearers assembled and gave their farewells to Gustave. He volunteered his diamond for the purposes of balancing nature and creating a new Bearer. What he didn't know was the splintering process and reuniting of the shards would expose the greatest threat to Bearers to date—Henry and the government. I salute Gustave's selfless contribution and his work as a Bearer."

The other Bearers speak out a salute in concert: "Gustave."

Crimson continues. "Gustave demonstrated his full cooperation in maintaining nature's will by first doing his duty as a Bearer, and second, being willing to sacrifice himself so his diamond could be reborn into a new Bearer—Calli Courtnae. Calli then went on to assist in the removal of Henry's diamond, in the internal shutdown of General Harding's facility, and in the elimination of Deus Ex. The rebirth of Gustave's diamond has been the greatest single event thus far since the inception of the Sanguine Diamond. I will take this opportunity to remind all my Bearers that you accepted the responsibility to protect humanity . . . even if that means giving your diamond for rebirth." Crimson pauses. No one makes a sound. "For now, let's celebrate the moment. For the first time in several decades, there are no immediate threats to our safety or to the safety of mankind."

Crimson then turns my direction. "Jonas and Calli, it is time to reunite the last remaining shard with the diamond. Come." She begins walking away from the group.

A broad smile stretches across Jonas's face. *Come on, Calli,* he says.

I stand and begin walking in Crimson's direction. Chris jumps to his feet and asks, "May I come, Crimson?"

She stops and says, "Of course, Chris."

He joins me at my side and together we follow her and Jonas away from the gathering. Thoughts from the other Bearers fill my head. The same division exists: some accepting, some disapproving, some angry.

I ask Chris. *Do you sense the other Bearers in your mind?*

A few of them, yes.

Can you read their minds?

No. Can you?

I'm not sure.

Crimson's mind merges with mine. *Calli, what you are experiencing is due to the Blue Diamond. You now have control over all the Bearer's mind-blocking abilities. You can hear the thoughts they think are private. Be careful with the knowledge you gain from Diamond Bearers' minds. Don't let anyone know you can get past their mind-blocks.*

Crimson leads us away from the group and down toward the lake.

Jonas asks, "Is it going to hurt?"

"Pain is a normal part of human experience," Crimson replies. "When you learn to identify your pains and determine which ones are life-threatening instead of just moderately annoying, you'll find you won't worry so much about hurting. To answer your question, yes, it will hurt a little."

Chris grasps my hand and squeezes it firmly. I turn to him and say, "I'm not afraid, Chris. I've been through this already."

Crimson stops by the water's edge and positions me next to Jonas. She looks intently at my chest and then at Jonas's. Then she turns us away from each other so we are standing a foot apart, back to back. She motions for Chris to come stand in front of me.

"You'll need to catch her after the diamond leaves her

body. Don't touch her until that point."

Chris nods and gazes at me in apprehension.

Crimson stands in front of Jonas and says, "All right you two, back up until you touch."

I step backward and bump into Jonas. Without warning, my shard rips through my heart and flies out my back, off to the side of my spine. The pain takes the wind right out of me. I realize the shard has torn through my lung in the process. I fall forward into Chris's arms, then he lowers me down to the ground, supporting my body. I will my injuries to heal and can tell Chris is doing the same.

Jonas receives the shard and collapses into Crimson's arms. His ability to use the healing power is not as refined as mine, but Crimson compensates by healing him with her power.

My connection to Jonas is gone. I feel his diamond, the same as any other Diamond Bearer, but not the quantum entanglement with his mind.

My body continues to heal and completes the process with Chris's help. I hear through the connection with Crimson's mind that she has invited Brand, Beth, and Anika to come join us by the lake.

The mind connection I have with the other Diamond Bearers reveals that some of them are curious about where the three "youngsters" are going. Others are feeling angry they aren't included in Crimson's activities.

Our friends arrive by our sides a few moments later. The blood on Jonas's back and on mine—and the fact that both of us are being supported because of our weakened states—are cause for concern. Their minds reveal their thoughts . . . even Brand's mind.

Anika hurries over to Jonas. "Are you okay?"

"Yes, I'm whole now," Jonas answers. He turns to Crimson. "May I touch her?"

"Absolutely."

Jonas pulls Anika into a warm embrace.

Crimson motions Brand and Beth to join the rest of us. Once we are all together, she instructs me to use my Grecian Blue and encircle the group with audio protection.

I speak to Chris's mind. *There's something I have to do. Be right back.* I stand and walk in a circle around our group, reciting the words under my breath, "No one will be able to hear. No one will be able to hear." Visually, I see a glittering mist form where I have walked. Once I have completed the circle, the mist connects, and I know I have secured the conversation we are about to have. I sit back down by Chris, and he wraps his arms around me and pulls me close.

Crimson addresses Brand. "You've demonstrated selflessness and a willingness to support the will of nature. That's why you've earned the right to choose to become a Bearer. Regardless of your decision, you will keep your Repeater stone until your death, or until the power fades from the quartz. I would like to request that you charge a topaz for me, if you don't mind. I'm curious about your power."

Brand responds, tongue-in-cheek, "All right, but if you misuse it, I'll take it away."

Crimson chuckles, then continues. "Anika and Beth, you have both suffered losses of the worst kind. Loved ones have been violently taken away from you, leaving you in a state of shock and indescribable pain. I advise you to embrace your memories of your loved ones and welcome the grief that accompanies your loss. It is both healthy and character building. Ignoring or covering up your emotional distress will only result in anger and vengeance-seeking behavior—neither of which are attributes of Diamond Bearers.

"Beth, I've had my eye on you since you were a young girl. I altered your vision, allowing you to see the auras of Unaltereds. I knew you would become friends with both Calli and Chris and would be a powerful ally. Your journey is only beginning. Even though the government compound has been shut down, an army of Unaltereds remains—some of whom know vast amounts of details concerning the clans and even Diamond Bearers. I would like you to find them and determine the extent of their knowledge. Your leadership skills make you the perfect candidate to head up my task force . . . if you want the job."

Beth smiles. "I'd be honored to work for you, Crimson."

"Excellent. I extend the invitation to Anika. Beth selected you to be on her team when hunting for Calli because of your work ethic. You may choose to accompany Beth and Brand if you wish."

"I'd also be honored to work for you," Anika says confidently.

"To Brand, Beth, and Anika, I say contemplate your choice of becoming a Diamond Bearer before deciding. Learn from Calli, Chris, and Jonas as the six of you begin your new lives as the younger generation of my Diamond Bearer task force. I'll visit after a while to learn your decisions about becoming Bearers. Now, please excuse us. I need to talk further with Calli, Chris, and Jonas."

The three leave the circle and walk toward the main gathering.

"As it stands, a limited number of Bearers know of the Grecian Blue Diamond transfer between Maetha and Calli. This will not change for some time, as I can foresee uprisings within the Bearers. I've blocked all of your minds concerning this information. You won't be able to share or accidentally divulge it."

Crimson continues. "Jonas, you and I are going to be spending a lot of time together. I will help you master the powers that have been given to you prematurely. Don't worry. You'll be able to visit Anika on a regular basis.

"Chris, I want you to continue to carry the diamond on your person until you feel you've mastered the powers, especially those of healing. Calli will help you learn how to control most of the powers. When you're ready, Calli will insert the diamond into your heart. Remember, the diamond will bring about the death of anyone who touches it, who isn't an Unaltered, so protect it.

Crimson addresses Jonas again, "Jonas, I need to speak privately to Chris and Calli now. Go join Anika."

Jonas nods his head and walks away.

Crimson takes my hand into hers and then places it on Chris's hand. "The vision you both viewed on the airplane is attainable, but don't believe for a second that the years between now and then will be perfectly smooth. You two are always welcome to visit me on Maetha's island in Bermuda, should you want to talk."

A question occurs to me. "Crimson, will our relationship, or that of Brand and Beth, or Jonas and Anika, ever be an issue concerning nature's will? Do relationships among Diamond Bearers ever get in the way of doing our jobs? I only ask because of the problems between Neema and Freedom, er, Henry."

"What have I told you about the power of two people in love?" Crimson asks.

"That there's no stronger power."

"Correct. Someone in love has the ability to harness the cosmic powers within the Sanguine Diamond and intensify them more than an average Diamond Bearer. That's why I gave you the Grecian Blue . . . and keep in mind I didn't know then that Chris would become a

267

Bearer. Even a Diamond Bearer in love with a non-Bearer can harness more of the Sanguine Diamond's powers than a regular Bearer can. Once I realized Chris would become a Bearer, and once I witnessed the interaction and teamwork between the two of you, I knew then that you two would become the most powerful Bearers.

"You see, Neema and Henry were in love once too. Neema's desire to create a Diamond Bearer couple, and Maetha's defiance of my wishes, was the key element in my decision to revoke Neema's diamond. A few centuries passed before the most advantageous opportunity presented itself. The only thing that prevented Henry and Neema from taking over the world when he became a Bearer was Henry's anger toward Maetha for keeping him alive throughout the plague. His anger was a welcome poison for their relationship, I felt. Their breakup brought an end to a potential annihilation of all Bearers. Henry had no idea what kind of power he threw away because of his inability to control his anger."

Chris asks, "What are you saying? Could Henry have killed other Diamond Bearers?"

"Yes. Now, before you let the wheels in your brain start to spin, know that this information is privy only to you two and Maetha. She understands the significance of two Diamond Bearers in love, which is why she had to be held accountable for making Henry into a Bearer against my wishes. I'm telling you this, Chris, because I sense that you have the potential to dwell on the anger you hold toward your father. Your disposition and character traits would never allow you to become like Henry, but your anger could minimize your ability to use the powers of the Sanguine Diamond. Accept the fact that you are who you are today because of everything that has happened to you thus far, good or bad. From this point forward, you shape your own destiny. For you and Calli to remain my strongest Bearers, you must master your anger, and not let it master you. You need to learn meditation. Calli can teach you."

She turns to me. "Back to your question about relationships between Diamond Bearers affecting their abilities to do their jobs, I will say that happiness strengthens relationship bonds. I've always encouraged my Bearers to have a significant other, someone to share their life with, and someone to love. I don't know if you've picked up on this yet, but a few of the Bearers are partners. Sadly, they don't have the same level of love the two of you share. If Beth and Brand, or Jonas and Anika develop deeper relationships, they will become strong couples, but not as strong as you two."

"May I ask why?"

"Certainly, Calli. You are the only one of your friends who has not suffered traumatic loss. Your parents weren't murdered, and your childhood was not abusive. Basically you've reached adulthood without the baggage your friends have. Believe me, you are rare, but this didn't happen naturally. I've helped you throughout the years, allowing you to make your own choices, yet protecting you from trauma. I prevented two automobile accidents, one airplane crash—even though everyone would have survived, I didn't want you to be afraid of flying. I prevented a home burglary that would have caused you to lose your sense of security. Your parents might have been murdered when Henry showed up at your home looking for you, if I had not protected them. Through it all, you've remained a grateful individual, cognizant of the differences between your life compared to other girls your age. You are not boastful or proud. You've remained humble. You grew up to become unselfish, caring, and in tune with nature's will. I'll never stop being amazed at how you are able to look at a situation and find a solution without the jaded attitude of so many other individuals. Your ability to harness more of the diamond's powers, because of your pure innocence and your love for Chris, is what makes you the strongest Bearer. With Chris by your side, you two will help rebalance the Diamond Bearers in preparation for what's to come."

"What do you mean 'what's to come?'" I ask.

"I selected you, Calli, protected and trained you for a much bigger purpose than what you've already accomplished."

"Bigger purpose?"

"I know you have more questions, but this is not the time to discuss what lies ahead."

Chris asks Crimson. "So, what do we do for now?"

"What do you do now? Are you asking me for permission or for orders?"

"I guess I'm feeling a bit overwhelmed and a little lost. I don't know what I should focus my time and energy on first, well, besides Calli. The government is not a threat anymore, and it sounds as if the whole operation will be swept under the rug. You said we're the most powerful of the Bearers, but I don't feel much different."

"You're overthinking this, Chris," Crimson says. "Shorten your sights and simplify your thinking. Your friends Beth and Anika could use your support at their parents' funerals. You'll have additional final arrangements that will need to be made concerning your father's estate. I took the liberty of looking into his will. He left just under five-hundred-thousand dollars behind, along with a home valued at a quarter million. Knowing how you feel at the present toward your father, I understand your desire to turn your back on everything. However, consider the good you could do with the money. We are always looking for safe homes that can be used by Bearers at the drop of a hat. Consider donating it to the group. I'd recommend you tuck the money away and use some of it to get an education. Calli's medical studies will be incredibly helpful to the Bearers in the years to come. Medical advancements will continue to shock and amaze even this old girl," she points to her chest. "As for you, Chris, I think you should consider remaining within the government. Perhaps attend officers' training and start climbing the ranks."

"Military, really?" Chris asks with more than a little disappointment in his voice.

"I'm not ordering you to do that, Chris. However, you already have so much experience and so many internal connections; it would be a shame to walk away from that. You've shown you've got what it takes to be an excellent secret agent. Imagine the advantage you'd have as a Diamond Bearer. The closest position to that is Merlin's in the Senate. If we had someone within the CIA or Homeland Security, think of the advantage that would give the Bearers."

"I'll think about it."

"I know you will. As for you, Calli, remember to keep secret what you hear from the thoughts of the other Diamond Bearers. You may discuss things with Chris, but with caution concerning who might overhear your conversation." She pauses and looks beyond us toward the gathering. "Now, I'm going to go join the others as they engage in a lively debate about what it was exactly that killed Deus. Brand is telling everyone she was locked in an infinite loop. He didn't witness it, though. Only the three of us did. I can see you two have no intentions of rejoining the group just yet, so I'll go add facts to Brand's assumptions—facts as seen through Calli's eyes, of course."

She walks away, leaving us beside the lake with the full moon above us, illuminating the water.

Chris takes his jacket off and drapes it over my shoulders to cover the exposed skin on my back. His unique scent fills my nose and causes my body to shiver with excitement. For the first time in a long time, my heart races without pain. Chris wraps his arms around my body and pulls me close to his warm chest. My arms instinctively react by wrapping around him. "I love you, Calli," he says against my temple.

"I love you too, Chris."

He tightens his embrace. "You know, we never got to know each other. We were too busy saving each other's lives and the lives of others. We got to see each other's inner qualities and characteristics and develop a deep love for one another before learning what each other's favorite movies are or if we have any hobbies."

"Yeah, I guess we did everything backwards." I reach up and slide my fingers along his jaw line and then push them up into his hair. I tug his head down and bring his lips to mine and kiss him gently. He lets out a low groan and intensifies the kiss for a moment before stopping.

"You drive me crazy, Calli. I almost can't control myself with you. Pretty much the only thing that has kept me in check lately is the fact that Jonas knew everything we were doing."

"Well, not anymore."

He lets out another pained groan. "I know."

I hug him tight again as a surge of energy sweeps through me. "We're both Diamond Bearers, Chris. Would you have ever thought in a million years this would happen?"

"No, but I look forward to spending a million years with you."

"What a cheesy comeback . . . but, I like it. Hey, *you* can extract *my* mind now, did you think about that?"

"Of all the things I've thought about doing with you, that wasn't one of them." His entirely serious gaze stares straight into my soul. He winks, sending excited tingles and thrilling electrical jolts throughout my body. "Do you want to go on a date?" he asks.

"What? We're ready to rip each other's clothes off, and you want to go on a date?"

"Yes . . . and yes. I'm simplifying my thinking."

"Where are you going to take me?"

"Anywhere and everywhere!"

Thanks for reading!

Thanks for reading my books! I hope you'll take the time to leave a review on Amazon or Goodreads. I'd really appreciate it.

Also, drop on over to my website and let me know what you thought of the series by using the Contact Me form. While you're visiting my site, sign up for my newsletter to be kept updated on the progress of upcoming books in The Unaltered series, and to receive exclusive freebies and news. Thanks again for reading my books. ~Lorena

Calli's story is only beginning. Read more about the world of Unaltereds in:

The Diamond Bearer's Secret
Book Five in The Unaltered series

The Diamond Bearer's Secret, book five of The Unaltered. Calli learns that everything she's been through since receiving a diamond has been in preparation for a much larger purpose. An event looms in the future that could end life as she knows it and her assistance is crucial. The problem is, the Diamond Bearers are dividing at a time they should be uniting and she is viewed as a young upstart by centuries-old comrades. They're not about to let her upset their ranks or move forward with plans that go against their thinking. They're unaware Calli can hear their grumblings and, through her, Crimson. Neither Calli nor Crimson back down. The ultimatum still stands: support nature's will or surrender your diamond.

Problems arise over an anonymous blog revealing critical information about people with powers. The blog must be stopped before the secrets of the Diamond Bearers are released. Unfortunately, the powers contained within the Sanguine Diamond don't include the ability to shut down a blog—nor do Diamond Bearers rooted in antiquated practices have a clue about how to address this life-threatening issue. Only those who understand how the virtual world works can fight against a virtual enemy.

With everything escalating around them, Chris and Calli still find time to get to know each other better. Will they like what they find? What other information will be found within the files from General Harding's compound? The more pressing question is, are Crimson and Maetha still keeping secrets from Calli?

Book 5, *The Diamond Bearer's Secret,*

is available on Amazon and Barnes&Noble.

ABOUT THE AUTHOR

Lorena Angell is the internationally bestselling author of the YA fantasy series, *The Unaltered*. Inspired by an interview from J.K. Rowling, Lorena began to write and published her first book in 2011. Since then, she's earned over 4,200 reviews (average of 4.5 stars), has been a #1 bestseller in over 11 countries and wants nothing more than to write more books for her readers.

Connect with Lorena Angell at:

www.LorenaAngell.com
Twitter: @LorenaAngell1
Facebook: The Unaltered Diamond Series
Instagram: the.unaltered.series